ORDINARY MISTAKES

Three stories of drama, intrigue and illusion

CATHERINE GILLING

ORDINARY MISTAKES

Three stories of drama, intrigue and illusion

CATHERINE GILLING

MEREO
Cirencester

Mereo Books

1A The Wool Market Dyer Street Cirencester Gloucestershire GL7 2PR
An imprint of Memoirs Publishing www.mereobooks.com

ORDINARY MISTAKES: 978-1-86151-475-2

First published in Great Britain in 2015
by Mereo Books, an imprint of Memoirs Publishing

Copyright ©2015

The address for Memoirs Publishing Group Limited can be found at
www.memoirspublishing.com

The Memoirs Publishing Group Ltd Reg. No. 7834348

The Memoirs Publishing Group supports both The Forest Stewardship Council® (FSC®) and the
PEFC® leading international forest-certification organisations. Our books carrying both the FSC
label and the PEFC® and are printed on FSC®-certified paper. FSC® is the only
forest-certification scheme supported by the leading environmental organisations including
Greenpeace. Our paper procurement policy can be found at
www.memoirspublishing.com/environment

Typeset in 10/16pt Century Schoolbook
by Wiltshire Associates Publisher Services Ltd. Printed and bound in Great Britain by
Printondemand-Worldwide, Peterborough PE2 6XD

CONTENTS

ORDINARY MISTAKES

CHAPTER 1

Luke stared at the darkness through the train window, still inwardly seething at the afternoon's events and unable to shake off his annoyance. That damn girl! That female, that distraction of elegant legs with that awful bright pink handbag. He slumped in his seat, thinking about it over and over again.

So half of it was his own fault. Who was he kidding - it was all his own fault! Of course. But logic did not help rectify the facts. How could he have been so stupid? He had seen the brooch in the shop window last week, the perfect present for his mother's birthday. An original piece, it was unique and the only possible choice. There was nothing else like it in the shop. He had set his heart on it and he had known his mother would absolutely adore it as well. So why had he left it until the last minute to actually go into the jeweller's to buy the present? Simply because he had not expected anyone else to buy it.

Now it was gone; his precious gift had been sold only minutes before. That girl who had swept out of the shop as he approached had bought it. Who would have expected a person with short spiky hair and the outlandish taste displayed by that pink handbag to pick the very gift he had set his heart on? He had thought of chasing after her to try to buy it back, but to accost her in the street like some apparent madman was not only impractical, it was also highly contentious. He might have found himself arrested. Besides, by the time he had looked outside, she was nowhere in sight.

His whole day had been ruined. He should have brought it straight away, but he hadn't. With sagging spirits he had acquired an inadequate substitute, his only solace being that his mother, the dear that she was, would not mind what gift he brought her. Which was not the point at all; it had been important for the gift to be special, because his mother was special.

Naturally this first irritating incident had managed to build into a whole series of minor trials. He was caught in the thick of the rush hour he had meant to avoid, which in turn made him late getting back to the flat to collect his travelling holdall. He had to rush his meal, yet stopped to watch the tea-time news headlines, although he had not meant to. He could not help being interested in land preparation for the proposed London Olympic Stadium at

Stratford. Then having shaken himself away from that, his keys decided to play hide and seek, delaying him further. As a result he was now having to take the late train down to his parents.

Luke stared at his tired reflection, shook his head and closed his eyes, hoping to shake off this mood before he reached home. Indeed the thought of home soon worked its effect, with its welcoming warmth and atmosphere of normal family life, with the sibling mayhem of his younger brother and sister echoing amidst his father's comments and his mother's calming control. Although this weekend the house would be buzzing with activity in preparation for the party tomorrow night, everyone would be getting under each other's feet. Robin and Janet would be skillfully ducking out of any chores, while relations and friends would be arriving from everywhere. His father would be in his element at playing host and his mother, bless her, would still be organizing and double-checking everything for a perfect evening. Luke managed a smile, determined that nothing on his part would spoil anything over this weekend for his mother.

Even the sight of Robin, impatiently pacing the car park, had added to Luke's improving attitude. Obviously Robin had been volunteered by his parents to meet him, and not with good grace, Luke noted. His younger brother was grumbling because of the alterations he had had to make to his own arrangements for this evening, due to Luke's late arrival.

Fending off the complaints, Luke tossed his bag on the back seat and slid into the passenger seat without any sympathy or sense of guilt at all. To have messed up Robin's plans for one evening was no great drama, especially when he knew perfectly well who his brother would have preferred to be with at this moment.

"Blame the pink handbag," Luke offered, as some recompense, as they drove off.

"So what was she like then?" his brother quizzed.

"Who?" Luke replied, not following.

"She obviously made an impression, despite the pink handbag."

Luke grunted, refusing to contemplate the idea. In fact he had barely had time to take in many of her features, except for those legs. Rather than continue this topic of conversation, he quickly reversed the tactic.

"Anyway, what was so important about tonight? Who is this latest girlfriend of yours? Do I know her?" he asked casually.

"I doubt it," Robin mumbled begrudgingly, unaware of the flush of embarrassment which coloured his face.

Luke smirked; he knew why Robin was reluctant to confide in him. Not much he did not know her! A little too well, in fact. It was never going to work, but Robin was grown up enough now to sort out his own relationships. Luke was not going to interfere, just as long as it did not become a problem.

"Are you bringing her tomorrow night? Have you invited her to the party?" he asked Robin. Luke actually saw him flinch, but pretended not to notice.

"No," came the reply, a little too quickly.

"Why ever not? It's open house. Or is it me you're afraid of? I won't muscle in, I promise," he teased.

"You flatter yourself! Why should she be interested in you?"

She had been, once. Luke nearly felt inclined to reveal what he already knew, but it was more fun letting Robin squirm a little longer. Robin was really doing his best to keep the two of them apart, and Luke felt it would interesting to see if he managed to achieve it over the whole weekend. The creases around his mouth developed into a distinctive flicker of appreciation at the thought of the fun he could have at his brother's expense. The smile was mistaken by Robin for some pleasant memory of Luke's present London lifestyle.

This gave Robin the chance to recover his composure and begin eagerly firing his own questions about the capital and its tantalizing nightlife. Luke feigned ignorance, wondering why everyone expected London to be so exciting. It had been hard work to establish his career in the business world. To begin with he had had to find a second job in the evenings to make ends meet. Now he worked long hours just to keep on top of its requirements, with the result that he had less and less time for a proper social life. In the beginning he had frequented the clubs and bars, and had been an avid theatre and concert goer. These days he merely attended the firm's functions or went to a restaurant, less and less enthralled by the city's many other attractions. Thus Robin's hopes of lurid details, as in previous attempts, had dwindled away by the time they reached home.

The house was unusually quiet on arrival and Luke was disappointed at not being smothered with greetings by anyone.

"So where is everyone?" he asked lethargically, following Robin upstairs to the room they were to share. Their sister was at the house of one of her friends, probably celebrating the end of term, and their parents were out entertaining the relations who would be using Luke's old room over the next few days, he was told.

Luke shrugged and yawned, throwing his bag on to the best of the beds. He had not anticipated Robin's reaction. His brother swiftly knocked it to the floor.

"I don't mind sharing my room with you, but you can have the fold up," Robin informed him abruptly.

Luke was surprised at this uncharitable outburst, and being the older of the two felt inclined to argue the point. He offered to toss a coin for it, but Robin was adamant. Luke's dark eyes flashed briefly, aware that his brother was tentatively squaring up to him, testing his newly-acquired adult status. Luke poked the ugly contraption on offer suspiciously, displeased at the prospect, doubting he would get a good night's sleep on it but concluded that it wasn't worth causing any friction between them and let it pass. Sadly, it looked as if those friendly, playful brotherly tussles of their youth were a thing of the past. Luke recognized that his brother was at that awkward serious stage. Although he acknowledged it, subconsciously it did not prevent a little mild retaliation, especially since he was getting the raw end of the deal bed wise.

"Have you stayed at her flat yet?" Luke asked as he unpacked his bag.

There was a shocked silence. Not that Luke had expected a straight answer.

"I take it she has a place of her own?" Luke added, to deflect his brother from realizing the full amount of Luke's knowledge concerning Robin's love life.

Robin let out a sigh of relief, thankfully concluding that the previous question had just been a fishing trip to try to find out more. Luke noted that he had not jumped in defensively with a contradiction, which would have trapped him into revealing more than he intended. His brother was learning.

The next morning, having changed into his old jeans and a casual polo shirt, Luke helped himself to an early breakfast in the kitchen. An unintended and unearthly one, as it happened, attributed to the wretchedly uncomfortable bed and his brother's grunts and tossing and turning since first light. Wide awake and crunching the toast with sadistic pleasure, he sat there considering various payback propositions for his brother. That bed was awful.

He glanced at his watch and pouted, annoyed at the hour; it was still too early to phone his friend Ben to beg him for somewhere better to sleep tonight. He would even settle for the lovely padded settee he remembered, if the spare room was still full of boxes. Impatiently he found himself looking at the clock almost every five minutes while he tried to occupy some time by reading yesterday's local paper, but he could not settle.

"Oh, come on clock!" he grunted.

"What are you thinking of, getting up at this time?" interrupted his mother from the stairs.

She must have heard him about; he had not meant to bring her down.

"I missed you last night. Make me a cup of tea," she purred, sitting down next to him.

Here, with no makeup, her hair a little ruffled and in her housecoat and slippers, was his mother at her best. Her appearance was natural and homely, her affectionate gaze watching him.

"You look tired. Are you working too hard? Are you happy being in the city?"

As always, the unmistakable maternal concern sounded in her voice; a mother remained a mother despite one's years and maturity. She read him so well. There was no hiding anything from her and she had the knack of sensing a problem before he had even recognized one himself.

He grinned weakly. Maybe his tiredness was due to more than the lack of sleep last night; he was not sure.

"Stop worrying about me," he replied. "Today is your day and I want to be the first to wish you a happy birthday." He leaned over quickly to kiss her.

"Enough of that," she scolded softly. "Now listen to me, Lucian…"

"Mother. Please. Just try to take it easy and enjoy the day, or you will be worn out by tonight."

"Lucian! Are you listening? "

She was the only one of the family who always used his

proper name, refusing to bend to the inevitable short form everyone else used.

"Janet will be having some friends around here later," she went on. "They are young and impressionable. Please don't tease them."

"Mother, whatever do you expect? I am always nice to everyone, including Robin's friends," he scoffed in exaggerated profound innocence, shocked at her implication.

Ignoring his remark, she tapped him smartly on the shoulder.

"You remember we have guests and although they may be tolerant, I expect all of you to behave. Now I'm going back to bed for another hour. No doubt you have plans of your own."

Indeed he did. He was off to find Ben as soon as practical and find a better bed for tonight.

In fact Luke did have his own private agenda this weekend. Besides finding Ben, he had his own method of curing any stress. He loved to visit old Mr Taylor on his allotment for a chat. Luke liked to see what he had grown, smell the freshness of his produce and learn all he could. It fascinated him, because this man shared the same satisfaction for the feel of the earth in his hands as his grandfather did. To dig and turn the soil, to bend his whole body into hard physical labour. To feel the sun on his back and the wind on his face, hot and dirty, it was the one activity which seemed to make him utterly content.

Later, when Luke returned to the house, he found that the

last few hours had totally relaxed him. The fresh air had worked its magic and he felt much more content. His whole weekend was planned; tonight after the party he would spend talking the hours away with Ben, trying to put the world to rights, no doubt. A late lie-in, a drink at the pub at lunchtime and the afternoon tinkering in the garage on his old motor bike. That all seemed like a really good weekend to him.

Entering through the open front door into the hallway, Luke began carefully picking his way through the mass of deliveries which had amassed during his absence. There were cases of drinks stacked along one wall, boxes of glasses, plates and cutlery hired from caterers, near the kitchen, baskets and various arrangements of flowers as well as brightly-wrapped presents bursting on every surface, together with an important list of instructions for any further deliveries fluttering on the small area of carpet left in front of him. Retrieving the detached paper, he stuck it back in the centre of the front door, giving it an extra thump to make it stay there. From the floor above he heard the unmistakable squeaks and giggles of Janet and her friends, the sounds betraying the mass of silly young females expressing their wild fantasies and infatuations, he had no doubt. It was definitely not an area for him to hang around in, and it was only the sight of their untidy pile of bags cluttering the stairs which slowed down his journey. There amongst the tumbled heap of insignificant baggage, lay - a bright pink handbag. It was identical to the one he had seen yesterday, the one carried by the woman who had snatched his mother's gift from under his nose.

He stared at the thing. Of course, this was obviously one of the latest fashion items, and he would be seeing plenty more of them about. That was just what he needed - to be continually reminded of yesterday.

Then, before he could clear himself out of the way, he was engulfed by a bustling rabble of teenagers bursting down the stairs, all of them flushed pink and chattering excitedly. Flattening himself back out of their way he watched to see who the pink bag belonged to and was surprised when a plump blond snatched it up and beamed at him as she left with the rest of the crowd. Luke grinned to himself. That chubby child bore no resemblance to the lithe female of yesterday, yet their tastes were the same. Unbelievable!

As he watched them depart, they suddenly scattered as a van reversed up the drive towards the house. The reversing bleep and large stack of chairs visible inside brought the ominous voice of his father from the front room, summoning Robin from wherever he was hiding, while Luke silently presented himself for secondment without fuss. At least his father was too busy with some of the day's arrangements to enquire into his work in London at the moment.

It had not taken long to transport them all to the back garden and around through the side gate. Once done, Luke escaped to find his sister Janet, whom he had spotted further down the garden. Engrossed by the fish in the pond, she had not heard his approach. Unable to resist the temptation, he crept up behind her and gave her a quick dig in the ribs, one of Robin's favourite tricks, making her jump, squeal aloud and turn around. Glaring and ready to hit out, she stopped once she saw the real culprit.

"Hello. Have you missed me?" he managed to say as she hugged him enthusiastically.

"I am glad you've come," she panted, keeping hold of his arm.

"How did the exams go? Do you think you passed? Is college next on the agenda?" he asked kindly.

"I want your support," she continued, tugging at him to move away. Dear me, what scheme did she have up her sleeve now, he wondered? What was he about to become involved in? He had not minded indulging her when she was younger, but Janet wasn't a child any longer, either, so he had no idea of the shock coming to him.

"Well," she began slowly, her voice dropping to a whisper, "I want to go backpacking with my friends, after the exam results next month. You know, staying in hostels across Europe. Really seeing the places as they are, before they change."

"They would need to be damn good results!" he could not help snapping at her. "Are you out of your mind? You know how dangerous trips like that are now. It's been in all the papers."

Luke was horrified; their parents would go ballistic at the idea. How was he going to make her see sense?

"But you went to Europe on that old motorbike of yours at my age." She pouted at him.

"The world was a safer place then, there's no comparison."

That seemed a lifetime ago; the four of them from the village, carefree and ignorant, with tents tied on the back of their bikes, had enjoyed a summer of pure escapism, but he shook himself free of such memories.

"Who was the tubby blonde with the pink bag?" he asked, expecting to divert her for a moment.

Unfortunately this deliberately tactless remark brought no chastisement and no defence of her friend. Janet stubbornly refused to be sidetracked.

"Emma wants to go as well. There's a group of us, six or eight maybe. We've been on holiday before together."

"A package holiday is not the same as what you intend to do this time. You're wasting your breath," he informed her firmly.

"You won't talk to Mum and Dad for me then?" she pleaded pitifully.

Her little face peering up to his, the sad puppy-dog expression normally used to good effect in the past waiting for him to give in. But on this occasion all her acting skills were not going to work. This was not some trivial matter at stake. He shook his head.

"Certainly not, not when I'm concerned for your safety."

"I'd hoped you would help us plan the best places to visit, but that's obviously not going to happen."

"Why can't you find a summer job instead, or wait until after college?" His voice was now a little calmer.

"We want to go now!"

Luke grimaced. This looked like being a long and tiring exchange. Janet, for her part, with all her feeble arguments for her cause, failed to win her case, while all of Luke's suggestions for alternatives were equally firmly dismissed by his sister. Apparently Emma's sister had a vast experience of all these various ventures and had filled them in on all the pitfalls she had encountered. Emma's sister had done this, Emma's sister had done that, and the endless examples and misfortunes thrown at him to make her point made him quite exhausted, to the extent where Luke felt he would quite like to strangle Emma's sister for her free opinions, her irresponsible advice and most of all, for her apparent influence on Janet. This unknown female had a lot to answer for!

The debate ended abruptly with Janet's declaration that Emma's sister would help them organize their trip, since Luke would not. They had already enquired about the ferry tickets and would be booking them soon, whatever the objections. So she would tackle her parents on her own, with or without his help. Heavens, she was growing up too fast, and becoming just as stubbornly unwilling to listen to reason. Luke was angry with himself for failing to persuade her, but he had to put a stop to this somehow.

"Don't you dare ruin mother's birthday this weekend. Don't you dare to mention this to either of them. I'm warning you! One word and I will personally put you over my knee and spank you in front of everyone," he growled threateningly.

"You wouldn't dare! "she sneered at him.

"No? Shall we test the theory?"

He had never laid a hand on her before, except in the

normal playful taunts of their childhood games, and she knew it. But Luke could not back out now. He had to act, had to make her understand he meant every word. He grabbed her. Bending his leg on the stone rockery, he easily pulled her over his knee, all her struggling making no difference to his very strong grip. He held her there and spanked her twice very hard, then with his hand raised ready to spank her again he made her promise to say nothing this weekend.

When he let her up she had tears in her eyes, and he knew he had been pushed into making a serious mistake. He felt sorry for his actions, but he had not had time to think of any other way to prove he was utterly serious. Yelling that she hated him, Janet rushed off back to the house, leaving him to hurry after her, head down, hands in pockets, with no idea how to patch it up.

A shout from somewhere inside summoned Janet to the phone, allowing Luke to catch up with her in the hall, where he leaned ominously on the table by her side waiting for her to finish. His unwelcome presence hampered her animated gestures of conversation, as every time she tried to elbow him out of the way or turned her back on him to ignore him, he simply moved around to face her again. Janet hung up abruptly, furiously thrusting the receiver down with more force than was good for it and dashed up stairs, slamming her bedroom door behind her, without giving him the chance to utter one word.

Still in the hall, Luke considered where to follow her or not, when the door bell rung close behind him. It rang again, a short sharp burst which he tried to ignore, until his mother's voice echoed from the kitchen to instruct anyone who was about to see who it was.

Reluctantly Luke turned the latch and opened the door, dreading the arrival of more caterers and deliveries. Surely they had enough supplies to feed the whole road for a month, he mused. When he saw the caller, he took a step back to make a more careful appraisal of the slim, lithe figure with spiky hair with striking blond highlights who stood before him. This was not possible - he must be mistaken. Was it her or not? He could not believe his eyes as he stared her up and down, trying to decide, He hardly took in the several dishes, covered in cling film, she was holding in her arms.

"Mrs Mathews asked me to drop these off." Her voice slowly registered in his unresponsive head. He could not take this in. He stood dumbly aside to let her go through, pointing to the kitchen.

"There's another tray on the back seat - would you mind?" she added in passing, nodding towards the open rear door of the old CV6 parked at an angle on the gravel drive a few feet away. Not that his brain was listening; instead it was whirling with questions, as she continued into his home. She was no neighbour he remembered, yet the casualness and familiarity of the conversation in the kitchen, where he heard his mother gush her thanks, indicated she was no stranger either.

"Oh, my dear, how good of you to bring these over," his mother was saying. "I do hope you will drop in tonight."

He still had not moved when she returned through the hall, for which she gave him a curious glare and a decided shake of the head. Clearly he was being categorized into some unfavourable group for some unknown reason. Her resigned sigh before she swept out of the front door indicated that she thought very little of him at the moment, although why she should be bothered to assess him at all when she did not know him he had no idea.

The tilt of her elegant neck and her golden, tanned back were displayed to every advantage by a thin strapped top, together with her perky step bouncing down the gravel drive and her slim hips swinging in an alluring rhythm, this time without a pink handbag in sight.

He strode after her to the car, anxious to ask if she had been in London the previous day. She bent out of earshot into the car, where she retrieved the tray from the rear seat and then kicked the door shut with her foot before turning to face him.

"I thought you were going to fetch these for me?" she declared, dumping the tray firmly into his hands.

He opened his mouth to defend himself, unable to find an excuse immediately, and the woman did not wait for a reply. She turned smartly on her heels, jumped into the driver's seat, revved the engine noisily and drove away into the village without another look. Luke stood there like some idiot with the tray full of food, still stunned by her appearance. The crazy car was as distinctive as the person in it. They were a perfect match.

Janet flounced down the stairs and thumped him on the shoulder, her sullen face glaring at the sight of him.

"Mind out.!" he complained sharply, as the tray was nearly knocked from his grasp.

"You will be pleased to know that Emma's mother has refused to let her go," she hissed at him.

"That is not my fault!" he retaliated with equal force. Thank goodness someone had sense in that family. At least one problem had been solved, although he still had to placate this teenager at some stage.

"What is going on out there?" his mother enquired from the other room, having heard the snarls but not the content of the exchange.

"Nothing important," Luke replied casually, giving a warning frown to Janet for her to agree.

His sister, surprisingly compliant, repeated his answer, her cheerful voice, belying the animosity she felt towards him. Well, that was a turn up for the books. At least he did not have to worry about her putting the dampeners on their mother's party any more.

The confusion and doubt of a few moments ago still whirled away in his head. Of course he could have asked his mother who she was, but she would have got completely the wrong idea and also jumped to the wrong conclusion. He could not have that. He wanted a peaceful weekend.

The birthday party soon engulfed them all. The family, uncles, aunts and cousins, friends and neighbours, gathered as usual to celebrate in style, people everywhere underfoot.

The place was full of cheerful banter, reminiscing, laughter and the clink of glasses. Some had settled into the huge buffet, displayed on the terrace, including Janet, who, showing no signs of her earlier sulking, was eagerly delving into the desserts. Other guests, prompted by the background music, had begun softly singing the old songs they thought they had forgotten, or dancing those slow old-fashioned dances of a distant past. Speeches were made, toasts given, balloons popped and the cake cut, to the accompaniment of a rousing cheer. His mother's face was flushed with happiness and his father revelled in the shared attention as they later waltzed together, their favourite dance.

It had all gone well so far. It was a successful night and Luke retired from his social obligations to find a quite recess for a while, to wait for Ben. Two long drinks later, hearing Ben's voice making its way through the chatter of the guests, he set out on a search and rescue mission for his best friend. As he was deftly winding his way through the active throng, with Ben in sight, an unexpected voice behind halted him.

"Lu-ci-en," a soft sound purred in his ear.

Luke immediately tensed himself against the familiar moves which normally followed that approach; the gentle breath on the back of his neck, the light touch of subtle fingers walking up and down his spine and his unmistakable shudder at the sensation it caused. The minx was trying to see how much she could still provoke him, as in her old casual manner she purposely brushed her head against his shoulder. He turned slowly, unwrapped her hand from his arm and placed her apart from him, fully aware of causing many a glance and raised eyebrows.

"Don't do that!" he hissed under his breath, to avoid others hearing.

"Why? I had to see if I still had the right touch," she whispered.

For Luke the past meant the past and luckily Liz, despite this show of affection, was simply amusing herself for the moment. She was not the type to want to renew past relationships either. Liz had been the ideal example of what good fun meant and by mutual agreement they had both enjoyed themselves, but they had both moved on.

"You devil, Liz! Shouldn't you be with someone else this evening? "

"Of course," she replied, rolling her eyes wide.

"Then go and dance with him!" he hissed at her, smiling too sweetly.

She sighed too dramatically, flouncing off yet clearly displaying her reluctance. Then she gave him one more quick glance, winked mischievously and laughed, her little performance over.

"Well, for someone who always profoundly denies having a reputation with the female population I would think that was a prime example of the opposite," Ben commented, arriving with some drinks.

Luke let out a long breath of relief and looked to the heavens. That had been a close call. He has not expected such a thing to happen, despite realizing that she would put in an appearance.

"Everyone knows you were an item once," said Ben.

"Two years ago!"

"I don't understand why Robin is still trying to keep their relationship a secret from you, unless he is embarrassed?"

"Well she has made sure it is no secret any more." Luke smirked and pointed across the lawn, where Liz had thrown herself into Robin's arms and was kissing him long and hard in front of everyone. Poor Robin, what was he letting himself in for? It was obvious Liz was too much woman for him to handle.

He turned back to find himself deserted. Ben had found more attractive company to talk to, but did it have to be that female? He did not blame his best friend for preferring the bewitching tanned neck and not least, the simply-cut dress which wrapped itself around that slim body. The pair of them stood chatting and laughing, an apparent rapport between them. Reluctantly he made his way across the terrace in their direction, loitering in close proximity and hoping Ben would drag himself away. But it was clear his friend was in no rush to leave her. He tried to catch his attention, causing Ben to stare back and mistake the glare for something it certainly was not. Ben introduced them to each other.

"Clare, this is Luke. Luke, this is Clare."

"We met earlier - when you came to the house this morning," said Luke.

"Oh, yes," she answered, merely acknowledging him. There was nothing for it; he might as well ask her.

"Excuse me, but were you at Lambert's in London yesterday afternoon?"

"I may have been," she conceded cautiously.

"You bought the very item I wanted. The silver filigree brooch with the cream stones. I intended to buy it for my mother's birthday present. It was lovely."

"Which was why I bought it for my aunt."

Totally indifferent to the information, she made no other comment. There was no attempt to appease his disappointment. Her lack of sympathy sent a flicker of resentment for yesterday surge through his mind. OK, so what was his next move?

"Have you know Ben long?" he asked, trying to change the subject

She nodded, without clarifying the when or where.

"I'm surprised Ben has not mentioned you before."

"Watch out, Clare. I should warn you Luke has a way with the females of this world." Ben teased, his mischievous face betraying the sort of wind-up that was coming.

"So I have heard," she said.

Did he imagine the disparaging edge in her voice, implying she knew more than enough? Not that it really mattered what she thought of him, or what Ben had been telling her. Although he was beginning to question the so-called loyalty of his best friend. For goodness sake! Where on earth had this apparent reputation come from? So he had dated plenty of female company in the past. None of them had been serious and his companions had always been tactful enough not to tell tales. Any dire exploits which might have taken place remained private. Maybe the lack of rumours about his personal life only added to the speculation about him, due to other people's assumptions.

"I blame his dark Mediterranean features for the attraction," said Clare.

Luke could see this developing into a destruction job if he was not careful, with obvious innuendoes about his past history being used by Ben to show off to this girl. He saw no reason to be goaded into having to defend himself, especially to strangers. Just wait until later when he had Ben on his own.

"I hope you are both enjoying this." That was the only ambiguous and curtly civil reply he could muster, as he curled his lip in a silent snarl towards Ben.

The signal that Ben had overstepped the mark had been received and understood, and he fell silent.

"Besides avoiding all your past girlfriends, I expect dodging the local adoring fan club must also be quite tiring," Clare continued.

Hadn't she realised the joke had finished? He did not need this! Not from this irksome girl. Ben's excuse for his behaviour might have been his wish to impress her, so what was her excuse?

"You must know all your sister's school friends fancy you," she insisted.

Luke was shocked. The idea of being the centre of teenage admiration wrecked his ability to repudiate her claim. His mind flashed back to the moment when he had been surrounded by those giggling young girls on the stairs. He hoped she was wrong.

Then dear Uncle Len, always unsteady on his feet, fell over, and the loud crash had everyone rushing to help him up, including Luke, which saved him having to continue this conversation. The elderly relation safely settled, the fuss over and calm restored, Luke then found himself whisked away to set the table and chairs straight again and become involved in further demands for the continuing family celebration. Luckily the former double act remained out of reach, mingling with others, which suited him for the moment.

When he next saw Ben, one hour on, he was on his own and with no sign of his former companion; Luke could not resist asking him sarcastically where his new friend had vanished to.

"Gone home," Ben replied.

"Bored with the company?"

"It is getting late." Ben yawned, not rising to the bait.

Luke checked his watch; it was late, but after the earlier stitch-up this evening, he could not help wondering if tonight's arrangements were still on offer.

"I am waiting - to give you a lift." Ben smiled.

Their friendship was back on track. They had hardly ever fallen out and never seriously or for long, which left Luke to make his excuses to his mother before they could get off to the cottage. There they finished off the night over a few drinks, first debating Ben's questionable performance this evening and then the familiar quest to put the world to rights, plus each other - not that Luke could ever find much to criticize in his friend - while Ben continued his favourite topic, the analysis of Luke. Ben's recurring observation was that after years in London Luke was no happier now than when he had first moved there. His words, echoing his mother's earlier comment this morning, began to indicate a conspiracy. Why were they so concerned with his happiness? He was content enough, or hopefully gave that impression, except that his disappearances to his favourite bolt hole, his grandfather's place in France, more and more frequently over the last few years, told a different story. Could he really find something as simple which pleased his own inner spirit? Luke wished he could.

"You hate being in the city and you know it. Everyone is enjoying life, except you."

Ben had found what he wanted already. He was here in his element and enjoying his work, without any doubts about his chosen career. He reveled in his passion for photography. It excited him; he loved getting the right picture, and his endless enthusiasm never faltered.

For Luke, it was not that easy. "You always get involved with other people's lives, without living your own," he said. "What do you want?"

Luke never admitted to himself that Ben was right and he remained silent, unable to give an answer to the question at the end.

Luke shrugged; he was ready for bed. He yawned and made his way upstairs. He did not want a deep and meaningful discussion at this hour. He never spoke of his own improbable dream and never acknowledged that he wanted it. Would that impossible, unreachable goal make him happy? He had always thought it would. Luke had a good job, with better than good money, which remained his sole purpose if he was ever to achieve his objective. Happiness would come later.

Luke woke late the next morning. He lifted his head a few inches, focused his eyes on the clock, grunted, and promptly turned over and snuggled down again. Savouring the pleasant sensation of a soft old-fashioned feather mattress and the wonderful large bed, he felt unwilling to wander downstairs, even when Ben told him he was cooking breakfast.

The previous clutter had been cleared from the spare room and moved into the proper studio at the back, and the room, with its wooden flooring, old furniture, rugs and small windows, simply oozed warmth and character. Everything about this quirky cottage appealed to Luke's senses, from the shelves littered with a collection of old cameras, books, lenses and atmospheric pictures to the obligatory tripod and camera bag by the front door, ready to be grabbed for a quick assignment. In comparison, his own modern city apartment seemed cold and uninviting, but then that place was never meant to be home, it was merely a convenience.

Luke stretched himself and finally made it to the kitchen, where the pair of them sat down to a hearty breakfast and lazily sifted through the Sunday papers and magazines which were scattered on the table around them.

"What do you think of Clare?" asked Ben.

"Who? Clare?" munched Luke, his head buried in the book he had just found.

"Spiky hair, long legs Clare. She is very photogenic. I have several photos of her. I took them while we were at the same design college."

Luke did not disagree about her looks. Why should he? His appreciation of the female form was not in doubt. His eyes were hypnotized, like others, by those long legs during the evening. Except that he refrained from commenting this time, being more interested in getting back to the page he was on; he had meant to finish this book the last time he stayed.

The day turned out to be one of those really hot summer days when the only thing to do was as little as possible. Ben lay in the hammock, rocking slowly from side to side, while Luke lazed on the lounger, in the courtyard at the back of the cottage. Both of them were content to remain there for the rest of the day, if necessary. It was too much effort even to talk, and with nothing to disturb his languid mood, Luke could imagine he was anywhere in the world.

Pleasantly dreaming away, his gaze encompassed the unexpected sight of Clare, who had drifted across to his line of vision to talk briefly to Ben. He watched her through the narrow slits of his half-opened eyes. He could not fail to notice her bright face, her laugh and the toss of her head while she talked. She was infuriatingly attractive. Was it only a few days ago he had cursed her tantalizing figure, disliking her for no other reason than that she had brought the gift he wanted? How childish was that, when it was his own fault for leaving it to the last minute! The corners of his mouth curled into a smile. So where was that terrible pink handbag he would always associate with her?

It was time to finally dismiss the incident over the brooch, and even forgive her participation in Ben's attempted character assassination of himself last night. What was the point of getting stressed? He felt in too mellow a frame of mind. He closed his eyes again and heard her steps making their melodic pattern across the paving, only to stop beside him. When they did not move on, he was forced to look up to find her there, leaning towards him.

"About yesterday. Did you really not know that Janet's friends had a crush on you?"

"I would not have set foot in the house if I had. Tell me, where did you get the information from?"

"I have my sources," she whispered softly.

Luke noticed the little grin and the merriment in her eyes and felt more than prepared to take any teasing she offered today.

"Lucian is a very unusual name. Very French," she continued casually.

"That was mother's fault. You know mother, well I assume you do. She named me after my French grandfather." He gushed like an idiot, before stopping himself. He would like to tell her more about himself, to tell her how at school he had been ribbed something rotten because of his name, to tell her anything amusing to encourage her to reciprocate information about herself. But he did not; he let the idea lapse. Especially with his best friend watching him like a hawk.

"I will be dropping around this afternoon to collect the trays from yesterday. Your mother said she would leave them in the kitchen for me," said Clare.

"That will be fine. The back door will be unlocked. Our parents are taking the other relatives out for the day, but Janet will be home. Just help yourself. I might be working in the garage."

"See you later then," came her parting shot, as she smoothed her dress and left them.

Ben looked across at Luke, while Luke stared straight back, the silent inquisition ending in a stalemate. Luke was refusing to pass any comment which would fuel any wrong ideas Ben might be harbouring. Ideas Ben clearly had on his mind, because he quickly mentioned that Clare would be coming down again next weekend to help him with his next project. Then, after a deliberate pause, he asked just too casually whether Luke would also be down that weekend.

Luke did not bother to answer, and all too soon their peace was obliterated by the tune from the mobile phone in Ben's lap, a reminder from friends who were joining them for a drink. They both stirred themselves sufficiently to walk the short distance to the local pub.

Once there, Luke heard his brother's distinctive voice amongst the scattering of other people there. He let Ben go to get in the first round while he headed for the safety of the bench by the wall, to avoid any likely antagonism. There he closed his eyes and pretended to be asleep, which seemed to be working, until Robin kicked at the bench deliberately to wake him up, forcing Luke to open the heavy lid of one eye to see what he wanted.

"That was a crafty move, staying at Ben's last night. It took hours to tidy up this morning," said Robin.

If that was all he wanted to tackle him about, then good. Luke had not even given a thought to the left-over shambles after the party, and being accused of laziness by his brother was no big deal, although he quickly challenged his brother to reveal just how much he had actually done himself to help clear up. The lack of reply indicated that Simon had done very little either.

Luke closed his eyes again and heard him walk away, which was just as well. It was too nice a day to have to face any jealous repercussions over the Liz issue. Not that there was ever any danger of Luke being provoked into revealing more than he should about his own previous relationship with her. His brother had a lot to learn, he could offer a few gentle tips - no - that was wicked. His mouth twitched. Another time, if Robin ever pushed him too far.

Later as he walked home, the family car rumbled by, the occupants giving him a friendly wave, off on their family excursion. It left Luke without any family obligation to fulfil, meaning he was perfectly free to indulge himself, tinkering on the old motorbike for the rest of the afternoon. Soon he was lost in grease, oil and engine parts, filters and cables, totally engrossed in his long process of restoring the bike back to working condition. The hours flew by, until a long shadow fell across the entrance and made him look up. It was Clare. She must have already been to the house, since she held the trays she had come to collect.

"Hello," she said.

"Hi, you found them then? Was Janet in?"

"Yes, we exchanged a few words. She had some friends in, they were playing music upstairs."

"I can't even offer you a cup of tea," he apologized, indicating the state his hands were in.

"Another time."

Under the pretence of needing to stretch his legs, he stood up to walk down the drive with her, idly wondering why he had not seen her about the village before and if there was any chance of pursuing this acquaintance further. For some reason he felt averse to asking her any direct personal questions after such a brief introduction.

Then as he slowed by the gate, anticipating their parting, Emma launched herself in a rush from the house, causing them both to turn. Emma, obviously startled by their presence, stopped, dithered uncertainly, clasped her arms across her chest and then dashed past them. Her strange behaviour bewildered Luke.

"Emma Mathews - what are you doing with my handbag again?" came Clare's outburst after her.

"You know Emma?" he asked, a little stupidly.

"Emma, of course. There, now you know my source of information. Emma blabs everything."

"Yesterday, she had your pink handbag."

"Oh yes. That's family for you. She always borrows my belongings without even asking, but what can you do?" she sighed affectionately. Then, without waiting or expecting further arrangements between them to be made, she waved her cheerful wave, walked that provocative walk out of the gravel drive and was gone.

Luke stood staring at the empty space as the obvious conclusion registered. How could he have missed the connection yesterday when Clare had brought those trays from the Mathews house? This girl, was Emma's sister. It was hard to accept. They were so different!

Of course, there was now another problem to contend with. Slowly as he stood there, he recalled the recent arguments with Janet where this same sister had figured so prominently. Emma's sister was encouraging Janet and her friends to go to Europe, despite any parental objections. He did not like the idea that this girl he had begun to like could be so irresponsible; it did not fit with the image he had just formed about her. It was very confusing. Maybe there was there another sister he could blame instead for influencing them? He hoped so. How was he to find out? The last thing he could do was ask Janet about Emma's family. That was inviting trouble. Besides, the way she still felt towards him meant he could not believe in anything she said anyway. Even his return to the house earlier this afternoon had been met by her threatening taunts, as proof of her continuing resentment.

"The weekend is nearly over," she had said. "The promise expires on Monday, when you will be safely out of the way back in London!"

Luke wasn't worried. His parents were sure to feel the same way as he did about the scheme. The whole idea was still doomed to failure. Their trip was never going to happen, he was certain of that. In which case, did he really need to be angry with Clare, if she was the culprit, for her support for their plans? They were just getting acquainted. Why spoil it by getting stressed out? Besides, he shrugged philosophically, there was every possibility that his sweet, manipulative sister might have exaggerated Clare's part in this scheme. He would not put it past Janet to say anything just to make sure she could to get her own way. The truth of the matter might be completely different.

CHAPTER 2

The first two days of Luke's week were mentally exhausting, and Luke returned to the flat each night with a thumping headache. He always worried if his decisions throughout the day had been shrewd enough for his employers. Yet they always seemed to come good. Which was why, no doubt, he had been approached recently by a rival business consultancy. Being head-hunted had come as a surprise. The pay was better, he would still be based in the centre of the city and the commute would be the same. But did he really want to work even longer hours, all days of the week, for more money? Actually, no. He had refused them once, but the company had not given up. Another upgraded offer had been made. He did not even want to think about the complications of settling into a new environment. He wanted to be left alone.

He eventually relaxed, stretching out on the large leather sofa, and listened to Ben's message on his answering machine. He was reminded that Clare would be back at Ben's place this weekend if he wanted to come down. He sat thinking about the idea, smiling at the welcome distraction from the stress of business. Clare?

Another weekend at home would be wonderful, except that in the end, a problem at his work decided a different course for his personal plans. He would not be going back to the village; he would not be seeing anyone. A sudden loss in an overseas investment had everyone working overtime the whole weekend to restore the loss in revenue it caused. Everyone in the office searched for files, documents and reviewed contracts to see where they could improve their business interests. Luke stared out of the window while everyone else seemed engrossed in their tasks. Why was he doing this?

If he wasn't going to get home, he decided he could at least put any free time he had to a more pleasant use - such as resolving his curiosity about Clare's precise place in the Matthews family. He had the whole week of evenings ahead to contemplate the best way to tackle the idea. Despite originally deciding that it was not important, he now looked forward to finding out a little more about her in anticipation of their eventual next meeting. So where did he begin?

He did not really want to ask Ben about her, but Ben and his mother were his only other sources of information. And both of them would be awkward to tackle, however delicately he might put the questions. He decided on Ben, feeling there would be more chance of a private conversation. If he phoned home, there was the possibility of either Janet or Robin overhearing.

There was no point in being tactful. However he began, Ben would jump on this sudden interest as something more than it was. And let him, Luke decided; he could withstand the teasing to get the correct information. So he just blurted it out.

"Clare Matthews - does she have any sisters?"

"That is a strange question."

"Well, does she?" he demanded, beginning to feel tense already, and knowing Ben would instantly pick up on the tone of his voice.

"Since when do you need to research the background of your next conquest? You are normally so laid back and casual in your approach."

"Does she have an older or younger sister? That's all I want to know."

Ben was more than puzzled how a sister made any difference. He did not understand the purpose for such a question, but nevertheless he considered that the information would be worth the promise of a beer from Luke the next time he was down. The fee was quickly agreed before Ben continued.

"Younger, although I don't know the age difference."

Luke let out a deep sigh, thanked him and hung up.

Having eventually gleaned what he wanted from Ben, Luke found his opinion of Clare changing every few minutes. He was thinking too much and too long about it. He considered his options. Despite all the confusing and conflicting information, Luke decided he was going to ignore the possible downside, and ploughed through the usual hectic workload of the day, eager for the following evening. He intended to phone Clare on the chance that she might consider meeting up. Except he didn't have her phone number. Ben had not offered it and he certainly wasn't going to phone him again to ask. It would only fuel Ben's intense curiosity further and cost him a great deal of endless innuendo.

He would have to phone home and ask his mother for Mrs Mathews number first. He paused on the last number as he dialled; he could not help wondering if Janet had dropped the bombshell to their parents yet.

His mother's voice was its normal calm tone as she answered, which indicated that the trouble had not surfaced so far. How long before it would? He did not believe his sister had given up, although he could not imagine what Janet intended to do. He shook himself free of his concern to make his request. His mother, happily unaware of the impending trouble, passed on the phone number without asking questions. Bless her.

He phoned Mrs Matthews immediately, before he changed his mind, asking politely if she knew where her eldest daughter might be this week. The lady chuckled, obviously used to such phone calls concerning her pretty daughter. Without hesitation she confirmed that she was working in the city at present and gave him the telephone for her flat in London, so he could contact her. Luke could not believe his luck.

He settled down to compose himself for his next phone call, intending to be friendly and casual without betraying his curiosity. His first call was met by the answering machine, which was disappointing. He left it for half an hour and then did the same again, with the same result. How often dare he phone and how late? He decided to wait until tomorrow. But the next two nights were a repetition of the first; every time he tried to phone all he had was the answering machine clicking in, forcing him to leave a message and his own number, hopeful for her reply, instead.

All he could do was wait, wondering who would call first, Clare or his poor mother once she found out about Janet's plans.

Sure enough it was his mother. Apparently Janet had not waited that long to plead her case for going youth hostelling and had done so most proficiently, by the sound of it. He listened patiently as his mother confirmed all the arguments against the idea, which were exactly the same ones he had put forward himself. She understood he had been approached for support and had refused, which obviously explained the reason for that falling out between Janet and himself that weekend. Yes his mother had noticed the change of atmosphere between them; she did not miss much, she told him. At the moment Janet was sulking upstairs, refusing to talk to anyone, complaining she was never allowed to have any fun.

"Lucian, dear," she began.

"Ye-es, mother?"

"Now you know you are going to your grandfather's next month."

"For a holiday, mother." He was already suspicious.

"Would you take Janet with you? It might satisfy this urge she has for travelling at the moment."

"No, no, no. A hundred times no!" Not for anything in the world, his mother could try all she liked, would he be persuaded on this. He would not do it. The last thing he wanted was Janet following him around and getting in his way. She would be wanting this and that, because she had always been pandered to, playing upon the fact that she was the youngest as she had done in the past. Janet would have to accept their decision and learn she could not have everything her own way any more.

"Besides, what is Robin doing this summer?" he asked.

His mother's voice dropped even lower as she relayed her other piece of information, that Robin and Liz were planning to go to Rome together soon.

"That was sudden. Friday night he would not even admit they were an item."

His mother waffled around diplomatically on the subject, trying not to be too critical but clearly not pleased with this additional development either. His brother and sister were both developing strong personalities and growing up so fast.

"I can't keep up with you all," she concluded at the end of their conversation.

The rest of the week proved mildly frustrating as he hurried back each evening from work, putting other arrangements on hold. He pottered about his showcase flat, anticipating the returned phone call from Clare, which as the hours and days passed, failed to materialize. Undaunted, he tried the number a few more times, but always the answering machine kicked in. He did not understand. She did not seem the type to deliberately ignore his call. It was no good, he would have to phone Mrs Mathews again, to find out if she knew where she was.

"Hello Mrs Mathews. This is Luke. I have been trying to phone your daughter in London, but I am not getting any answer."

"Oh, I am sorry Luke. I can only guess she has had to go down to the coast for her agency. It is involved in some publicity for the theatres, or something like that. I can never keep up with her. She enjoys flitting about the country so much. I'm sure she will return your call when she gets back."

"Thank you Mrs Matthews. You did not mind me phoning?"

"Not at all."

Luke sighed. He had waited in for nothing, although it had given him plenty of time to think.

Although there were no doubts that Clare was indeed Emma's only sister, he had not convinced himself that Janet had told the truth about her and refused to believe anything detrimental about Clare until facts proved conclusively otherwise. Having missed her last weekend, he wasn't sure if she would be back in the village again this weekend, but it was worth a trip home on the off chance to find out.

Luke caught the early train home on Friday afternoon; not that he ever needed an excuse to pop home, because his mother was always delighted to see him. His mood was decidedly mellow as he anticipated a relaxing few days. As he pushed open the front door, his mother's beaming face put him instantly at ease. His father gave him the usual nod, with a sceptical frown. His brother was out and Janet - well Janet actually smiled with delight, which was not a good sign.

Once the welcoming banter had waned and everyone had reverted to their own quiet routine, Luke prised himself from the armchair to risk the temporary privacy of the hall to try to phone the flat again. He still had not managed to contact her, and again no one was home, so he was left with the evening free to find a comfy corner and finish the book he had borrowed from Ben as compensation. Not that Luke was particularly bothered too much, he was still glad he had come. If she did not turn up he would still enjoy his mother spoiling him and find more time for work on the old motor bike in the shed.

The next morning started badly; his father wanted a word with him straight after breakfast. With his mother and Robin absent, a serious argument developed, with only Janet as a witness. Apparently his father had heard of his refusal of the offer of a better job elsewhere in the city, from a colleague in the firm that wanted him. Luke's father could not understand his son's reluctance to better himself, and began a lecture upon his lack of ambition. Ambition? Luke reflected that this career had never been his choice, it had just happened. He had drifted into it and somehow got caught up in the necessity to prove himself at every level.

It was time to clear the air and stop the parental ritual he normally endured.

"I am sorry father, I appreciate your concern, but it is my choice."

"The wrong choice. You are wasting a good opportunity."

"Look father, when will you remember this is my life? To be perfectly honest, I am fed up with your continual advice and interference."

"I am only trying to help you better yourself. You clearly need someone to point you in the right direction."

Luke raised his eyes to the ceiling and let out a deep sigh, refusing to be pressured. Then he looked at his father again, to find that the serious expression had not changed.

"They have recognized your ability. You could learn a lot more. It would be a mistake to turn them down."

"Then it will be my mistake. I can live with that, it's no big deal. What is all the fuss about? One job is much like another."

"I don't understand your attitude."

"Father, for the last time this is none of your business. I refuse to discuss it any further."

His father went off in a huff, leaving Janet to store all the information in her memory for future use against him, although he had no doubt it would not take long for her to relay all the details later to Robin, and with great relish. He expected some comment, but she went sweetly on about her task in the kitchen, humming a tune to herself as she finished putting everything away and even offering to make him a cup of coffee. Janet was being far too nice altogether. He looked at her sceptically.

"Have you given up the idea of this youth hostelling holiday?" he asked.

"Not yet."

Her perky little smile betraying a secret ploy was matched by a scowl from Luke. What was she up to? He could only let it ride until for the moment.

He decided to phone Mrs Mathews again, just in case Clare had put in an appearance.

"Hello Mrs Mathews. This is Luke. Do you know if Clare is coming down this weekend?"

"Luke? - Clare? You wanted Clare? Clare is here," answered a confused voice.

"Clare is there? Could I speak to her please?"

"Er - yes, I'll fetch her."

He heard the receiver being laid down and her voice calling Clare. A muffled exchange of words and then, "Hello," came her cheerful response. "How are you?"

"I am fine. I tried to phone you last week. I left several messages on your answering machine."

"Oh, I haven't been back to the flat yet. I've been down at the coast on and off during the past two weeks, occasionally escaping from the awful hotel they booked us in to come up here overnight instead," she confessed brightly, the innocence genuine, he could tell.

Luke pulled a face. If she had been here at times during the week, why hadn't her mother told her about his call? It was very strange. Mrs Mathews had always been so reliable, according to mother. Never mind, he decided, he was speaking to Clare now. Then again Mrs Mathews could have been too occupied dealing with Emma's tantrums. No doubt, like his sister, she was still trying to obtain permission for their holiday.

"What did you want?"

The question caught him off guard.

"Are you here for the weekend? The cup of tea is still on offer."

She laughed. "It will have to be another time, unless you want to come to Ben's cottage later. You can make me a cup there, while I try to decide on the best photographs for an exhibition."

Ben had given her his spare key, so she could mull them over while he was off out somewhere, she explained.

"See you there later then."

Luke sauntered around to Ben's cottage. When he could get no answer at the front door, he went around to the back, where he could hear her singing to herself inside the studio. Luke called out before he entered, so as not to startle her and once inside he found her studying piles of pictures scattered over several tables.

"Good, you can help me," she murmured, beckoning him to join her.

There were photographs of every size, from which she attempted to find the best, moving some to one row and then taking them away again, chuckling at some, turning them this way and that, considering them and then discarding one or another. Clare showing him the occasional one for comment whilst he simply stood there pretending to look at the pictures.

"Ben said you were at the same art college."

"Yes, but I studied exhibition design. It was a good choice, it takes me all over the place these days."

He had come here to talk, but so far he had said very little, not that she had appeared to notice, as her fingers drummed absently in time with the background music.

Then Clare made him turn his back for a moment, telling him she had a surprise to show him, it was one of Ben's most treasured pictures in his collection. He heard the rustle of paper as she rummaged in a folder and turned around when he was bid to view a large black and white portrait now propped up against the wall.

He had not known what to expect, but it was never this. It rendered him speechless. It was of Clare, her hair longer and pulled loosely back over her shoulders, with little wisps softening her face and long tendrils trailing about her neck. Dressed in a simple blouse and a long skirt, she stood framed under an arch. His eyes soaked up every inch of the picture. The image was breathtaking, magical. It had captured every detail of her skin, her hair, the finest fibre of the material. It was utterly stunning. It was one of the most romantic, evocative pictures he had ever seen. He could not stop looking at it and then back at her. Here with the reality of the light catching her features and her golden skin, it was an unbelievable sensation. Why hadn't Ben showed it to him before?

Clare chatted on, mentioning it had won some prize at college, while Luke nodded, fully understanding the reason why. He was still at a loss for words and the effect of the inspiring picture in front him did nothing to help. Walk away, he told himself, this is entirely foolish, stupid!

Luke never made the cup of tea he had promised.

Instead he hurried away as soon as he could justify his departure from her company, having forgotten everything he had originally intended to ask her. He made his way back through the village looking for some distraction, and fortunately found Robin and some others playing football on the green.

He eagerly joined in the impromptu match, the sheer energy and physical contact being an ideal requisite to drive everything else from his mind and clear his head. It had been ages since he had enjoyed a good old-fashioned kickabout, especially against his brother, who was on the opposing team. The wild scramble, with shouts and yells at each other, as they pushed and ran, tackled and passed, with all the normal unsporting antics left Luke breathless, panting and soon desperate for a brief rest. Clearly Robin was the fitter, since he was still skilfully in control of the ball. Although Luke's legs were getting heavier by the second, he was urged to chased Robin across the grass until he tripped over his own feet and fell over, glad of the chance to stop.

Waving his apologies he walked off the pitch to claim the role of spectator, whilst Robin continued the match, until eventually the game petered out and the players dispersed. Luke had been waiting around for his brother, so they could go home together for lunch, but Robin walked off ahead of him unwilling to share his company. Luke could not understand this odd attitude as he hurried after him.

"Hey, wait for me."

Robin did not look back, he continued striding on, except

his eyes were cast to the ground as if he had all the troubles of the world on his shoulders. Luke could not imagine what the problem was and having caught him up, he quietly kept pace with him until Robin's steps slowed as they got nearer home.

"I hear you and Liz are going to Rome soon," said Luke, attempting cheerfully to ease his mood.

Robin stopped and hesitated.

"Come on. What's wrong?"

"About Liz."

Luke waited.

"You don't mind?"

"Mind? For God's sake! Robin, that was a long time ago. You seem happy together. Are you?"

Robin nodded, but his expression remained glum.

"Then that is all that matters," Luke said encouragingly.

"You - you wouldn't tell Mum and Dad about where you met Liz? Where you both worked? Would you? I want them to like her," he eventually managed.

Was that all that was bothering his brother? Nothing serious then. Although not knowing the extent of Liz's revelations to his younger brother, Luke still had to be extremely diplomatic.

"Crumbs, Come on Robin! How could I do that without revealing my own decidedly disreputable involvement in that place. You know me better than that. I would never deliberately cause trouble for you, whoever you were seeing. I know when to tease in private and when to keep my tongue in company."

"Thanks," Robin responded, giving him a weak smile, content that this secret stayed between them.

"By the way, there was no need to be so defensive that other weekend about you two being together, I had already heard the news from another source," Luke confessed kindly.

"What I don't understand is how on earth you two met."

"That is simple, in the rain at a bus stop, in Eton."

"Eton?" Luke could not imagine what either of them were doing there.

Robin grinned. "We had both missed the bus and with a long wait ahead, we went for a coffee. She was easy to talk to. We make each other laugh."

"Do you mind if I ask what she is doing these days?"

"Liz is in hotel management. In Windsor. Quite an improvement of prospects since you knew each other."

Luke was impressed. Now it was out in the open, his brother showed signs of becoming totally at ease.

"And what about you? I imagine the restoration of historic homes is quite demanding."

"I'm still only a technical assistant. I just help organize the schedule and find the right craftsman. I enjoy it. Every building is different, with different problems. "

"I'm pleased."

Luke nudged him affectionately and they walked on home together. Dirty and exhausted, they both trudged into the just-cleaned kitchen to a hail of complaints from his mother. Then, clean and changed, Luke strolled downstairs, to find Janet waiting on the bottom step, still smiling and then dancing around him, bursting with news.

"Emma is going to ask her sister to come with us on holiday and see if that will make a difference to all the objections," she beamed, her smile a mile wide.

Lucian cleared his throat. Personally he could not see the Clare he thought he knew agreeing.

"Mmm. All I advise is that you don't get too excited. She may turn you down yet. Besides, who in their right mind would want to play nursemaid to your unruly lot is beyond me."

Janet ignored his comment, refusing to believe their expectations might still be scuppered. No wonder she was so happy all of a sudden, although he had to admit, their parents' main argument was on shaky ground if Clare did volunteer to go with them.

He left her to her fantasies and went to answer the phone. It was Ben, back at the cottage. He was excited at what Clare had prepared for the exhibition and begged Luke to come over and share in the appraisal. Luke tried to excuse himself, explaining that he had called in earlier and it had looked fine then. Unfortunately Ben was not taking no for an answer, and after some more persuading, Luke found himself returning to the cottage.

"I am so lucky. Clare's agency is interested in sponsoring an exhibition at a London gallery," Ben beamed, enthusiastically grabbing Luke by the arm and dragging him into the studio, which had been transformed since this morning. Everything was neat and tidy, the photographs were lined in sections with the discarded ones in boxes on the floor. Ben praised the content of the layout and selection.

"Clare has a great talent for picking out a balance of different subjects, don't you think?" he said.

"If you say so. You're the artistic one, not me," Luke mumbled.

Luke was all too aware of the very scene earlier as she sorted the pictures in front of him, a scene he had tried to dislodge from his mind. As if that were not enough to torment him, Ben headed for the folder propped against the bench and Luke knew he was about to endure that breathtaking black and white picture of Clare for a second time. With great flourish, Ben swept it from its wrapping and leant it against the wall, exactly where it had been placed earlier.

"Stunning, isn't it? It is going to be one of the centrepieces," Ben reflected, staring wistfully at the picture. How could Luke avoid the overwhelming haunting attraction which caught him afresh? It made him speechless once more.

"It captures everything, doesn't it? The perfect image of romance. It was the picture which won me my first national competition and decided me on my career."

Unable to ignore its beauty, Luke was stuck there for an hour, making all the right encouraging noises about Ben's opportunity and lingering over a drink, to keep up the pretence of everything being normal, while he felt quite exhausted by the whole experience.

When at last he trudged home, he had not expected to be met by a jubilant Janet, who threw herself at him, hugging him profusely again and again. Luke felt tired, what now, his brain whirled. What had he done to warrant this attention? The answer seemed to be - nothing.

"Emma's sister is going to come with us. Now we'll get our parent's consent."

"There is still no point in jumping the gun, the matter not quite a fait accompli, yet," he warned.

Janet did not care what he said, she was simply delighted their plans were coming to fruition.

Luke felt more than disappointed in this latest development. It was hard to believe it had only taken a few hours for Emma to persuade Clare to spend her holiday with them. The only reason he could find for such a sudden decision was the obvious sisterly concern to ensure their safety. If he had had the energy, he would have been almost tempted to go and wish her good luck. She deserved a medal if it was true.

Later that evening, as he vegged out on the settee and watched the television with the rest of the family, he could not be unaware of his mother fidgeting around him, trying to catch his attention without the others noticing. Yawning, he stretched himself and headed for the kitchen, following his mother, who disappeared in front of him. Puzzled, he found himself dragged to the table for another conference about Janet, who apparently was determined to pursue her plans.

"Mrs Mathews came around before tea. Have you heard the latest? Emma's sister has offered to go with them, which squashes most of our arguments immediately. What do we do?"

"Are you sure this is not just a little fabrication on someone's part, to change your minds about letting them go?" said Luke.

"Janet would not lie so blatantly. Do you think it isn't true?" his mother mumbled, a little stunned.

"I can't believe anyone in their right mind would take on such a responsibility. Not even if she felt she was doing it for the right reason, to give you and Mrs Mathews some peace of mind. To attempt to control the unbridled enthusiasm of a group of young headstrong girls abroad would test any one's sanity."

His mother looked as if she was giving this a lot more thought, presumably deliberating the impossibility of Emma's sister being able to keep an eye on them all. The whole situation was taking a different slant, it seemed.

"If only she would change their minds instead of encouraging them. Is that why you wanted to talk to her last week? Mrs Mathews was surprised you knew her older daughter. That was very kind of you dear."

Diplomatically Luke remained quietly at the table, while his mother continued to debate various theories to herself. His only concern came when she stopped deliberating and took his hand between hers, a sure sign of something difficult about to surface. He waited, unable to anticipate where this was leading.

"Would you talk to Emma's sister for us? I know she is home this weekend. Would you please, please find out if she is intending to go with them or not?" She paused. "And if she is, try to make her change her mind."

"Are you joking? Oh, No. No chance," he gushed quickly. Make her change her mind, how? It was bad enough arguing with his own sister, let alone anyone else's. Why didn't Mrs Mathews talk to her own daughter? It couldn't be that hard, his own mother certainly had no difficulty in trying to manipulate her own children, especially him, he professed. His mother tut tutted.

"Why doesn't my father have words with them instead?" he suggested. His mother looked horrified. He didn't have the patience or manner to handle this correctly. Her head tilted slightly as she looked knowingly at him. He was going to lose, he could feel it.

"Lucian, you have such tact and a charming manner when you want. Why shouldn't she listen to you?"

"Why should she?"

"If all else failed, I am sure you could use those mischievous flirting skills I hear so much about."

"Mother!"

"Why Lucian, you haven't inherited your grandfather's good looks for nothing."

He blushed, he knew he did, a grown man embarrassed by his mother. Who had she been listening to? She made him sound like a cross between Romeo and Casanova. For God's sake, he wasn't like that!

"Why do you think Liz still likes you? Why do they all like you?" she asked.

Luke shook his head. Instinctively he knew all the sweet talking in the world wasn't going to work on this modern, independent woman. Whatever he said or however nice he was to her, there would be no twisting Clare around his little finger.

"Please try," his mother pleaded.

He looked at his dear mother. How could he refuse? He promised he would try his best, but he could not work miracles.

Luke spent a restless night trying to think this out, wondering how he could broach the subject and test out how much of Janet's story was true. He would just have to play it by ear as he went along. The problem was that a certain picture kept drifting into his mind and confusing the issue. He found himself unable to reconcile all the conflicting aspects of Clare's spunky personality with the softness of that picture Ben had taken.

Sunday breakfast over, he looked at the clock. Best get it over and done with, he decided. He made a phone call and headed out of the door without letting on what he was up to. He was sure this wasn't going to work anyway, even somewhere private and on neutral territory would not make much difference to the difficult assignment.

Anxiously he waited at the pub, sitting at one of the benches on the front green, looking up and down the road for her. Not many minutes passed before she breezed along the road and threw herself down opposite him, resting her elbows on the table and with her chin resting cupped in her hands, she looked him straight in the eye.

"Is this instead of making me a cup of tea?" she joked.

This was not going to be easy; in fact it was impossible

to start. If only those pretty features were not so pretty, those eyes not so expressive, her too distinctive hair not so spiky and her bright smile so good at undermining his ability to keep a grip on the subject. He dropped his glance to study the wooden table top, to avoid the distraction, only to be faced with that awful pink handbag. He took a deep breath. It was now or never.

"I heard there is a new development in Susan's and Emma's holiday plans," he began, trying to sound casual.

"They never give up, do they?" She laughed.

Luke felt himself bristle, surprised at her somewhat flippant attitude and to make it worse, she was still smiling at him.

"They are growing up so quickly. Travelling always broadens the mind. It will be a good experience for them. Besides, now they have a chaperon to look after them, that should be less of a worry for the parents," she added.

So it was true, she was going with them. He had to admire the responsibility she was taking on. She was just what they needed, a modern confident, assertive woman and too feisty altogether. Too feisty for him to bother with his original intention of asking her not to go with the youngsters that seemed like a total waste of breath.

"I am surprised that anyone would volunteer to escort them," he muttered.

"Is this all you want to talk about? I just came here for a pleasant drink, not a debate."

Luke went to the bar and returned with the drinks, reluctant to continue. This was not going the way he wanted, but he could not let his mother down.

"I'm concerned about the whole scheme," he told her seriously.

"Lighten up Luke, it's a lovely sunny day. There must be more pleasant things to talk about."

"It's important."

"Goodness, you are being over protective. Europe will be a great learning curve. They have to become independent some time. Just be grateful they only wanted to go to Europe and not off around the world," she teased, sipping her drink.

"No doubt your own glamorous European experiences have influenced the decision," he told her bluntly.

"What? Now just hold on. My experiences? You are blaming me for their holiday plans!"

"They clearly admire you," came his sarcastic remark, before he could stop himself.

"Maybe. I don't know. It doesn't matter. At least they will learn a thing or two about tolerance and understanding. A quality you seem to be sadly lacking, no doubt because you are stuck in your mundane job in the city," she retaliated, quite prepared to trade insult for insult.

Lucian drew breath, aware that they were attracting some attention. He had not handled this well. What could he do to defuse the situation?

"Their manipulation to win parental approval for their madcap scheme has been quite brilliant," he said. "I didn't think they could do it."

"Are you accusing me of having a hand in that as well?" A steel tone edged her lowered words.

"I did not say that," he added quietly.

"No, but you implied it. Heavens! I think you have a nerve to criticize anyone. You should be grateful that someone is prepared to take care of them on this trip. Who else has volunteered to go with them?"

"If they had not been encouraged, they might have found something less adventurous to do with their summer. And we would not have been put through this turmoil."

"I didn't come here for an inquisition." She swore quietly under her breath, deliberately loud enough for anyone to hear.

He glared menacingly at her and Clare, equally defiant, stared back. This continued until, deciding she had had enough, Clare got up and stepped away from the bench. He got up to go after her, but thought better of it as she turned and squared up to him.

"You're a bully. I know you threatened Janet," she snarled at him.

"To stop her ruining the birthday party!"

Why was he explaining? She was the one who should be explaining her actions to him.

"And you are too... too annoying and unreasonable to talk to," he snapped back at her, but it was too late to take it back now. So much for his decision to avoid the public indignation of verbal abuse.

"Me, unreasonable! You're a fine one to talk."

Then Ben suddenly intervened from nowhere. "Hey, what is going on?"

"Ask your friend," came her seething reply.

Luke attempted to block her departure, but she warned

him decisively to get out of her way. She refused to listen to any more of his insane conjectures. At this, Luke threw his arms up in a gesture of pure frustration. He gave in and stepped aside, defeated as she walked off. As he had anticipated Clare was not the type of woman to be intimidated or influenced by him. If Clare had made up her mind to do this, then nothing on this earth was going to change it.

His mother had been quite understanding over his failure concerning Emma's sister and even began to accept the youngster's plans with good grace. Meanwhile Luke returned to London and easily slipped back into the familiar routine of not going home on the weekends. Luke did not ask after Clare; there was no point, she was out of his life even before she had become part of it. If he wanted more, he had lost his chance. The only person who remained highly amused at the situation was his best friend Ben.

It was a month later when Luke received a sudden summons from his grandfather insisting he came to France immediately. He had a proposition, if he was interested. Luke could hardly wait to get there, as he remembered affectionately every childhood holiday spent on his grandfather's farm. The journey made him impatient and anxious, while the French countryside drew him closer and closer to its heart.

Luke stood with his grandfather and his neighbour Bernard looking over the parcel of land which formed a triangle between their two properties. The small farm was for sale and if they could combine the three plots and reorganize the field structure to make it more productive, it would be to their benefit. The prospect of a co-operative scheme indicated a much better future for them all, they explained.

"Are you absolutely sure you want to do this?" said his grandfather. "It's a big step. I don't want you to regret this a few months down the line."

Luke smiled a wide smile and sighed contentedly. Yes, now he knew, all his savings had been for this. He did not want anything else. He had never been so sure of anything. It was so right. This was exactly what he had wanted, his previous unacknowledged dream; just to stand and look around, to believe it could belong to him. That he could own it. He had never dared hope this opportunity would appear. A shiver of inner satisfaction filled him and lifted his spirits beyond belief.

It would take everything he had, scraping together all he could, selling the flat and its contents. It was an immense financial commitment to take on, but Luke did not hesitate. Although the challenge ahead would have been daunting to any sensible man, instead Luke felt regenerated, as if a great weight had been lifted off his shoulders.

"Are you prepared to give up that rewarding life in London? It will mean living here permanently and sharing the work load," his grandfather emphasized.

Luke was smiling even more. France was to be his home. He had never felt so - so alive. The decision was easy. The small rural community, its surroundings and this place were all part of him. Every year he loved renewing all the acquaintances in the village, chatting and sharing his time with the locals.

Bernard nudged his old friend.

"I think you have your answer. Look at his face."

Luke returned to London bursting with excitement and desperate to share the momentous news. His passion might have surfaced late, but now it filled him, stirred him, as nothing else ever had. He had never felt so happy and so refreshed.

He phoned Ben and then his mother. Ben showed little surprise and told him it was about time too, while his perceptive mother, confessed he should have realized where he really belonged from the times he used to enjoy working in the fields alongside the itinerant labourers who appeared every summer at his grandfather's farm. How was it mothers were so astute? Well, his was.

"Why didn't you mention the idea before?" he asked her.

"Lucian, you were not ready. You had to work it out for yourself."

She laughed and made him promise to come home soon to tell her everything in detail.

Buoyed up by his plans, Luke could hardly wait to get everything moving and sorted. His flat was already on the market. He could easily survive the daily drudge of getting to the office for the annoying six weeks' notice he was obliged to give, especially when his ultimate goal was so tantalizingly within reach. He cancelled his gym membership and ducked out of all other social invitations, set himself a minimum budget to survive on and began counting the days. In his limited spare moments, he cleared all his unwanted clutter and took it to the nearest charity shop. He sold most of his CD's to one of the market stalls, and despite the flat looking quite sparse, the whole process felt therapeutic.

The only slight pause in his excitement came when Robin phoned out of the blue, wanting to call in at the flat, since he and Liz were going to a show in town. Instinctively Luke saw the possible awkwardness this could present, since he did not know how much Liz might have told her brother of her time spent living here with him. He tried to avoid their visit by offering to take them for a meal instead, but they had some romantic restaurant booked for after the theatre, leaving him little choice except to agree.

They arrived arm in arm like any young lovers, the familiarity between them relaxed and uninhibited, with Robin's face declaring his happiness more than any words could express. The pale-skinned blond boy had an unmistakable air of confidence. He had matured, and Robin's lazy, amicable demeanour confirmed the development in their relationship.

"I hear you are going to France," Robin chirped.

"I hear you are going to Rome," Luke replied, with equal encouragement.

While Luke found something for them to drink, Robin joked briefly on his new minimalistic style in the flat and the apparently frugal living arrangements.

"It is no sacrifice. I cannot wait to escape London," Luke commented.

"I doubt father will be happy about your news."

"I don't even want to think about it."

Robin did not pursue the matter, quickly turning to focus on the evening ahead and enthusing over the other West End shows on currently. Liz in contrast was a little quieter. Having idly gazed at the décor, she gave Luke the occasional curious, questioning glance in respect of some of his favourite items and other various missing pieces.

Robin soon checked his watch and waved the tickets at Liz, indicating that they should make a move. Luckily Luke's apprehension had proved unnecessary, and no awkward remarks had been voiced. It was only when she was leaving that Liz whispered that she hated to see the flat almost empty. She gave him a light, friendly kiss on the cheek and told him she wished him well, only to have Robin gently scold her for still flirting with his brother as they made their way to the door. At which they both laughed.

Luke could not believe the bond of trust they had displayed. He phoned his mother to relate this latest development, only for her to astonish him further by revealing, rather reluctantly, their intention to live together. So although they had been an unlikely couple to begin with, their commitment to each other seemed pretty secure.

Luke's remaining frantic days at the office were over. The last few boxes of unwanted items had gone out for the dustbin collection, the keys of the flat were in the hands of the estate agents and the transfer of his money to his intended destination had been dealt with. Luke reflected that, that was that then. He was about to start a new way of life.

With all his worldly goods crammed into two holdalls, Luke headed home to relate the full details of this dramatic move to France to his mother, since she had begged him so eloquently to do so more than once. Sure enough, the moment he arrived she whisked him into the kitchen, their usual place of conference, for a lengthy chat. She was eager to know everything and had already scolded her father, his grandfather, for not warning her what they were both up to. So there over a cup of tea and a biscuit, he slowly explained what had happened and their plans.

The adjoining farm, bordering both his grandfather's farm and the Bernard farm, had come on to the market. Luke had put an offer in on it, and it was now his. The papers had been signed and the ownership transfer had been completed. The three of them had gone into partnership as a co-operative, with the intention of combining the fields. For the moment they would use the existing outbuildings, but since it was practical for Luke to share his grandfather's farmhouse, the other farmhouse would be left empty with the possibility of converting it later to a holiday home for more income. Every word was bringing Luke closer in his mind to the actual moment he would be there. He could have gone on and on, but there was no need; his mother's continuing benevolent smile reflected the pleasure she felt for him. Having her support meant a great deal.

As he expected, his father had been impatient to talk to him. Here it comes, Luke sighed as the onslaught began, his father asking him exactly why he had quit his very highly-paid job in the city. He was furious. Why, his father demanded at full volume, had he thrown away a highly important position?

"I told you last time. It was not important to me."
Luke took a deep breath and began to put his case very distinctly. He was tired of his father expecting him to do something he was not cut out for. It was simple enough: he was going to France, to farm. His father refused to believe it, it was a ridiculous turn of events, in his opinion. "The carefree holidays where you played on the farm, generally getting dirty and having fun, is no basis for thinking you can turn your hand to farming," he thundered.

Luke reflected. He acknowledged his childhood had been a wonderfully happy time, the time he had enjoyed the most, with Lucy, a neighbour, and his childhood friend. He had climbed the trees and the ladders, rolled down the hay and chased the chickens, made fortifications out of the packing cases and ridden on the large farm horse which pulled the carts over the fields. That welcoming, friendly atmosphere still encompassed the whole place today and with her father Bernard and his grandfather as his mentors, Luke knew what could be achieved.

"I have two experts on hand to make sure it does not fail," he said.

Farming, there was little profit in that, he father stuttered, desperate to make him see sense.

Luke smiled and repeated his previous declaration, that he was going to France, to farm. Nothing was going to change his mind.

His father looked his son up and down, obviously convinced that Luke was completely mad. Then with his preliminary outburst over, he paced the room back and forth, desperate to find further inspirational arguments to air. Surprisingly, none were forthcoming. He poured himself a stiff drink before plonking himself down in his armchair, seemingly incapable of further attempts to attack Luke's plans. Luke did not really expect this to be the last he heard on the matter from his father, but appreciating the temporary lull, he made a welcome escape from the house while he could.

Having heard via the local paper shop that Ben had returned from his latest photo assignment, Luke set off to Ben's cottage to bend his ear by expounding the various possibilities for his own future plans. His intention was countered by Ben's ability to tease him about the high-profile life he was abandoning in London and all the social benefits he was leaving. Their lengthy banter continued over a drink and ended with Ben reminding Luke that he had to be back in time for the photographic exhibition in London next month. Luke promised and suggested he even might drag his grandfather across with him. It would be nice to have him visit them for a change.

Luke had barely sauntered in from the village when his mother casually mentioned that he had just missed Mrs Mathews, who had called in to update her on their daughter's progress over a cup of tea. Apparently their chaperone, Mrs Mathew's eldest daughter, sent regular reports on their travels and all was going well, much to everyone's relief.

"She showed me the beautiful brooch Clare had given her. It is silver filigree…"

"With a circle of pearls," he sighed, finishing the description for her.

"Why yes, how did you know?"

"Because it was the one I intended to buy for your birthday, but she beat me to it." The disappointment was heavy in his voice.

"Never mind dear. I love the one you did buy," she murmured soothingly.

"I don't understand. I thought Clare intended to give it to her aunt. I wonder why she gave it to her mother?"

"Clare did not give it to her mother. Clare gave it to her aunt."

"You are confusing me."

"I don't know why, when Clare is Mrs Mathew's niece."

His mouth dropped open as the words struck home. Clare was Mrs Mathew's niece? Oh God. How did he manage to get that so wrong?

"I thought Clare was Emma's sister. Mrs Mathew's daughter," he said, his voice drying up.

"What on earth made you think that?"

The pink handbag had made him think that. The affectionate scolding of Emma had made him think that. Her defence of Emma's plans had made him think that. Nothing had indicated anything different.

"I saw her with Emma. Their banter certainly indicated sisterly teasing. Oh, mother! I thought Clare had been responsible for encouraging Janet and her friends to go to Europe. When I met her to tackle her about their plans, I assumed she was the sister because she made it clear she supported their trip. We had a very heated argument and we did not part well."

"Oh Lucian! No wonder Clare complained of your intolerable behaviour to her aunt. I thought it strange at the time."

"So who is Emma's sister?"

"Jane. I don't think you have ever met her. Mind you, she is the same age as Clare and they do share a flat and work together sometimes. I can see how you might have made the mistake. Oh, this is so funny. I must phone Mrs Mathews immediately." She laughed heartily and headed for the phone.

Luke did not think it funny at all. He was still taking it in. Clare was not Emma's sister, not all the things he had thought. He was angry with himself for the mistake. He had spoken too rashly, and there were no excuses. Every angry word returned to haunt him. He had alienated her because she had defended their spirit of adventure. She had been merely admiring a characteristic she valued. He now saw her in a different light; she was bright and funny, refreshingly different, enjoying the world and everything in it. She had accused him of being stuck in a rut at the time; well she had that right, he sadly acknowledged. He could not imagine how badly she still thought of him, if she thought of him at all.

This latest news had certainly put a dampener on his day. He went out to clear his head, but it was not that easy. What else had he got wrong about her?

Impatiently he waited for Ben to drag himself back from the pub, to tell him all about the mistake he had made over Clare. Ben's response was typical. He thought it highly amusing; the explanation for their alienation was a classic, and one Ben meant to taunt him with for the inexhaustible future. This was not the response Luke wanted, and he walked out into the courtyard to lean over the stone wall and stare into the water by the bridge, Ben following him.

"I don't like making mistakes," Luke admitted.

"That is why you are so good at your job. But they are business factors you can control. People are another kettle of fish. If you want to apologize to her, she will be in London this week. I have a meeting with her at the gallery."

Luke scuffed at the dirt with the toe of his shoe and began picking up small stones and throwing them into the quiet ripples. He didn't think that was a viable proposition. He doubted that this independent, astute female would let him within speaking distance to apologize in person, whatever the location. Public humiliation was not something he was used to and to be honest he did not particularly want to face an angry and indignant woman who had every right to rebuke him.

"It was your fault I made the mistake I did. You said Clare had one younger sister," said Luke.

"But I didn't say it was Emma, did I? Clare's sister Anne lives in America, with their father. You simply did not ask the right questions."

Luke had not known what the right questions were. He pouted, flicking another pebble into the water. Ben laughed again. It was not the first time Luke had made a complete fool of himself. Ben repeated the old adage that he should have known better than to jump to conclusions. But what other conclusions could he have come to, considering the information he had been presented with?

By the sound of his voice, it seemed to Ben that Luke was giving up before he had started. Which was a pity, in his opinion.

He walked back from Ben's cottage by instinct, without noticing where he walked or who he might have passed on the way. He had to sort this out, to think, to put things into place. He had been so occupied with France recently that he had not thought too much about her, and now all he could think of was that glare of hate at their last meeting. He still had the number for the flat, which Clare and Emma's sister shared on a scrap of paper folded in his wallet. It would be safer to phone. He would take that chance. Would she be in? Would she speak to him? Well, here goes.

The dialling tone rang briefly, and Clare actually answered. He could not believe his luck and before she could hang up, he gushed his apology over and over. She had not cut him off yet. At least she was listening to him, which was a relief, since it allowed him to slow his garbled words down to make a little more sense.

"Ben has just explained it all. He thought it was very funny. I do not," she told him firmly.

What! Well that was damned quick, he did not expect

69

his so-called best friend to be so hot off the mark. Luke felt betrayed. How friendly were the pair of them?

"I am sorry for everything I said," he told her. "I thought you were Emma's sister. You seemed so keen on them travelling. It was easy to assume you were."

"You assume too much. I travel a lot. I believe it has never done me any harm. In fact most people enjoy it." Her terse reply almost stopping him from continuing.

"I am sorry. Please - can you forgive my stupid comments?"

The silence was difficult to define as he waited tensely, expecting the angry ear-bending derision he was owed from such a feisty modern woman. He heard her sigh; she did not answer his question.

"Is that is all?" she asked.

Then, as if assuming that was the end of it, she simply and casually hung up on him, leaving Luke confused by her obvious indifference. He had got off too lightly. It did not feel right. There was no understanding some females.

Needless to say, Luke decided not to visit the gallery with Ben; he saw no reason to receive the same dismissive treatment from Clare a second time. Philosophically, he doubted if they would ever be friends after this, and besides it was way too late to dwell on what might have been when his whole future lay elsewhere. A future he had longed for.

Once in France, Luke soon settled into his grandfather's home. It felt as natural as if he had always lived there. His smart casual clothes hung in the vast spacious wardrobes, the solid traditional furniture a reminder of the past. He loved every inch of the vast stone farmhouse. It was so wonderfully different from everything he had left behind. Likewise his days were completely different from his previous existence. The stress of battling the city bustle, the rush and noise and crowds, were forgotten. Here he looked forward to each new day; he woke and was up with the sun. He could hardly wait to be outside doing something. He was impatient to embrace his new life.

"Slow down, my boy. You cannot rush nature," his grandfather would tell him over breakfast.

There was so much to do, but although it was logically impossible to have everything ready by next year, the three of them managed to grub out most of the old hedges and plough some of the smaller fields into larger, more economical ones. Of course driving the tractor had been harder than Luke had imagined, but he soon mastered the knack of its temperamental controls and engine.

"You can't expect it all to be done in a day," his grandfather reminded him, taking the tractor keys out of his hand and propelling him into a chair. Exhausted, he slept like a log, but always woke eager to continue.

Luke naturally fell into the role of farmer. The endless days of hard work sat easily on him and he often finished the day simply leaning on a wall or over a gate, gazing at the view of the surrounding rolling farmland with satisfaction as the alterations slowly took shape. Even when there was little to do he walked the fields, simply taking in the pleasure it gave him. He never regretted the decision he had made.

He belonged here. It gave him a warm and comfortable feeling. Indeed he knew his life here would never be dull, rustic or predictable; besides having his grandfather and Bernard around, there was Lucy, Bernard's daughter, to keep him on his toes. At weekends the delightful Lucy came back from Paris to encourage their schemes.

Lucy! The sight of her here always brought the widest of grins. As youngsters growing up they had had a habit of always falling in with each other's plans, however silly. They had always considered themselves as part of one extended family, and they still breezed in and out of each other's homes just as they had always done, without formality or ceremony. Lucy, who made him laugh. Lucy, who knew him for what he was, the good and the bad; his past history, the relationships he had mastered in London, although she had become less than sympathetic over the recent years, no doubt bored by his lack of judgment. She had been the one person who scoffed at his self-doubts, informing him that any female in her right senses would prefer a contented, hard-working farmer to an unhappy London businessman.

It had taken every penny he had to buy the land, but they all knew they would need a new tractor to plough the larger fields next year. None of them liked taking out loans from the bank, so Luke was keen to find any extra work in the village to aid their funds. He was willing to spend every spare moment he had tackling anything. He became one of the labourers helping to restore the village hall, learning about roofing and guttering as he went along, scrambling up and down ladders and over the tiles. Once that had been completed, he found himself co-opted onto other village projects, which gradually expanded his knowledge and furthered his friendships with more of the inhabitants.

In addition to this, Gus the mechanic, another old childhood friend, had managed to enroll him as a paid assistant for two extracurricular classes at the village school, no doubt because he had his own children there. The first involved helping the students improve their English and the second found him, for some unknown reason, running up and down the sports field trying to keep control of the children playing rugby. How he had been roped into this he could not remember, but it had resulted in an instant acquaintance with most of the village children, which was not a bad thing, he decided. He quite liked their habit of waving to him on their way to school or sometimes running up the lane later to ask questions as he worked on the farm.

Then out of nowhere he was offered part-time and holiday relief bar work at the local hotel, although he had weakly protested that he was out of practice, having only done bar work to boost his income when he first went to London.

"At least you will be safer working here than in that dive of a night spot where Liz worked," Lucy quipped.

"As a waitress," he said, quoting the official version Liz preferred.

"As a hostess."

"And part-time singer," he added.

"A very diplomatic definition! Which must have suited you both," Lucy mused wickedly.

Luke had no regrets. Liz had been great fun. Besides having confided his every personal detail to Lucy over the years, there was little point in making any excuses about any of his relationships.

As Gus gave Luke a lift home one afternoon, they saw two children rushing down the centre of the road towards them, wildly waving their arms.

"Lucian! Lucian! Monsieur Daney!" they both shouted at the same time.

The children looked hot and almost out of breath.

"Melanie lost her hat. She is in the river."

Having no idea exactly what they meant, the two men abandoned the car to race on foot to the river bank. True enough, there she was, her shoes and socks lying on the grass, while she had paddled out into a shallow patch of the river, to grab at her hat. Before she could bend down to reach it, the current swept it away into the deeper and faster water. Not to be put off, she was back off the pebbles in an instant and chasing it along the river bank towards the broken little wooden jetty ahead.

Luke could see immediately what she intended to do and yelled at her to stop. Not that she did; she skipped along the rotten planks as light as a feather and stood on one of the posts at the end, watching for her hat, oblivious of the danger.

"What are you doing to do?" Gus yelled, grabbing Luke's arm as he started after her.

"What do you think? The river is deep there. She could fall in."

Luke carefully tiptoed along the outside frame of the old rotting jetty, determined to keep his balance by grabbing at the overhanging tree branches to help him.

"Melanie. Don't you dare move," He growled at her on his approach.

"I don't need your help. I can swim" she pouted indignantly.

"Not in this part of the river you don't. The currents are too strong." By now he had gingerly reached one of the other posts, fully aware of the creaking warnings of the rotten wood he had crossed, which promised to give way at any moment.

"And not in your school uniform," he added as he made a grab for her arm and pulled her towards him. A plank splintered under their combined weight, and sweeping her off her feet under his arm, he made a run for it, grabbing at the branches with his other hand, whilst the whole frame began to sink beneath them. A few feet from the shore, the branch broke and he made a desperate jump. He managed to throw Melanie forward onto land, while he hit the water and the splintered wood. He scrambled up the bank, soaked through and his arm ripped by the woodwork, to face an unrepentant Melanie staring at him.

"I did not need rescuing!" Melanie declared.

Luke glared at her, aware that this was all the thanks he was going to get.

"Are you all right?" Gus enquired, more concerned about Luke than Melanie, who did not have a scratch on her. Luke shrugged. He would be once he was out of these wet clothes and his grandfather had seen to his arm. There was no serious harm done, although he would like to shake Melanie until her teeth rattled for her stupidity.

"There was no need to make such a fuss," she insisted to both of them.

"Oh, no? Of course not! The jetty has merely fallen into the river and been swept away. Just as you would have been," Luke replied sternly.

By now Melanie's schoolfriends had joined the scene, having gathered up her socks and shoes, and stood perplexed looking at Luke in his sorry state.

"What happened?" one of them asked him.

"Never mind, I am taking you all home now. I think we have had enough excitement for one day," said Gus. "And in particular I want to talk to Melanie's mother," he added meaningfully, glaring at the child.

"Is Melanie in trouble?"

"What do you think?"

The others giggled.

"I didn't ask you to play the hero," Melanie told Luke. She was fully aware of what was in store for her when she was delivered home. Apart from the scolding and punishment from her mother, she had lost her school hat. That would be another punishment from their teacher. She was sure she could have reached her hat if Lucian had not interfered.

"And I could think of quite a few reasons why I wish I hadn't," he retaliated, holding his aching arm.

Luke squelched his way home, while the others

disappeared in the van. It seemed that Melanie was getting to be exactly like his sister, he concluded. Heaven help them all.

There was something comforting about the familiarity of being accepted into the local community. Luke felt so content here that he almost did not want to go back to London for Ben's exhibition, but he had promised and his grandfather was looking forward to travelling with him to visit the rest of the family. The other consolation was that Luke would have a few days at home to try to finish bringing his old motorbike back to full working order. He also had a box of books he wanted to bring back, not that it looked as if he would get much chance to read them the way he had his life organized at the moment. Not that he minded; he was quite happy with the way things were going.

CHAPTER 3

Luke returned with his grandfather from France for Ben's opening, both of them staying with Lucian's parents for the duration. And whilst his grandfather preferred to come up to town for the last day of the show, Luke had agreed to go up early.

Luke had arranged to arrive in the afternoon for the private viewing before the main evening event and he found Ben in a flap, walking around and around nervously wondering if everything was really in the best place. Luke could not fail to be impressed by the Knightsbridge gallery, from the modern etched glass panels of the entrance doors to the topiary-shaped shrubs at the entrance, the shining marble floor and the large coloured slabs setting the photographs into sections. Added to which, the reception desk was hosted by some very immaculate smart-suited personnel, reflecting the status of the gallery, also further confirmed by the other equally efficient staff who stood by to distribute drinks, nibbles and brochures as required.

The location was perfect. It was bound to attract the best clientele, and was so professionally organized.

"How did you manage it?" he asked Ben in admiration.

"Clare, of course. Once the gallery had agreed to show my work, her expertise took over. She has all the right contacts. She even arranged an item on the local TV and radio news."

Clare was responsible for all this! Luke was learning more about her every day, and he knew enough about the business world to realize that she must have used some real influential clout to have brought this off so successfully. Once again, it seemed he had underestimated the ability which went with that extraordinary personality. He had expected her name to crop up eventually, but he refused to show any obvious interest and intended to pass it off as best he could.

"No doubt they will be taking their commission out of any profit I make. Have you heard from her?"

Luke shook his head and shrugged philosophically. With Ben and Clare in touch so frequently, he thought Ben would have known the situation.

Luke stayed for the evening to give him moral support, although he kept an eye out for the other distinctive and so far elusive guest, with the intention of avoiding both her and her portrait. Gradually the foyer and gallery filled; people milled around the framed photographs, and several curious individuals were talking to Ben. Thankfully they were asking him the right questions and Ben was now in his element talking shop, and seemed to be managing fine. Luke preferred to watch and assess the assembled gathering as they wandered from picture to picture. There were some truly beautiful people about, as well as the seriously wealthy elite parading their cheque books and plastic, more interested in being seen in the right place than in the work on display. The gallery became a hub of chinking glasses and chatter and Luke, when required, became very adept at subtly ushering the invited guests around the gallery without encountering Clare's photograph. As the hours passed he could not help wondering when the prime architect for this this event would put in an appearance, but he resisted the trap of asking the obvious. More importantly, several magazine arts editors were genuinely requesting interviews with Ben, and the desk staff were carefully making appointments for next week.

The evening had not been unproductive for Luke either. He had easily noticed the tall brunette on the front desk and had on more than one occasion opened the door for her, for which she had smiled at him, enabling him to smile back. The frequent glance in his direction naturally led to him exchanging words with her and having lost none of his charm or talent, he almost secured a date for a drink after closing on the last day. He had left with a 'maybe', which pleased him.

By the end of the evening as Ben and Luke sat in the quiet, emptied halls and echoing gloom ready to let security lock up, Ben felt mentally exhausted by the whole experience. He had the rest of the week to endure, although thankfully it should be quieter now the opening night had passed. He sighed. It had been a success, and Luke promised to bring his parents and his grandfather to see Ben's work at the end of the week.

Luke returned on Friday to be met by a distraught Ben, who had been completely overwhelmed by the number of people who had found their way to the studio. Suddenly the flavour of the month, he had not been prepared for the instant recognition or the exposure. The aura of admiration frightened him. He was just a photographer. The gallery was hinting at the possibility of another exhibition, but he desperately wished for some common sense to prevail as they reached the last day.

Even as they talked, people were still calling into the gallery and of more interest to Luke, the brunette was still on the front desk. He was just about to go and talk to her when Clare breezed in through the front door. Clare! She looked better than ever, her hair now with bronze highlights amid a sophisticated short bob and wearing a fluid soft silk dress and jacket, the material sliding smoothly over her hips as her beautiful long legs balanced on pencil-thin high heels. It was no wonder he caught his breath while she slipped her designer briefcase in behind the reception desk and checked the messages before making her way to the gallery to mingle with other invited guests.

Heavens, he had never realized the impact the sight of her would have on him. All he knew was that he needed to avoid her, to get a grip on himself. Accordingly, at any sign of her coming in his direction, he pretended to study one of the pictures with total, absorbing interest. His strange behaviour had naturally been noticed by Ben, who rebuked his attitude as rudeness and instructed him to be pleasant. Who was Ben kidding? Pleasant? How? It was not just his choice. She had already judged him in the past and found him wanting.

"Don't be so stupid, she won't bite, go and talk to her," Ben instructed, forcing Luke towards her as he called her over. Detaching herself from one of the staff, she came to join them, making it too late for Luke to escape. She was everything he remembered, the long lashes around her delightful brown eyes, the perky small oval face, the soft, light voice and that becoming glimpse of a smile that lay on her lips. Let alone those damned provocative hips. How could he tactfully extradite himself from her company?

Surprisingly, she enquired how he was without any indication of any awkwardness between them.

"I am sorry about my mistake in the summer," he managed to offer.

"It's done and dusted, as they say."

"You mean it?"

"Of course. I soon saw the funny side afterwards. Life is full of mistakes. There is no point in dwelling on them. Life has too much to offer."

"Could we start again?" he asked, coming to his senses.

"Start what?" she teased, with an infectious grin.

"Being friends."

"I am not sure being friends with you is safe."

"Then can we at least not be enemies?"

"I might consider it."

He could tell she was still teasing him, but he had hoped for a better reaction, especially since she had obviously forgiven him ages ago. Even though he had not forgiven himself.

"Send me a postcard when you decide," he sighed.

"Oh Luke. What is the matter with you? Cheer up. Don't take life so seriously."

"Sorry. I just wanted to make sure things were patched up between us. I would hate to be in your bad books."

"Then I suppose I will have to reinstate you into my vast list of friends."

Luke offered his hand symbolically and they shook on the deal, the act making her laugh.

"You are looking well. Still as ruggedly handsome as ever I see," she chirped cheerfully.

"And you are as distinctive as ever," he purred with some satisfaction.

Clare tilted her head, giving a carefree toss of the new hairstyle and a slight raise of the eyebrows as the only acknowledgement of his rather vague compliment.

"Could I take you for a drink later, or a meal? To make amends for the mistake, while I am in town tonight?" he offered. He knew a nice Italian restaurant near-by.

"Honestly, there is no need."

Unfortunately, at this point they were interrupted. Luke felt a slap on the shoulder and a glass of wine was thrust into his hand by his father, who had just arrived with his mother and his grandfather. Indeed his grandfather, the old rogue, swept his arm under Clare's elbow and whisked her away to have her explain some of the pictures to him, despite knowing full well that Ben was the only authority on the subject matter in the place.

"There, that was not as difficult as you thought, was it?" Ben commented, nudging him.

Indeed Luke had been surprised at her ability to make him suddenly feel a whole lot better.

Somehow during the following hours Luke managed to exchange an occasional smile with Clare, while she attended to the other company on and off. It was encouraging enough for him to want to ask her again if she would have dinner with him tonight. Frustratingly, she was difficult to get alone, until finally he seized his chance to drag her away from the latest small group by making the excuse that she was wanted at the front desk. Escorting her aside, he quickly made his pitch.

"May I take you out for a meal after the exhibition closes tonight?"

"Honestly I can't tonight."

"A bistro then, a drink?" Luke offered unwilling to fail now.

She shook her head and sighed, without giving a reason. Common sense and his past experience of corporate functions, business lunches and wining and dining, had him wondering if she might have had enough of all that in the lead-up process and during the week of this exhibition. She might prefer something much simpler.

"Plain old fish and chips then, and a walk along the river, very refreshing at this time of year." he suggested brightly, feeling very pleased with the idea.

"Freezing, you mean. I am not as hardy as you," came her animated response. She pretended to shiver.

Luke had plenty of other suggestions waiting to be explored, but Clare stopped him in his tracks before he went any further.

"I am sorry Luke, but I do have a prior engagement. I am going to the theatre with Ben."

Luke stared at her as she turned away with a smile. If she was going out with Ben tonight, that meant a meal or a drink afterwards with him as well, and even if it was only as friends or in appreciation for her participation in this exhibition, Luke took the hint. His mission with Clare had failed, but in retrospect there was still the brunette at the front desk, whom he had chatted up at the beginning of the week. He could still enjoy a pleasant evening.

Except that when he asked, he now found himself blown out by her as well. She refused to even consider have a drink with him, which left him to reflect on his utter incomprehension of the female nature. So much for these sophisticated London women. It left him little choice; he would have to return home, with the rest of the family.

The next morning found Luke considering the prospect of trudging around to Ben's cottage to find out if he was back from London. Apart from maybe messing about with his old motor bike, he had nothing else planned for today until this evening, when everyone was going to the Autumn Dance at the village hall.

As he made his way to the door he was delayed by an impatient Janet, reminding him of his promise to take her out some time ago as a birthday treat since he would not be here on the actual day. She had chosen where she wanted to go and it was to go to Brighton today, she declared. Luke, however, was not in the mood to play congenial benefactor when it clashed with his own arrangements, or to honour a promise at such short notice. He refused, on the grounds that she could go to Brighton any time. Her further explanation of the college party tonight merely confirmed his aversion to the prospect:; endless thumping music, crowds and too much drink, had not been the civilized treat he had in mind. He told her she had no chance, however much she might persist. Janet sneered, muttered something and left him, to stomp upstairs to bang her bedroom door and put on some loud music as a protest. Luke ignored the display of pique, whilst his father came out of the front room and shouted upstairs for her to turn it down. It went quiet and Luke slipped out of the door before his father decided to have another discussion about his prospects.

Luke left for Ben's place; he might as well.

"Hello the house," he sang out, walking straight into the cottage just as he had always done if the front door was open.

"Hello yourself," came the unexpected female reply, as Clare stuck her head around the kitchen door. "Ben is off out with his trusty camera - you know Ben. I think he is trying to shake off the adrenaline rush of the last few days, to get back to normal. It's going to be hard. Now he has taken that irrevocable step into the limelight, it won't be easy to stay the same Ben we all know."

Clare! He followed her back into the kitchen and stood

watching her washing up the crockery in the fluffy bubbles. She looked perfectly comfortable, and her familiarity with the location of everything indicated her regular use of the place. That was not a good sign, he decided. The casual friendship between Clare and Ben began to look a lot more than just that. Although it really should not matter to him, should it? He had no right to feel this way. Why punish himself over an attraction which could never be within his grasp? She was not part of his life. She would never be part of his life. His life was in France. Dull common sense told him that hers would never be.

He enquired cautiously if they had enjoyed the theatre and whether they had both come down last night. Clare confirmed that the show was brilliant and to be recommended, if he had time to see it. As for the second question, she revealed they had come down at such a ridiculously early hour that she had crashed out in the spare room, rather than wake her aunt for a bed. So she had stayed the night here with Ben. The information did nothing for his tentative composure; rather it felt like a kick in the stomach. The silence of his conclusions from these observations was too obvious and made her turn her head.

"Are you put out by my being here?" she asked directly, before he could hide his expression.

"No."

"Liar," she said softly.

In truth he felt jealous of seeing her here in Ben's kitchen where she gave the impression of being as naturally at home as if she had always belonged there. A simple perfect mellow scene, so in keeping with the atmosphere created by that black and white portrait of her, could not be ignored. It was too easy to dream, to imagine her together with him like this in the French rustic farmhouse he owned. The other French farmhouse, which he had never intended to make into his home until this minute.

"I don't know why you should be."

"I am finding it hard not to wish you were in my kitchen instead."

She could not hide the appreciative smirk his comment brought, although she was quick to scupper his idyllic ideas.

"Don't get any wrong ideas about me. I am not the domestic type," she warned. "I do not intend to cook, sew or clean for any man. Been there, done that, a great mistake."

A deep inner sigh sank through Luke.

"How is France? Are you still happy there?" she asked.

"Definitely."

She threw him the tea towel, indicating that he could dry up. Now on safer ground, he went on to relate his argument with his sister and the horror of the wildly unsuitable event she had chosen. He could not see himself among a crowd of students, in a dark, smoky hall, jumping up and down to loud rock music. He wondered why Emma had not wanted to go with Janet, but any such remark could easily be taken as criticism, and he did not want to risk that.

Clare failed to suppress a giggle.

"Which part did you find so amusing? Me playing the heavy as a chaperone or being completely out of my depth with the music?"

"Neither. I'm waiting for the day you meet Jane, Emma's sister, my cousin. She will be home this weekend. You forget, you all owe her a great deal. After all she made sure the girls came back safe and sound."

He was hoping to avoid anything which put him on dangerous ground concerning any of her family. He did not want to think about Jane. It was not the past which bothered him, it was the present, the now. Here, with that female so close.

"Are you coming to the dance tonight, at the village hall?" he asked, quickly changing the topic.

"I expect so. Ben is playing in the band, isn't he? Will you be there?"

"I expect so," Luke answered, deliberately mimicking her phrase and making her laugh. That was a good sign, he decided, but before he could build on his advantage the tune on his mobile interrupted them.

He was still looking at her as he answered, but his concentration was soon fully focused on the panicking voice at the other end. It was his mother. He could not make out what she was trying to tell him at first, but it soon became obvious that his sister had gone off to Brighton on her own and by the note she had left, she planned to hitch hike. His father had already gone out, having taken his grandfather into town for lunch, and she could not reach him. She did not know what to do. They needed to find Janet.

He switched the mobile off. How could Janet be so destructively inconsiderate? He could kill her for doing this, worrying their mother in this way. If she had also done it deliberately to ruin his own plan to go to the village dance tonight, he would gladly wring her neck and still might, depending on how long it took to find her. Not that he had worried too much about going to the dance until a few minutes ago, but the prospect of Clare being there had made all the difference.

Nevertheless he had to find Janet, but how he was to do it was not so clear. No one had transport. His father had the family car, Ben was out in his two-seater and Robin's old thing had fallen to pieces beside the garage.

"Do you have your car here?" he asked Clare hopefully.

"No. I left it in London. We came down in Ben's."

The whole world was against him. What was he to do? He would have to get back home first.

"Will you save me a dance tonight?" came his parting request as he left.

"Several, if you like," she answered, smiling at him and making him stop briefly.

"Really?"

She nodded. Goodness, did she mean it? He wanted to say more, but he could not wait; he had to go.

Luke sprinted back to the house. The old motorbike in the shed was his only hope, although he had not finished its repairs. He almost gave up the moment he dragged it out; the throttle cable was stuck, and the thing would not start. He shook the cable, rubbed grease and oil on various parts and hoped. He tried to kick start it, again and again, skinning his ankle in the process and making him swear aloud, aware time was important. He finally revved the dusty machine into its full, deafening performance and realized he dared not switch it off in case he could not start the temperamental old crock again. He shot off, the wheels spinning on the gravel, heading for the main road. Surely she could not have gone too far? As long as he could find her before she reached the motorway. This new-found independence had a lot to answer for.

A few miles down the trunk road, he thankfully spotted Janet standing in a layby ahead in the typical student stance, her arm extended and thumb up, with a cardboard sign bearing the word 'BRIGHTON' printed in black felt marker held across her front as she faced the oncoming traffic. The traffic was light, Luke felt pleased to note, otherwise he might have missed her.

As he indicated to pull in, the gleaming vehicle in front of him suddenly turned into the space where she stood, to halt with the passenger door level with her. Horrified, he saw her bend down to the open window, her hand already reaching for the door handle. He had to stop this happening. Twisting hard on the throttle, he screamed past the car to skid to a halt in front of the sleek bonnet. The engine still running, he left the motor bike on its side, dashed towards her, yanked her back and slammed the partially-open door closed before she could step inside.

"What the devil are you doing here?" she yelled at him.

"Taking you home, before you get into more trouble than you can handle," he gulped in breathless snatches.

A burly man got out of the driving seat. From the way he stepped around the front of the car, he had every indication of being a good Samaritan and quite able to take care of himself. He was also clearly upset at the treatment of his immaculate car.

"Is he bothering you? Do you want me to phone the police?" he asked Janet, very pointedly lifting the mobile from his pocket.

The man sounded quite concerned, showing every intention of protecting this young girl from a dishevelled, scruffy motor bike yob. Luke shot a defiant glare at his sister. Here was her perfect opportunity to lie and make it very difficult for him, since he had no ID on him, nothing to prove who he was. Confrontation with this stranger was not the answer; he had to appeal to him. He stepped back, relaxed his shoulders and sighed.

"This is my sister Janet, who is too young to understand the dangers of hitch hiking to Brighton. My mother sent me after her, to fetch her home."

The scowl on Janet's face and her gritted teeth towards her brother fortunately confirmed Luke's statement. The man seemed to accept the explanation, but just to assure him completely Luke offered the man their home number, insisting he satisfied himself. The man nodded, got back in the car, pressed the digits and began talking, while an indignant Janet pouted and thumped Luke in the chest with every ounce of strength she could muster. The man in the car nodded that he was satisfied, reversed a fraction, tooted his horn, waved and drove off.

"I hate you!" she spat.

Luke merely smiled very insincerely at her. He was

quietly relieved that it had not been some young tearaway in a sports car who had stopped to pick her up and then given her a lift regardless of anything he might have said.

Eager to get home, Luke picked up the bike, the engine just about still ticking over, and told her to get on the back, which she refused. Neither of them had crash helmets, she argued, so they were breaking the law, and she would not ride pillion. Of course she was right. He had left in such a rush that he hadn't even given it a thought. He did not mention his lack of road tax or insurance either, but he was damned if he was going to push the bike all the way home. Police or not, he did not care if he got fined, he was so angry. He pulled her on and moved off with such a jerk that she instinctively grabbed him around the waist for safety.

The journey back began at full speed and Luke aimed for every rut and bump he could find, to punish Janet for being so naughty, until the engine spluttered, stalled and chugged slowly to a halt. The petrol gauge showed empty. Luke grimaced. He had not checked it before he left, so he coasted the bike as far as he could. His hand automatically delved into his pocket for his mobile to summons help and rummaged hopelessly. He was sure it had been in his pocket, but it wasn't there now. Either it had fallen out when he threw the bike to the ground, during the ride over those bumps, or he had dropped it by the shed when he was trying to start the bike. Just great! There were no petrol stations this side of the village, no way to contact roadside assistance, not that he had his card with him. He knew he could not risk leaving the bike. Despite its dilapidated performance and condition, he did not want it stolen.

Janet sat on the bank, indignant and refusing to suggest anything useful. He was left with no other option than to consider the very thing he had really, really not wanted to do. He ended up pushing the heavy machine homeward with his ungrateful sister in tow. It took ages, the machine getting heavier the further he had to push it, forcing more and more rest intervals. His arms, back and legs ached as he struggled on, determined to get home in good time, to recover and be at the village dance later.

At the first phone box, which allowed him another pause to get his breath back, he made Janet use her precious money to phone their mother to explain the delay. Then, taking over the phone and forcing some begrudged coins from his sullen sister, he found himself still unable to summon any local help.

Taking a deep breath, he set off on the last leg, with a complaining Janet trudging reluctantly behind. His muscles ached like crazy and her moaning in his ear every inch of the way made the idea of throttling her very, very tempting. They eventually reached the front drive, and leaving his mother to deal with Janet, he began the frustrating search of the shed area for his mobile phone. He had no luck. Clearly he had lost it. Then, dumping the bike back in the shed, he went to scrub the worst of the remaining oil and grease off.

Later, after everyone was home and had eaten together and were getting changed for the evening, Luke managed to tackle his grandfather concerning the lunch his father had

had with him today. Doubting his father's motives, since he had never come to terms with Luke's transition to European farmer, Luke suspected a hidden agenda.

To his utter surprise, it turned out that his father had offered to put some money into their venture, rather than pick holes in it. Luke was horrified. The farm was his dream, his life's ambition; the whole co-operative project was already in progressing well and in their own control. Luke immediately told his grandfather that he totally resented the idea. No way did he want his father becoming an investor, with the threat of him muscling in, criticizing their plans and demanding some participation in it.

"He is only interested in the profit he could make," Luke exclaimed wildly.

His grandfather patted him on the shoulder and smiled.

"You need not worry. It will never happen. You and I are too much alike. Why spoil a good team? Besides, I know exactly how much the land means to you."

Satisfied, Luke went to lock himself in the second bathroom, to have a long restful soak and ease his tired limbs. He heard the others leave in the car, his parents taking Janet with them, to keep an eye on her after the earlier episode. They were not waiting for him, since he had said he would make his own way there. The house was wonderfully quiet and he had the luxury of having the place to himself, so he took his time dressing and choosing his clothes before walking to the village hall. He was looking forward to this evening immensely.

Outside the village hall, the forecourt was decked in

strings of bright coloured lights, strung across from corner to corner, whilst inside everything was in full swing, including the local band beating out some good dance music. The place was packed, to the point that Luke could not see Clare at first, only to pick out her distinctive figure near the stage, engaged in some friendly banter with his grandfather. Her welcoming smile was encouraging. At least she was not dancing with anyone else yet.

"I thought you weren't coming," she said.

"Blame the bike," he grinned, knowing she would understand, having seen it. "I'll tell you about it later."

But he never did. It was unnecessary, because she seemed content with his company and not averse to staying by his side. What pleased him even more was the fact that she barely glanced at Ben, who was fully occupied on stage with the other members of the band. Luke asked her to dance and she agreed. His touch on her skin remained deliberately light and unassuming. As they stepped out around the floor, he discovered he had never enjoyed dancing so much, especially when his partner moved so elegantly in his arms, smiling all the while.

The surrounding couples, like themselves, came to a halt to wait for the next tune to begin, and the pause was just brief enough for his grandfather to whisk her away from his grasp and into the following waltz. Luke stared after them. What was his grandfather doing? He tried to claim her back, but she remained with him for two more dances after that, giving no indication of needing rescuing. She appeared perfectly happy in the old man's company. Drat it!

Then, just as he had hoped to sweep her back into his arms, the music stopped and the band took a break. The interval had begun and people were making for the buffet area. Luke was not going to risk missing another opportunity to have her to himself. Finding her amongst the queue between the tables, he took the plate from her hand, put it aside and dragged her into the entrance lobby.

"What is the matter? What are you doing?" she asked.

"Nothing is the matter. I... just want to talk somewhere a little more private."

He did not say any more. Surely she must have some idea what he had in mind. They had been getting on so well together.

"I wondered if there was any way we could see more of each other in the future."

"And how do you imagine that would be possible, with you permanently living in France these days?"

How could she be so practical?

"We could work something out. You are great fun to be with."

"I thank you for the compliment."

He waited for her to say more and raised one eyebrow questioningly, smiling and hoping.

"OK. Yes I enjoy your company as well," she conceded.

In that moment he really wanted to kiss her. In fact nothing was going to stop him, he decided, right or wrong. Before she realized what was happening, he bent his head and gently kissed her on the lips, a kiss which surely left her in no doubt as to how he felt about her. He did not have the right words; besides this demonstration surely made it unnecessary. Didn't it? She stared at him for a moment before pushing him back slightly from her. Luckily she did not appear too angry or upset.

"What was that for?"

"To prove you how much I like you," Luke grinned.

"Do you kiss every girl you like?"

He knew he should not answer that.

"Goodness Luke, such fanciful behaviour. Whatever are you thinking? We may like each other, but we cannot cultivate a relationship out of thin air."

He did not want to understand her objective opinion.

"Have you seen Janet?" a concerned voice asked from behind.

"Not now mother," he snapped, not taking his eyes from Clare's face.

He stood there, trying to think of something he could say to change her mind. Truthfully he had not thought past this moment, let alone the complications of trying to make it work after today. But he did know how he felt about her, especially with her this close.

"For goodness sake, go and find your sister," Clare instructed him very calmly.

Not this time. Someone else could find his damned sister!

His mother's agitated prowling continued and she peered out into the darkness. Together with Clare's repeated insistence, Luke was forced to concede. Damn his sister. As it was, it did not take long for Luke to find her.

She was on her own in the car park, lurking about in a very odd manner, and when she saw him coming she sat down on the wall. What was she up to? She gave him a silly sheepish grin, a look that told you she had been naughty. Her eyes were a little glazed, a fixed smile appeared for no reason and her head wobbled slightly from side to side, like a nodding dog. He bent down for closer examination and smelt the beer on her breath.

"Oh, Janet how much have you had?" he scolded quietly. It had obviously been too much.

He could not leave her like this and gently he pulled her to her feet, which was not an easy task since her legs were like jelly. Her attempted steps were very unsteady as he guided her across the car park. Then the inevitable reaction hit her. With her face turning as white as a sheet and a retching in her throat, he hurriedly pushed her head over the nearest waste bin. Unfortunately he was not quick enough to stop her managing to throw up over his sleeves as well. Yuk. He shook his head, while he supported the rest of her.

"Hello, looks like we definitely arrived at the wrong time." Robin's merry voice echoed in the cold air. Robin and Liz stood huddled together, their faces beaming. "Look," beamed Liz, waggling the engagement ring on her finger in front of him.

Wonderful! He congratulated them, and he did mean it. Although it was difficult having a proper conversation with them since Janet began to shake, and then gave another heave. Robin stepped forward to help Luke support her and the two men exchanged meaningful glances in recognition of their own past experiences.

"Liz, do me a favour," said Luke. "I can't go back in there like this. Would you ask dad for the car keys and tell him we are taking Janet home? Could you also find my jacket, please?"

Liz disappeared briefly and then returned waving the keys, his jacket under her arm and some damp paper towel from the toilets. Whilst Robin went to fetch the car, Liz slipped the jacket over his shoulders and then set to, wiping his shirt and Janet's face as best she could. As she finished, she stood up and to his surprise kissed Luke softly on the cheek. To thank him, she whispered, for his discretion in not telling Robin too much detail concerning their past together. They exchanged a smile and if his hands had been free he would have given her an extra hug of reassurance. She deserved to be happy - everyone did. The past is the past. Her happiness was never at risk from him.

They were full of news on the way back to the house. They had just flown into Gatwick, done a little shopping in London and caught the train down and a taxi here. They had been excited and desperate to surprise everyone, which would apparently have to wait until later since they were presently involved in assisting with the Janet problem.

Luke became even less sympathetic towards his sister when he discovered his missing mobile phone in her open bag on the floor of the car on the drive home. And once indoors he was certainly in no mood to take care of her. Ignoring her wretched state and the sight of her kneeling on the floor propped over the toilet, afraid to risk moving, he decided it served her right. Leaving her to her plight and quite willing for the others to take care of her for a while, Luke happily showered and changed and set off back to the village hall again.

He managed to park the parental vehicle back in the same space and hurried into the hall to look for Clare. He thought he would easily spot her, but he could not find her, and then his grandfather kindly informed him that she had left with Ben a short while ago. Damn, damn! She had probably thought he had deserted her and no wonder. He would have to go after her to explain.

"Are you sure you should?" his grandfather asked. She had left with Ben after all. Luke ignored the implication, dismissing it as easily as he had the nagging idea when it first crossed his mind, earlier in the day. He sprinted around to Mrs Mathews' cottage. If she was not there he was going to be a damned nuisance at Ben's place instead. He banged on the door hard and Clare opened it, almost immediately, as if half expecting him, and informed him, in a very harsh tone, that she did not want to talk to him and ordered him to go away. He refused, putting his foot in the doorway.

"Go away, or I'll call the police," she threatened.

"Fine, go ahead. I have already risked breaking the law several times today."

He shrugged, neither bothered by the idea nor expecting her to actually do it, at which she kicked his foot out of the way and closed the door in his face. He banged and banged the front door knocker to the point where it almost came loose in his hands, but he was not going to give up.

God knows what the neighbours thought. Several peered out and then closed the curtains, prepared to ignore the noise, while Clare stubbornly refused to answer the door again. Sod it! This was getting him nowhere, and it was beginning to rain. He had a choice; he could give up and go home, but that was not an option really. Or he could either stand out here in the rain getting drenched for ages.

Or risk trying the back door. The back door won, and skirting around the back of the rows of cottages, he climbed over the back wall and knocked the dustbin over as he dropped down, making a heck of a din as the lid rolled across the paved garden path to announce his arrival. The lights went on at the back, upstairs and down, here and on either side. He accepted the strong possibility of being arrested as an intruder, but then he heard the key being turned in the lock, which gave him hope.

But it was young Emma who opened the door. She posed deliberately provocatively in the door frame, purposely blocking him from crossing the threshold and enquiring over her shoulder, to Clare, if she should let him in.

"If it stops him disturbing the whole village, so some of us can get some sleep, you had better," came the comment from the other girl, who pushed past with a bundle of ironing in her arms. Luke did not wait for Clare to counter the instruction. He stepped quickly into the bright kitchen to find himself facing a trio of females.

"Let me introduce Emma's sister Jane," Clare volunteered, with a flourish.

Jane. Jane? He took a good look, because it instantly

registered that this was the very attractive female from the front desk at the gallery, the brunette, the one he had asked out for a drink. Jane gave him a tormenting smile of acknowledgement, her eyes dancing with mischief. He wondered if he was in trouble with her as well.

"Not who you expected?" Clare hissed sarcastically, stepping up to glare unflinchingly at him.

"Er - no," he managed.

"No!" she declared, turning on her heels and marching into the lounge. Aware that Jane and Emma were both eyeing him up and down, and making no move to join their cousin, Luke followed her, mainly because he did not know what else to do or say at this precise point. God, women were so confusing, especially this one.

"Whatever you want to say, make it quick and keep your voice down. My aunt is trying to sleep," she said.

He could hear Emma and Jane scuffling their feet in the hall, their sniggers and unintelligible whispers indicating they were both going to listen to every word. In the past he would have gone to close the door, but having attempted to display his affection for her once, the prospect of any more witnesses did not bother him.

"Why did you leave the dance? I tried to get back as quick as I could" he began.

"How was I supposed to know if you were coming back? You didn't bother to tell me."

"I know this evening was messed up..."

"Messed up? What a brilliant understatement. There you were being so very attentive one minute, then you abandon me half way through the evening? That was embarrassing."

"I'm sorry. I can explain."

"Explain? Why bother? Your past reputation obviously has not changed. You made me feel like a complete fool. You disappear to look for your sister, then one of your ex-girlfriends sneaks off with your jacket from the hall. I saw her put it so carefully around your shoulders outside, before she kissed you and whispered in your ear. What was I supposed to think? Chatting up Jane last week and Liz tonight. What does that indicate about your idea of friendship? Obviously not much at all!"

"You don't understand. Please, it was not what you think, you have it all wrong. It is all Janet's fault. Janet had just been sick over me in the car park. Liz was helping me. I needed my jacket. I went home to change with Liz and Robin, who then stayed to look after Janet."

"Well, I fail to see why the kiss and the intimate whisper were necessary. You didn't exactly fight her off."

"You're jealous!"

"Jealous? No. Annoyed, yes. Annoyed at you for your behaviour and annoyed with myself for thinking you would be any different."

Different from what, he briefly wondered.

"Rats on you," she declared. "Just tell me this. Was I just a casual fling to amuse you for a while until you went back to your home in France?"

Luke frowned, he was not pleased she thought that of him.

"I did not think you were like that. What cruel game are you playing, Luke?"

"I – am not playing any game," he protested.

"No?"

"We were getting on quite well. I hoped you would come to the farm for a holiday."

"That is not going to happen, any time soon."

She shook her head and remained silent, not even looking at him any more, and he realized there would be no point in pressing the point any further. It was very late and time to call it a day. Emma and Jane had long since given up and left the hall, too tired to listen any more. Matters had gone from bad to worse to indifferent, but he decided he was going to be sensible and come back tomorrow.

By mid-morning on the Sunday Luke had run out of chores to keep him occupied. It was no good; he could not wait any longer. He needed to find out where he stood with her. He sprinted around to Mrs Mathews' cottage, approached the front door and knocked gently this time, unwilling to upset the inhabitants again after last night.

He was a little apprehensive of how he would be received, but there was no reception committee waiting for him, no complaints and no sign of any of the others. Jane had gone off for the day, and Emma and her mother were out for a while. What a relief. At least they could talk privately. But she was looking sceptically at him, the condemnation written on her face.

"I can't imagine what you want," Clare sighed, leading him into the front room.

"To explain properly about what happened at the dance. You never gave me the chance last night. I had to go home to change after Janet had been sick over me. I came back immediately to find you. I am not the heel you think I am."

"Not so fast, mister. You are still very carefully avoiding the reason for Liz kissing you."

Luke screwed up his face, wondering how he was going to pass off Liz's gesture or the reason behind it, innocent as it was.

"Really Clare. That was Liz being Liz," he shrugged.

"Not good enough." She ignored his indication for her to sit.

"I don't know what you want me to say."

"Then this conversation is going no further. You might as well leave."

He was stumped. How was he to get out of this?

"OK, have it your way. She was merely thanking me for something."

"Go on."

"That is all I can say. I cannot betray a confidence."

"Does your loyalty extend to all your past girlfriends?"

"If they ask it, yes. In this case, definitely. There, are you satisfied?" Luke snapped.

He noticed her hesitate, apparently toying over the matter. He hoped she valued his discretion and his honesty. Luke was not going to lie, nor was he going to share the private details of Liz's past, or his own imperfect relationship with her.

"Don't get any strange ideas in your head. You're not off the hook yet," she murmured.

He threw the newspaper out of the armchair in front of him and sank into it

"Are we still friends? Do we stand a chance of becoming more than friends?"

Clare shook her head and seemed completely composed when she answered.

"I doubt it very much. Dear Luke, let us be honest. We might grow quite fond of each other, but no relationship is ever going to work. How could it, with you living in France and me in England?"

"It could," he blurted out, surprised by her frank observation. Logic was the last thing he had expected. And whilst he could not find the right words to argue in his favour, she seemed quite articulate at presenting her case.

"Besides, I have a career. A very good, exciting career. I do not share your dream. I am not the type to settle for the domesticity of rural life."

"But, but..."

"Why fool ourselves by pretending otherwise? A part-time meaningless affair, with both of us trying to make sacrifices, would never make either of us happy. Be sensible," she continued.

He gulped and stared at her. He had never expected to hear the unemotional truth put so bluntly. His grandfather had often commented on his inability to understand women, despite his attraction to them. Didn't this just prove him right?

"You are so aggravatingly beautiful. I meant to sweep you off your feet," he sighed, not knowing what else to say. He was putting this badly. He stopped.

"I am sure you did, Luke. I am flattered by your interest, but it is just as well you are going back to France to live your idyllic dream. We each have our own lives to live."

There was a long silence as they both looked at each other.

"I'm sorry, but there is little point in continuing this conversation," she said finally.

Luke was stunned. Reluctantly he walked to the door.

"I wish…"

"I wish it was different," she acknowledged, as she paused on the step beside him, before closing the door slowly.

Luke could not take it in. Naturally he retreated to Ben's, hoping for a sympathetic hearing. Ben told him bluntly that he was an idiot, because Clare had already been headhunted by an international company. Why should she sacrifice a marvellous career opportunity to kick her heels in the countryside for him? Luke did not find this reason for her rejection any easier to swallow and he refused to be cheered up despite every ploy his friend tried, including the news that he had been offered a show in Paris.

Luke tried to smile, tried to show some enthusiasm, but he was not in the mood for anything, nor was he in the mood later for the champagne celebrations that evening, to celebrate Robin's and Liz's engagement. Somehow he forced himself to manage some convincing false merriment so as not to spoil their happiness, although the late night spent listening to their excited future plans was torment and he could not help being envious of their devotion and loyalty.

His only comfort was the prospect of his escape to France tomorrow. Luke could not wait to get back to France. He needed to get back to the farm, to his other life.

CHAPTER 4

With the decision to put off the work on the spare farmhouse intended for the holiday rental market, Luke threw himself into the more important task of restoring the outbuildings and working the land with his grandfather and Bernard.

"No regrets?" his grandfather asked during a pause as they worked alongside each other.

"None," Luke beamed broadly.

"Are you sure Clare is out of your life?"

That was a question his grandfather had kept asking lately. Luke nodded. Although that niggling hollow pang of regret would stir itself at odd moments, realistically he had accepted that Clare would remain a 'might have been'. If things had been different... but they weren't, so what was the point of dwelling on it?

"I need not have worried then," the old man muttered, knocking some of the mud off his boots.

"Grandfather!"

"I could see the danger of you being seriously diverted by that pair of long legs rather than concentrating on the farm. Not that I would have blamed you." He smiled wickedly.

Luke gave a weak grin. Her career would always have been a problem between them. Besides Clare, admitted that she never wanted to be part of the hectic rural existence he loved. No, he was happy enough here with everything he had wanted and longed for for so long. At last their plans were coming into fruition, which was enough to keep him focused. Romance could wait.

Thank goodness he had Lucy around to keep him amused and distracted. With Lucy he could relax. He did not need to try to impress, be on his best behaviour or pretend; she already knew him for what he was, so he could be himself. A light-hearted tomfoolery always developed between them, ending with helpless laughter. Even recently when she strolled out to feed the chickens, she had tried to push Luke into the pond for no good reason. Luke naturally had given her a playful shove back, and unable to resist the temptation, he had grabbed the hosepipe trickling into the trough and turned it towards her. Within seconds a battle had developed as they fought for control of the hose, during which the force of the water bounced off the side of the metal trough to spray them both with a torrent of water. Her hair had tangled on her wet face and the water dripping from his own did not stop their tug of war. She had playfully screwed up her face at him and he had begun to pull her closer and closer, whilst she doggedly kept hold until they were only inches apart. Luke had found himself staring at her, his usual carefree mood gone. He had stepped back from her. Then Lucy had remembered the washing machine and dashed off.

"You should be more careful," his grandfather said sharply under his breath as Luke passed into the kitchen moments later to find a towel. Luke had failed to see the reason for this comment and presumed the older man had simply despaired of their childish behaviour.

With renewed energy Luke spent days laying out and digging over the proposed kitchen garden beside the spare farmhouse. He had it all planned, with soft fruit, fruit trees and all kinds of vegetables, his intention being to specialize in supplying quality stock to restaurants. It would take a few years to establish everything, but it would add to their diversity and their income.

Late autumn found Luke busy on the farm, as well as dashing into the village to help with the forthcoming annual village festival. After having spent most of the afternoon up a ladder with Gus the mechanic putting the loose slates in place and fixing new guttering pipes and brackets to the village hall roof, a tired Luke had dragged himself home for a relaxing soak in a bath after an exhausting day. He had the whole of the farmhouse and the evening to himself, since his grandfather and Bernard had gone off to the village to play cards. After a meal, he flicked off his shoes and collapsed on the settee to stretch out and enjoy the CDs he had set to play. He had worked hard today and he had no intention of moving now he was settled with his favourite chocolate bar at hand to sustain him for a while.

So he took no notice of the door opening or the clip-clop of the steps which entered the room, followed by the bag being tossed on the floor near the arm chair and the shoes beside it. Lucy peered over the top of the settee, told him he needed a shave and headed off to the kitchen, where he heard the kettle being filled and switched on.

"How come you are home from Paris early?" he yawned.

"Time off for good behaviour," she replied, returning just in time to see him stuffing a piece of chocolate into his mouth.

"How come you have got that all to yourself? You pig."

"Get your own," he attempted to say, with his mouth full. She naturally made to grab for the remaining bar, which Luke swiftly snatched out of her reach by the narrowest of margins, having anticipating her move.

"Spoilsport," she quipped, as the kettle boiled and she disappeared back into the kitchen. He heard the cupboard doors and drawers open and close, the clutter of things being moved.

"Where did this fruit come from?" she called out.

"I bought it lunchtime," he managed, before popping the last bit of chocolate into his mouth and successfully throwing the screwed-up wrapper over his feet into the bin by the fireplace.

"Why?"

Luke did not answer, hoping the fruit's presence would be hint enough. The cushion which came hurtling across the room to catch him in the middle of his chest, making him grunt, seemed to indicate that the message had well been understood.

"You expect me to bake a pie?"

"I just hoped," he muttered.

"I'll do it tomorrow."

Luke could almost taste her apple and blackberry pie. He hated to be disloyal, but her pastry was better than his mother's, and that was some admission. He always devoured her pies as if he hadn't eaten for days. They were so deliciously scrummy that he never left a crumb on the plate and the taste lingered in his mouth for ages. How he loved Lucy's baking - and so did half the village, since they had already requested some of her desserts for the forthcoming festival.

Lucy returned and pushed his feet off the end of the settee so she could sit down with her coffee, completely ignoring the vacant armchairs.

"Where's mine?" he yawned.

"Get your own, as you put it," she joked, nudging him playfully and deliberately clipping the top of his unruly hair.

He did not bother. He closed his eyes and yawned again; it had been a long day. He did not blink, did not move, and his eyes ached. He had some vague recollection of her enquiring how the preparations were going and when were they going to start on the farmhouse, but nothing else until his grandfather woke him some hours later. Lucy had left him to sleep and gone home, taking the fruit with her. He could hardly wait until tomorrow for the pie.

The next day Luke and his grandfather deliberately found chores which took them through Bernard's yard several times. The mouth-watering aroma from the kitchen was enough to keep them near the farmhouse in hope of a sneaky taste. Luke unloaded the timber posts from the truck to store them in one of the outbuildings, while the other two men found a similar excuse to stack the reclaimed stone blocks from the demolished walls into a neat pile at the side of the barn. But much to their disappointment Lucy seemed determined to torment them by continuing with her own routine and not letting them into the kitchen.

It was not until the evening that Lucy finally decided to stroll down the lane from her own home, with the pie. She entered the house just as Luke received a phone call out of the blue from an excited Ben. Ben had the date for his Paris exhibition and of course he wanted to make sure Luke would come. It would be in a few months' time, and since they had some catching up to do, he suggested Luke stayed in town for a couple of nights. That way Luke could act as his guide and they could explore some of the sights together.

"Of course," Luke agreed, in a hurry to end the conversation. "I wouldn't miss it."

His mind was firmly elsewhere. His eyes were following the pie through the house, anticipating the moment he could tuck into it. No wonder the village was in such awe of Lucy's culinary skills.

Lucy returned from the kitchen waving the bar of chocolate tied with a ribbon which Luke had left there for her as a reward. She had obviously overheard the conversation and was keen to see the exhibition as well, especially since she worked in Paris during the week. Immediately she made plans to meet Luke on that day. Not that Luke was going to refuse her company; it suddenly made the whole prospect much more appealing.

The village festival arrived, and early evening found him dashing down to the village hall to deliver Lucy's contribution before managing to get back to shower and change and collect Lucy for the evening dance itself. As she skipped out of the front door to join him, Luke realized he had never been aware how pretty she was. She looked utterly stunning. She gave him a twirl for his approval and he nodded his appreciation before gallantly opening the car door with a flourishing gesture, as seemed fitting.

With the attractive Lucy on his arm, Luke felt delighted by the whole event. He relaxed to the music and let the time drift by. He did not know how long they had danced together before he found himself aware of no other experience than just being with her. He had never held her so long or felt her in his arms like this. How could he never have noticed the texture of her hair and the smell of her perfume? The mellow tones of her voice melted into his head and softly echoed around the room - or did he imagine it?

At the half-time interval Luke headed for the men's room. He splashed cold water over his face and then leaned on the sink to stare at himself in the mirror. Did he look any different? He could not tell. When had this fondness for Lucy become more than friendship? What had made it happen? Had she laid her head on his shoulder too long? Had she relaxed into his chest too much? He felt swept away by a sensation which made him shiver involuntary.

He returned to the hall and his partner, determined to shake off this shock to the system. Her smiling face was tilted towards him as usual as they danced. He could feel her eyes fixed on his, and any words he had just dried up in his mouth. He was not handling this well. Her mouth was so tantalizingly close, her soft lips were silently tempting him. How he wanted to kiss her! Here with Lucy in his arms, he struggled to appear normal. He only hoped she couldn't she feel his heart pounding, it thumped so loud.

The remaining hours were strained, as the intensity of his feelings threatened his composure. He could not wait to take her home, yet as was the way at these functions, there were many locals to delay their departure. He stood by the car watching her chat to everyone, his pulse racing. She hugged him in appreciation for the evening as she eventually joined him, her face beaming with pleasure.

"I love you, Luke! You made me so happy this evening."

He mumbled back something about also enjoying the dance and her company, but he wanted this evening over. He wanted her safely out of the way and out of sight, otherwise he might make the mistake of saying he loved her too, although his words would not be in appreciation of their companionship, but sincerely, in the true sense. He could not give in to such ideas. Think of the consequences, he scolded himself.

Luke did not sleep well that night, as he tried to shake off the bizarre notion which dominated his mind. He could not ruin their unique relationship. He must not let this happen. This was Lucy, they were friends, almost family. They still breezed in and out of each other's homes just as they had always done, without formality or ceremony. Ever since they had been youngsters growing up, they had had a habit of falling in with each other's plans, however silly, but that had to change. The village dance had altered everything. He gulped. God, the village would lynch him if they suspected his attraction to this precious woman!

Luke spent the next morning working in the vegetable plot, eager for anything to keep himself busy and stop himself thinking. But the weekend always brought her into life one way or another, and today was no exception. She passed by with the milk and the newspapers, waving out to him and thanking him again for last night, her face still beaming. He nodded, returned the casual wave and continued his digging. The only relief to his silent agony was the knowledge that she would be back in Paris tomorrow, giving him a whole week to conquer this madness.

Although Luke should have known a week was never going to be long enough, it soon passed without him having resolved anything. Luke had always looked forward to Lucy coming home at weekends. Now he suddenly dreaded the weekends, dreaded having to fend off those innocent little touches. He felt physically scared by the usual display of familiarity between them.

Lucy was quick to pick up on the change in him, and determined to have an answer to his sudden odd behaviour. Having eventually cornered him in the barn, she did not hesitate.

"I do not come home to be ignored," she declared, hitting him hard in the shoulder.

Luke did not flinch, he could endure any blows if it saved him having to explain. Grim-faced and tight-lipped, he refused to look her in the eye, knowing he had to remain silent.

"Oh, Lucian, tell me what is going on in that thick skull of yours." She had softened her approach to making him open up. She automatically reached out slowly to touch him, causing him to draw a long deep breath.

"Don't do this, Lucy!" he snapped, pushing her hand away. God, this was insane! He abruptly grabbed his jacket and informed her he was going for a walk.

True to form, Lucy simply followed him; she did not give up that easily. Something was wrong with him, and she could not understand why he was so miserable. Out of habit she attempted to slip her arm into his as they walked, but he refused to allow the familiar gesture. As a result they walked in silence, an awful nagging silence for him, idly picking their way through the autumn landscape and scuffing the crisp fallen leaves, until Luke stopped by one of the old wooden farm gates. Dejected, he leaned on it to look out across the rolling fields, attempting to watch the birds, the clouds, the sky, everything except the girl who had climbed on the gate beside him.

There together in the quiet of the afternoon, Lucy eventually broke the silence.

"What is wrong? Tell me," she whispered.

Luke stood like a statue, every muscle in his body tense, refusing to look at her, his jaw set, staring at the ground. How could he?

"Lucian, I can read a defence mechanism when I see it. Especially yours."

She jerked his chin to make him look at her. His eyes forced to look into her own dark deep brown eyes, the truth impossible to hide.

It escaped.

"I am in love with you."

"Oh dear, why now?" came her soft sympathetic voice, not surprised or horrified at his confession.

He shrugged, diverting his eyes once more.

"Poor Lucian, such bad timing."

"I know. I am trying to deal with it."

She leaned close and kissed him on the forehead, forgivingly, as if he were a child.

"Lucian, I gave up on you a long time ago. You are a muttonhead! I waited every year for you to come back as a child. I have waited every year since for you come to your senses. I only came home at weekends because of you. I was so fond of you. I thought you were the only one meant for me. All those wasted years, before I found the man I love. You left it too late," she murmured gently, in a whisper.

Dumbfounded, he gulped. All this time! How could he have been such a complete fool as not to have known how she felt about him before? How could he have missed the signs? She was the only female who knew how he thought, who knew and accepted his faults, his past history. Why on earth should she have loved him? What had he ever done to deserve her love?

Lucy had always been just... Lucy. She had always subconsciously been part of his life, but nothing more until recently. She had accused him once of never saying what he thought of her, since she had patiently put up with all his revelations over his other girlfriends and relationships over the years without complaint. He had nicknamed her 'lovely Lucy'. Well, 'lovely Lucy' had now put a huge crack in his contented little world.

"I can't bear it," he admitted, looking her straight in the face.

"You know anything more serious between us is out of the question."

"Of course I do. But - it is not that easy!"

"Then it is best I stay in Paris at the weekends for a while."

He nodded and she left him alone, totally alone to let out the deepest of sighs, to empty the breath right out of his lungs and lean exhausted on the gate.

As the weeks passed he did not know which was worse; seeing Lucy or not seeing her. He had certainly not been prepared for the effect her prolonged, deliberate absence made on him. She refused to come back at the weekends. Thus Luke worked out of habit, sullen and preferring his own company, often pushing himself into extremes of unnecessary hard labour, but he knew he was beaten; there was no way to ignore the obvious. The intensity of his feelings for her refused to lessen. Nothing helped. What a mess! Life was so complicated, what was he supposed to do? How was he to get through this? Weren't the continuity and the people half the reason he was here? And maybe subconsciously, because of her.

"That is the second time you have tried to put the milk into the kettle and water in the milk jug. I don't need to ask what is on your mind. I knew this would happen," his grandfather remarked. His kind face crinkled. No wonder the old man had told him to be careful recently; in his wisdom he had obviously seen the danger signs. Yet the whole idea had come as a complete eye-opener to Luke.

"I didn't see it coming. It just crept up on me."

"Lucian, it is just as well you recognized your feelings in time. It could have ended disastrously for everyone," his grandfather offered philosophically.

His father was still moaning regularly at Luke over the phone about his old motorbike and the clutter left in the shed at home. With a short lull in the farm work, Luke decided it was seemed the perfect excuse to see the family for a few days. If he could sort out all the paperwork for his motorbike, he could ride it back to France this time.

His mother was sitting at the kitchen table as usual, with her afternoon cup of tea and reading a magazine, when he returned from the garage.

"How is Lucy these days? You haven't mentioned her since you have been home. Nothing wrong, is there?"

"Why should there be?" he asked sharply.

She peered over the top of her glasses at him, raised her eyebrows and looked at him, until he was forced to turn away from her knowing expression. He did not really want to discuss the matter. He had come away to try to forget it for a while.

"You were always close, it's a wonder you never became more involved."

"Lucy isn't ever going to be another of my conquests, mother," he sighed, unsure of her implication.

"I never thought she would be, dear. She is too good for that."

Luke closed his eyes and shook his head, exhausted by the fight to put the whole issue at the back of his mind.

"Oh, Lucian! I despair of you."

Even his mother could see the signs! This was too much.

The bike was taxed, licensed and more importantly it had passed its MOT. He had sorted out all his old tools and packed them into the two large metal panniers at the rear. Everything he could find he took with him, even the bag of oily rags. He gave the old shed a final glance and set off.

The bike rattled and jolted its way off the ferry, through the port and the suburbs. Luke soon wound his way onto the open quieter roads, where the old thrill of the bike's throbbing energy quickly returned. He raced along, opening up the throttle, leaning hard into every bend, throwing the bike at every twist of the road, the wind tearing at his jacket. The speed and exhilaration were therapeutic, and the throaty sound of the engine and the vibration of its old frame had him more content than he had been for ages.

When he stopped for petrol, his arms and legs were throbbing, but it was a wonderful satisfying tiredness. This long journey was refreshing, exciting and the best tonic to ease his recent anguish. This was the answer, this other kind of indulgence would pull him through. He was winning the battle with himself. Every mile onwards made him more and more sure that however hard it was, he would bury his wretched, illogical feelings for Lucy. If he did not, Lucy might never come back to the farm and Bernard would miss seeing his daughter. And it would be his fault. It was inconceivable that his illogical hedonism should have such an unfair impact on others.

His grandfather was pleased to see him back so soon, although he reluctantly told him that Clare had phoned him earlier, wanting him to phone her back.

"The number is on the pad," he said.

Clare? Luke could not think why on earth she should phone, and instantly dismissed it as unimportant. He never did phone her back. Instead he immediately phoned Lucy to make sure their date for seeing the exhibition together was still on. It was. That was all that mattered.

Only a few weeks ago, with the man in Lucy's life still away, he would not have thought anything of innocently spending time with his childhood friend. Now he realized he had to be extra careful.

"We need to talk," he pleaded, slightly nervously. He had so much to say to her.

"Of course. After the exhibition," she replied softly.

Luke arrived in Paris, checked into the hotel, changed and made his way on a chilly November afternoon to Ben's second exhibition. The building had originally been one of those neoclassical-styled museums, with a huge portico and fluted columns and a mass of steps to the massive entrance door. A complete opposite to the modern London gallery, and quite daunting, almost oppressive, as if daring anyone but the serious connoisseur to enter.

He entered in search of Ben, but could not find him immediately. Instead he discovered someone else. There barely a few feet away, stood a very distinctive figure; Clare.

He stood dumbstruck. What the hell was she doing here? Why now? To be reminded of her was a jolt, and his heart sank. He looked her up and down. Her slim, tantalizing hips, her long legs, her bright dancing eyes, her bright perky smile and the toss of her head were exactly as he remembered. He could kill Ben! How dare he do this? Had he asked him to bring her back into his life? Had he asked him to interfere? Luke was angry - well more than angry, inside he was seething, but he took a deep breath and made an attempt to be polite.

"What a surprise. Are you here helping Ben with his exhibition?" he asked politely.

"Of course. Who else would he trust?" She advanced seductively, the movement of those long limbs almost hypnotizing him. She was now so close, too close, making him nervous to the point that he retreated backwards - very quickly. Heavens, where was Ben?

"Why didn't you answer my phone calls? I have been trying to contact you."

Luke made no excuse and did not counter with any polite conversation, because his only concern at that precise moment was the problem of how to prevent Lucy meeting Clare. This had every prospect of being a very awkward encounter for everyone. All he could think of was Lucy, seeing her here and getting the wrong impression.

"I wanted to ask your advice. I have been offered a job in France," she announced cheerfully.

He ignored the remark.

"What do you think?"

He did not want to think. Clare, delicious as she was, was not for him any more.

"I'm sorry, I can't stay to chat. I am meeting a friend," he said. Then he checked his watch and headed towards the door in quiet panic mode, his only concern at that precise moment being Lucy. Lovely Lucy, whom he would not hurt for the world, was due here any minute and Clare's presence here made him feel completely at a loss as he stood in the cold outside.

"I shall expect you in a smart suit, in Paris my escorts must be presentable," Lucy had informed him on the phone only yesterday. He had promised not to disgrace her, although he had not taken her request too seriously at the time, and how he wished his problems had remained as insignificant as that. Goodness knows what Lucy would think of this development.

He stood on the top of the steps under the grand columns of the front portico, waiting and fidgeting anxiously and watching the road below for a sign of her. A black limousine caught his attention as it glided almost silently to a halt at the bottom of the steps, the chauffeur stepping smartly around to open the passenger door for the elegant woman inside to alight. Yet elegant was not an adequate description for the unique and unmistakable class and style of Paris haute couture. This was Paris fashion at its very best, understated but oozing refinement, nothing else compared with the exquisiteness of Paris fashion, it stood out a mile. Then the captivating sight demonstrated her stunning lightness as the graceful steps tripped hurriedly up the steps, towards him. The smart dark hair flicked at the ends, fresh from some salon and the beautiful face with its dark lashes, now tilted questioningly at him hoping for some recognition.

"Lucy!"

"Who were you expecting?" she scolded, looking around to see if anyone else had arrived.

Luke could not find any more words. He could not stop staring at her; he had never seen this version of his friend before. The state of shock seemed to amuse her to the point that she was forced to take control of the moment. Placing her arm gently into his and turning him towards the entrance, she prompted him to escort her into this vast interior.

Once inside, she pause briefly. "My dear Lucian. This is Paris, this is my domain," she purred. Then, for no reason, she reached out and touched his face, tenderly tracing her finger down his cheek and across his mouth, stopping him from speaking. It almost stopped him from breathing. How could she do this to him in public? This slight, intimate gesture simply filled him with the feeling he had done his best to bury over the past month.

"Come on. Let the show begin," she whispered, guiding him into the hall. He had no idea what she meant, but as he wandered about with the most desirable woman in the building on his arm, he could see she was fully aware of the sensation she was causing. Like many others, he could not take his eyes off her, even though she was on his arm. Within seconds he found himself playing the silent, astonished escort, while she produced her own knowledgeable comments and observations on every photograph they encountered. Her evident understanding on many of the subjects left him struggling to find any adequate response, because the pictures faded into insignificance.

Luke did not understand what was happening, and only became aware of her purpose when he saw that they were heading directly towards Ben and Clare. He tried to divert her attention, to hang back, but she purposefully made for them, so that Luke had little choice except to start the introductions.

An enthusiastic Ben had scarcely exchanged a few words of greeting when Lucy turned to Clare and introduced herself in a perfectly friendly manner.

"Hello. You must be Clare. I have heard so much about you. About the brooch and the mistake of thinking you were Emma's sister."

Luke watched them both, while neither of them looked in his direction once.

"Now tell me. What happened to the pink handbag?" Lucy asked softly, as if in confidence to an old friend.

"I gave it to Emma in the end," Clare muttered, caught unawares by the direct question.

This was a Lucy Luke had never seen before. Far from being surprised by Clare's presence, she had instead quickly indicated that Luke had no secrets from her. Her subtle demonstration had subdued a normally assertive Clare on the spot.

Luke had barely drawn breath when Lucy turned her attention to the next task, mentioning the picture of Clare his grandfather had seen in London and the one Luke still seemed so intent on avoiding.

"Now show me, where is this infamous romantic portrait which drove Lucian to distraction?" she asked, sweeping her arms through Clare's and Ben's to propel them forward and leaving Luke to follow in their wake. Luke just wanted the floor to open up and swallow him. This could only lead to disaster, and he had a feeling that he would be the one to come off worst.

"So this is the romantic masterpiece which torments you?" she mused, glancing backwards towards him. She studied it hard, taking every detail. She nodded and accepted that it was very good before lowering her voice to Ben to express her only concern; whilst agreeing how clever it was to reproduce the image in black and white as a contrast to the original painting of Hughes's 'April Love', she said she still preferred the exquisite and emotional value of colour in the original Pre-Raphaelite work.

Luke slowly absorbed her innocent remarks. Surely it couldn't be true? Yet as he stood there, an astonished Ben complimented Lucy on her surprisingly keen artistic eye and confessed that she was right. He was not denying it.

The whole thing had been staged, and he admitted that it had taken ages to set up the correct detail and lighting to match the painting. They had been rumbled, and now Ben pleaded just too, too dramatically for her not to broadcast it too much.

The picture did not matter to Lucy, and she easily waved away the incident. But for Luke, the fact that this photograph was just a carefully-contrived copy of an existing painting had stunned him. It was difficult to accept. He had agonized over it, worshipped it, absorbed its every delicate detail ever since he had seen it. He had always imagined that there was part of the real Clare in that engaging portrait, and now the magic had been ruined. It really was only a piece of paper, and nothing more. The truth shook him even more than the performance Lucy had given, and he stood rooted to the spot, until Lucy gently put her finger under his dropped jaw to close it before moving on.

Lucy was firmly in control of the proceedings as she continued her tour and conversation with Ben, leaving Luke bewildered and standing like there a dummy. He did not even notice what had happened to Clare. He could only watch Lucy as she concluded her tour of the gallery, until she indicated she was leaving and he joined her at the exit, offering somewhat clumsily to take her for a coffee. She declined. She had to go on to another appointment, she told him, and the limousine arrived as if on cue the moment they went outside.

"What was that all about?" he asked as he escorted her to the car door.

"Lucian, work it out for yourself," she purred.

Then the car drove off out of sight, leaving him to stare after her, completely confused by Lucy's revelation and exactly what had actually happened. He went back into the museum, still bewildered, to find Ben waiting for him, while Clare thankfully had wandered off somewhere, probably as confused as himself.

"Wow!" exclaimed Ben, who appeared to be in mild awe of Lucy, "That was some female," he continued, waving his hand in front of him as if to cool his burnt fingers. "Now - just remind me again, who is she?"

"My neighbour. We are childhood friends. I have mentioned her before, lots of times," Luke said, still trying to see through the subtle display he had witnessed.

"Mmm I know – But she was very tactile, for a friend," Ben suggested.

"Rubbish. That was just Lucy being Lucy," Luke lied.

"Does she works in Paris?"

"During the week, as an editor for a Paris magazine."

"A Paris magazine or *The Paris* magazine? There is a difference. *The Paris* is an influential magazine. It adorns every coffee table of note, even London clientele. She must work for *The Paris* magazine. Who else but someone from that background would have been so knowledgeable?"

Luke shrugged.

"Don't tell me - you didn't realize? Luke, you dummy! She is fantastic."

Ben's admiration was obvious. And Luke could not blame him, especially after this last demonstration by Lucy.

"I am sorry for you," Ben added.

"Why?"

"Because with a woman used to such culture, I cannot see you ever managing to drag her away from Paris."

Brilliant! That was just what he wanted to hear - further innuendos. It would be no good protesting that they were really only friends after Lucy's clear signal to indicate the opposite. If only Ben knew the truth of the impossible situation. The place suddenly felt overpowering and unbearable. He had to escape and began to head for the cold outside, but a feisty female, clearly recovered from Lucy's spell, blocked his way. Clare was waiting to challenge him, with that daggers-drawn glare on her face.

"As handsome as ever and still displaying all the charismatic devilish charm the ladies love, I see. And now with enough nonchalant self-confidence to attract even the Parisian elite these days," she taunted sarcastically.

He did not even reply. Already mentally tired, he simply waited for her to finish. He did not care what she thought of him. It did not matter.

"A rural farmer indeed! Your life can't be as dull or as rustic as we'd all assumed," she continued.

"Have you finished?"

"No. Your transition into the French way of life has been miraculous. And in my opinion, despite her elegant sophistication and the silent warning that you are off limits, I don't see any evidence of future domestic bliss lasting too long between you two."

"First of all I don't need your opinion, and secondly why should you care?" Luke hissed.

She had drawn her own conclusions, and Luke was not about to correct her false assumptions. If she had the nerve to be jealous, it served her right. Having totally dismissed his previous overwhelming attachment to that damned haunting portrait in the gallery, this glaring assertive female before him now suffered the same dismissive fate.

"Care? who says I care. Why should I?"

"Why indeed?" he snapped.

Her dislike of him showed and in the brief silence as she struggled to find a suitably disparaging response, Luke turned his back and left. The quicker he could end this scene, the better.

He set off on a walk, a long walk. He wanted to be alone to work all of this out, but he could not. He eventually returned to the nearest coffee shop and sat staring into space, his mind trying to make sense of the previous few hours, the coffee getting cold in his cup. Besides everything else, Lucy's sophisticated performance bothered him enormously. He remembered how people had automatically parted in deference to let her view the pictures, and that she had been fully aware of the sensation she caused. Maybe Luke did not know her as well as he thought he had. Maybe her life in Paris was completely different. He felt really low, and stirred the cold coffee again without even considering drinking it.

Yet when he was joined at the table, he knew the woman

who drew her chair close to his and gave a satisfied sigh. It was the Lucy of old, in casual clothes, who borrowed his spoon to stir her coffee and tilted her head to claim his attention. He did not even ask how she had found him. Instead he asked her how long she had been interested in art and photography, when she had never given any clues of this other side to herself at home.

Lucy smiled into her coffee for a moment, before bending close and confessing she knew nothing about either. It was all a bluff. The arts editor, having had a preview yesterday, had helped her and told her what to say.

"Lucian, I am merely a cookery writer. It was all bravado. I could not do it again," she confessed in a whisper.

Which made Luke question the necessity for such a performance, since there was no one there she needed to impress, least of all a load of strangers, Ben or himself. Lucy laughed and shook her head. She had not set out to impress anyone.

"Then what on earth was today all about?"

"You haven't worked it out. Why should you? It started out as one thing and changed to another. Once the art editor mentioned Clare being there with Ben, his description matching your past vivid details too perfectly, I wanted to see her for myself. Lucian, she is decidedly distinctive."

"So were you."

"Not that you ever noticed me that way until recently, you philistine," she sighed.

Luke smiled weakly at the affectionate, forgiving and bewitching expression, which merely enhanced the utterly stunning creature she had become. She stretched out her hand across the table and intertwined her fingers in his.

"If only you had loved me half as much as those other girlfriends," she murmured close to his ear.

"Don't, this is hard enough."

She gave him a sympathetic smile and shook her finger at him before continuing.

"That damned portrait had a lot to answer for. Once I knew it was a copy of an original masterpiece I had to make you see the picture you fell in love with was false. True, it is an excellent picture technically, but the content was not a real interpretation of the actual person. It is posed, it is a lie. That is not Clare."

He suggested that the fact that he had confused the two made little difference any more, as neither were now important. It was part of his past he could easily forget. Her mischievous grin and her bright dancing eyes watched him and waited. Didn't she believe him?

"And finally I wanted to make her jealous. I wanted her to see what she had lost," Lucy confessed.

"Why would you do that? It is not as if I was interested anymore."

The rhetorical question remained unanswered and they both slumped into a tired silence. The comfortable silence of old had returned.

It was getting dark outside and the owner pointed to his watch, indicating that he wanted to lock up soon. Where had the time gone? Linking arms, they walked out into the cold night air, with Lucy snuggled up tight against his shoulder.

The familiarity felt comforting. Luke escorted her back to her well-appointed apartment, but declined to go up for a drink, consigning himself to returning to the hotel overnight.

The morning in Paris was wet, damp and dull, and Luke, not having slept much, was not in the mood to be sociable. With the three of them staying at the same hotel, there was no avoiding Clare completely and as he stared out of the hotel window over breakfast, he was fully aware of her doing exactly the same at the far end of the room.

"I suppose I am to blame for this," Ben mumbled, as he stopped on his way to join Clare.

"Not one of your better ideas," replied Luke.

Ben's glum repentant expression acknowledged his mistake. After getting over his admiration of Lucy, he had felt guilty for putting Clare through that experience. He had thought he had done the right thing in trying to bring Clare and Luke together again, and he had not expected yesterday afternoon to go so disastrously wrong.

Luke gave him a blank look and shrugged. He was not going to discuss it any further. He had already made up his mind to change his plans, and was catching the train home in a few hours. There was no point in hanging around, as everyone here was miserable except Lucy. Lovely Lucy! He had been such a fool where she was concerned.

Luke packed and paid his hotel bill at the front desk, his overnight bag at his feet as he checked the timetable for the trains.

"You are going then?" Clare asked from behind.

"It is for the best," he muttered.

"Ben was expecting you to spend some time together. For you to show him the city sights."

"A good tour bus will see him right. He will understand."

Close up, she looked as tired as he felt. Maybe she had not slept well either, but it was not his fault. Ben should not have invited her.

"Why did you come yesterday?" he asked.

He had expected her to be evasive, but on this occasion she astonished him by her frankness.

"To see you, of course. To see how you were doing. I thought we could get together and catch up over a meal or a drink."

He could not imagine why.

"You obviously did not feel the same. There was no hidden agenda, but I didn't expect you to rub my nose in it by flaunting your latest rich prize in my face," she stated calmly.

"Since I had no idea you would be there, that supposition seems invalid. Don't you agree?"

Why on earth was he arguing with her? He did not need to defend himself to her any more.

"Your friend made it perfectly obvious that you are well and truly spoken for. Or was that merely a ploy to shake off any unwanted past female baggage?" she retaliated.

Women! He was not even going to try to fathom how she came to that wild theory. He could feel himself getting tense, but he certainly had no intention of defending or explaining Lucy's actions to Clare. He took a deep breath and picked up his luggage.

"I hope you enjoy Paris," were his parting words. No smile, no sincerity, he just wanted to escape and go home.

"You're back early. I thought you intended to do some shopping while you were in Paris?" said his grandfather, noticing the lack of extra bags and parcels.

Luke made his excuses. He had not been in the right frame of mind; too many shops and too much choice.

"You didn't bother then?" the older man concluded.

If he hoped for further information, he was out of luck. Luke dumped his travel bag at the foot of the stairs, threw his jacket on the banister rail and disappeared into the kitchen to stare out at the yard, the outhouses and the fields beyond. Tomorrow he was going out on the motorbike.

Luke had spent two hours racing his machine around the concrete runways of the old disused airfield that Gus tested his vehicles on. Dirty but pleased with himself, he returned to find his grandfather pacing the kitchen.

"Your parents have just invited themselves for Christmas," his grandfather complained.

Neither of them had expected that. They had planned a peaceful Christmas, just pleasing themselves, lying in late, mooching about the house, eating when they wanted and sitting by the roaring fire with a book and a drink in the evening. Now they would have to be attentive and entertaining. They would have to get extra food in, with all the trimmings expected of a traditional English dinner.

"I hope mother is going to do the cooking," Luke muttered.

If they were to be here in person, they would have to adjust their choice of presents as well. They pulled a face at each other; they would have to put a revised shopping list together. The daunting task of beginning some proper Christmas shopping was something neither of them had anticipated. And it looked as if he would be the one designated to go back to Paris at some point to complete the task. Yuk!

Lucy phone him mid-week, bursting with excitement. She had to tell someone. He didn't mind did he? She was so happy, but all this had to stay a secret from her father and the man in her life. She wanted to surprise them both. Could he guess? She hoped to produce her own cookery book.

"I'm not surprised. Your editorials are brilliant," he told her.

Luke had bought a few copies of *The Paris* and read the considerable cookery section. It was full of fancy photographs; there were reviews of the finest restaurants, new eateries, recipes and a whole segment on various cooking techniques. He was genuinely pleased for her, as she deserved more recognition.

"I will let you know how it goes," she finished.

And she did; every few days she kept him updated on the progress. Her chief editor had been behind the suggestion. There had been lots of phone calls, as he demanded meetings with various publishers. The next phone call from Lucy reported that the negotiations with them seemed to be going nowhere. Her mentor was not satisfied with the vague intentions and lengthy delays. She sounded low. Another call to Luke, days later, had her sounding much better. She was in high spirits. Her boss had used his fast and over-persuasive selling technique to make them consider his suggestions seriously. He had made them realize what they would miss out on if they did not get in first. He warned them about other interested parties and expressed his surprise that no one had approached her before. Lucy paused, not wishing to boast, before admitting that her established expertise on *The Paris* had been the decisive factor.

"More episodes next week," she bubbled, finishing the call.

The phone rang in the hall. What was Lucy going to tell him next? His grandfather was getting quite suspicious about all these furtive calls. Except for once it was not Lucy, it was his mother greeting him with the news that Janet had invited herself for Christmas as well. Oh no! Luke hadn't had to deal with Janet for quite a while. No doubt she had by now honed her feminine wiles beyond his comprehension. Would he still have the knack to out-manoeuvre her little schemes, or would he even be able to recognize them? Goodness knows what she was up to these days. He hadn't realized how out of touch he had become.

His mobile on the hall table played its tune.

"Don't think you are going to enjoy Christmas, you rat. I am going to make you suffer," Janet snarled at him.

He held the phone away from his ear. What the hell was she so fired up about?

"I heard what happened at Ben's show. Clare went there so she might see you again. I can't imagine why she bothered. Emma told me how upset she was."

"This had nothing to do with you, Janet."

"I hope you feel guilty for making her totally miserable."

"You had better behave while you are here. I won't have you ruining everyone's holiday," he snapped, pressing the off button.

No, it was only his holiday she wanted to ruin. The holiday season was certainly looking bleaker by the minute. It would be manic, the house full of family and his younger sister set to reprimand and threaten him at every opportunity. Just what he needed. 'Thanks Janet', he mouthed at the phone.

In Paris the lights were decorating the big stores already, the merry baubles twinkling away in the windows, inviting even the most hardened passers-by to stop and gaze in wonder. Luke felt more relaxed as he lost himself in its magic, but with half a day gone, he had not got very far with his list. Of course a certain female's company and advice would have made the whole project much more enjoyable. He knew Lucy would be bound to be busy, but it would not hurt to ask. Yet when he phoned her office hoping to offer her lunch first as a bribe, he found she had gone to the airport. Which meant only one thing; the man in her life must be back in the country. That was that then, so Luke decided to abandon the shopping and headed for the nearest café instead.

There he sat stirring his coffee, munching a baguette and staring through the window, content to merely engage in the pastime of people-watching. Then suddenly one of the passing crowd caught his attention, forcing him to take a second look. He twisted his head to follow the hurrying figure. There was no mistaking her distinctive movements, despite the thick winter clothes she wore. It was Clare. Then she was gone. He shrugged; it had nothing to do with him.

He took out his list again and studied it, concentrating on where to go next. By the end of the afternoon he had several bags and felt quite pleased with himself as he headed back to the hotel where he had booked in for a couple of nights. In the past he would have begged the spare room at Lucy's flat to save money, but that was no longer an option.

That evening alone in his room, against his every intention to do otherwise, he found himself considering Janet's accusation. A week ago he had not given Clare any mind. Now it was Janet's's fault he was even thinking about her again. He could not believe that the same determined, practical, modern individual he remembered from their last conversation together had been upset. To make Clare miserable had not been his intention. It had been months since they had even spoken. How was he supposed to have reacted at meeting her again? What had he been expected to say? He had assumed nothing had changed, but he had never meant to deliberately hurt her feelings. Should he try to apologize or not? Would it make any difference?

Last night he had decided to leave it alone, but despite all the reasons to the contrary, here he was at the same hour, sitting in the same spot, prepared to wait in case he saw her again. He wandered to the door several times to look further down the street and then sit down again, gathering up his parcels which had fallen over every time he moved. He sat and waited and waited, for two hours, but there was no sign of her.

He gave it ten more minutes and then another ten, mentally arguing the stupidity of his actions every time he checked his watch. Eventually he accepted that the whole idea was useless. He had made the effort to do the right thing; that was good enough. He was going home, and put the whole matter out of his mind.

Back at the farmhouse, Luke could not help bestowing a weak half-hearted grin on his grandfather as the older man cheerfully checked the number of parcels Luke had acquired this time. The old man's delight was evident as he sorted out the items for the correct recipients and made several trips upstairs to stow them away in his various hiding places in his bedroom. His activities encouraged Luke to do likewise, yet with a lot less enthusiasm, he discovered, as he dumped the last into the bottom of his wardrobe.

A few days later, Bernard came bustling up the path, his face beaming from ear to ear and his eyes wide, eager to tell them the news. Chuckling and smiling, he was hardly able to keep himself still. He walked around and around, bursting to share his happiness. His relief and pleasure in having Anton home and safely back in France for the festive season was evident for anyone to see. Another family would be reunited for Christmas, and Luke could only guess at the overwhelming wealth of affection and utter contentment which would fill their house.

He did not expect the same here with his sister in attendance. He absolutely dreaded the day she would arrive. What excuses could he find to keep out of the way? If he had had more notice he might have been able to escape completely. He even considered offloading himself on Robin and Liz in in Italy, but that would not be fair; they did not need him interrupting their own little private sanctuary. He prowled the house trying to come up with some plan.

Then at the last minute, a miracle happened. He was delighted to hear that Janet and Emma were going skiing with Jane over the Christmas instead. He was reprieved.

With that problem out of the way, Luke relaxed, anticipating a very pleasant Christmas. Except there was one shaky moment to dent his expectations. During the normal exchange of banter between the Bernard neighbours during the festive season, Anton deliberately pulled Luke aside for a private word.

"I don't blame you for being in love with my wife, but you know what would happen if you overstepped the mark," Anton confided.

"As if I ever would!" Luke replied, firmly and very quickly.

He had been astonished that such a warning was necessary. He had known Anton for nearly as long as he had known Lucy. As children they had played rugby in opposing village teams. They had climbed trees together, swum in the river and generally enjoyed the rough and tumble of being boys. Because of their natural respect for each other he thought Anton would have known him better than to have spoken of this matter at all.

Anton nodded, accepting his assurance. He smiled, his face crinkling, obviously amused at the uncomfortable situation Luke had found himself in.

"I can only thank you for not falling in love with Lucy earlier. Otherwise I might not have stood a chance," Anton concluded in his usual lighthearted manner. Giving him a friendly nudge, he ushered Luke back to the others.

Luke sheepishly tried to accept the kind remark, but felt a little miffed and embarrassed that clearly Lucy kept no secrets from her husband, even the very delicate ones. He had hoped that 'lovely' Lucy had passed off his declaration without the need to mention it to anyone. Obviously not, and he did not blame Anton for wanting to make sure that any such fanciful inclinations remained squashed in the future. Luke sighed. No doubt he would have done the same if it had been the other way around.

Once the discussion was over, the topic was never mentioned again and Christmas turned out to be peaceful, pleasant and very enjoyable. Christmas Day found his parents happily pottering about the rambling farmhouse, both of them quite content to relax and sink into the old comfortable furniture and to snuggle up with the cushions, read and forget the hectic routine of their normal

Christmases at home. Cards and board games filled the hours before a cold meat, pickle and cheese supper. Boxing Day had Bernard, Lucy and Anton coming over in the afternoon to continue the festive mood. All of them were merrily chatting and of course discussing her book. Both of her men were so proud of her; the book had been ready for the Christmas market and they both had their signed copies to treasure. Then Gus and his family had called in for a couple of hours, to boost the already cheerful assembly. The children chased around and explored the large farmhouse while the adults sat, ate and toasted the coming year.

The New Year was a quiet period. There was not too much to do and Luke settled down to check over the accounts, double-checking everything and reviewing their incoming expenses and taxes. It was necessary to plan well ahead. Meanwhile the older men were overhauling all the machinery in the barns, and Lucy and Anton had returned to Paris. It was obvious none of them expected to see much of Lucy now her husband was home on leave.

It was a month later when she resumed her weekend visits.

"You have a visitor," his grandfather shouted from outside.

Yes, here was Lucy, tripping into the house as normal. How he loved her smile. You couldn't help but return it. Her eyes were wide and shining. Apparently the book launch had gone well, and she had had newspaper interviews published, in the city and locally, and even a live interview on the radio. Although she had naturally told her father and

Anton, she felt she had to come and tell him personally. She had never felt so happy; she wanted to hug everyone. Luke did not mind that at all as she swung him round and round.

"And what are your future plans, now you are a famous author?" he teased her kindly.

She had no idea, she was still revelling in this wonderful sensation. She was so animated that she could not keep still.

"Come on, I need to walk," she said. She grabbed Luke's arm and dragged him outside, where to his amusement he found that she was not capable of merely walking. She skipped every step of the way around their usual route, unable to contain the excitement she felt. The world was wonderful, the sky so blue, the sun so bright and the scenery so perfect today, she purred.

"Eventually I suppose I want my own small intimate restaurant, somewhere in the provinces. Somewhere in a pretty setting, overlooking a river or the countryside." She sighed dreamily as they leaned on the top gate. Then she shook her head and changed her mind.

"I am happy whatever happens. Maybe I don't need a dream," she said.

Luke looked affectionately at his friend. He could see how truly and wonderfully happy she was.

"And you? Is this enough for you?" she asked, turning to look at him.

"Who could not be happy with this? It is all I ever wanted. I am happy here, more than happy, thank you."

"You are a fool!" she scolded.

Luke was startled at her sudden remark.

"This lump of dirt," she continued, kicking the ground hard with her foot, "has a lot to answer for!"

He did not understand this. She had never been so seriously disparaging about the land before.

"Do you mind? This lump of dirt is my future."

"Yes I know, your wonderful obsession, your precious dream. I admire your commitment to have taken this on. And this farm may satisfy you at the moment, but will it be enough in the future? Isn't it time you considered more than the next few years? Once you have put all this into shape and established your routine through the seasons, what then? There is more to life than this. You need to put down proper roots. You need to grow."

Luke stared at her. He didn't like her words. He had plenty of time to think of his future, in the future. He did not want a lecture. But Lucy had not finished.

"It is time you saw beyond that pleasant comfort zone you cocooned yourself in. Besides the farm, what are you doing with your life these days?"

"I have enough to do, thank you."

"Helping Gus in his garage, tinkering with machinery and worked shifts at the village inn. Helping with the children in their after school activities. You are merely finding things to fill your days. You seem to have forgotten about romance. Lucian, do something before it is too late."

It was all right for her; she already shared a wonderful relationship with a man who had no sign of embarrassment or inhibition in his overwhelming display of affection for her. For no reason at all, Anton often simply swept Lucy effortlessly off her feet, slowly put her down and nuzzled her neck affectionately, their eyes never off each other. It was obvious the way they felt for each other.

Was he jealous? of course. What did she expect of him? It was not that easy.

"Stop playing at being a farmer," she said.

"I am not playing at being a farmer."

"Aren't you? All your work and plans are futile unless there is someone to share it with. I would hate see you end up a lonely old man."

Blown away by her outburst and harsh criticism, Luke was utterly speechless as she simply left him there to consider her assessment of his prospects. How dare Lucy make him re-evaluate the worth of his only ambition? It had always been enough for him, before. Was she right? Was his life in fact empty? Her words became an unwelcome invasion over the following days. They had hit home hard. This was a reality that he hadn't been prepared for or wanted to consider.

He found himself reduced to a great deal of soul-searching as he recognized the truth of her observations. He was just filling in time, in his spare time. Although he found things to do - the occasional meal, local concerts and further afield the cinema - he shared his life at a distance; he was not close to the friends he had in the village. And as for female company, it was so casual it might as well be non-existent. Even Gus's mission to set Luke up with every eligible female in the area had not been a success. He had never given up on the simple hope of sharing every day with someone permanent in his life. Of wanting someone of his own about the place who shared his dreams. He wanted that stability he saw with other couples. He wanted to be happy.

Even when he retrod the stony lane up to his favourite spot to lean over the top gate, to restore the satisfaction he had always felt being here, it failed to work. His normal exuberance, his expectation of nurturing the land, of seeing things grow and the progression of the changing seasons, had been overshadowed by her candid observation.

For once, and for no reason at all, he felt like getting drunk, in private, and he had the perfect opportunity of an empty house with his grandfather and Bernard away at an agricultural show. The mix of wine and strong alcohol, which he hated normally, had successfully blotted out the awful process of thinking and the headache the next morning was well deserved and somehow satisfying as he struggled to open his eyes. It had been worth it and he felt content, despite the awful crick in the back of the neck and a stiffness caused by falling asleep on the settee and later rolling onto the hard floor overnight. For a few hours he had managed to forget the doubt Lucy had put into his mind.

Braving the bright daylight which made him squint the next day, Luke made the effort to finally replace the hinge on one of the farm gates. It had needed doing for some time. As he fiddled about and fixed the last screw in, he became aware of one of the village children, sitting on the wall, who had obviously been watching him for some time.

"You don't look very happy. Something wrong?" chirped Melanie, too cheerfully, scrambling down to join him and studying his handy work. Children were the same everywhere and always too quick to spot things, but he was not sure his patience was up to coping with any inquisition today. Normally this one and her friends would scoot along the lane on their bikes, calling out to him and waving. Apparently today he was stuck with her full undivided attention as she sat down right beside him and annoyingly began humming or tra-la-la-ing, whilst throwing pebbles down the stony lane at intervals.

"Don't you have homework to do or something?" he muttered impatiently.

"All done, without any help," she boasted.

Her usual trick in the school holidays had simply been to creep up on him, yell 'boo' and run away, giggling. What a shame she couldn't be content with that now.

"Please go home brat," he growled.

She shook her head and beamed broadly at him, reminding him precisely of his mischievous sister's expression when she intended to torment him. Somehow that had to be avoided at all costs. He picked up his few tools and quickly removed himself from the impending danger zone. He was satisfied to hear, within seconds of his departure, the sound of Melanie's huffed resignation and her steps scuffing the ground back down the lane towards the village. Thank goodness for that.

There had been several messages left on the pad by the phone. He flicked through them; Lucy, then Lucy again, wanting him to phone her for a chat. Luke thought not. He had not quite forgiven her for her objective criticism and he was not precisely in the right mood to contend with any more of Lucy's overwhelming excitement and enthusiasm, while he felt the opposite. Instead he went off for a few hours on his beloved bike.

The next weekend Lucy was home again. She found Luke working in the kitchen garden.

"I'm leaving Paris," she told him as he dug over the plot.

"But - they worship you in Paris," Luke muttered, the words almost drying up in his mouth.

She explained that the book was selling so well that she had been offered a contract to write her own series of cookery books to include her recipes. She would have full control and be able to work from home, once she and Anton had found a home, of course. That was her next step, finding a home for them. She could not wait; everything was wonderfully falling into place, she gushed.

"I would have thought you were too important to the magazine for them to let you go."

"Nothing is more important than making a home and having a family eventually." She paused. "I take it you have not recovered from my observation on your personal life?"

"I doubt I ever will."

"And you haven't done anything about your love life since?"

He shook his head and smiled.

"You could always try internet dating."

"That wouldn't do much for my reputation," he scoffed.

"You do not have a reputation any more. You're out of touch. What am I going to do with you? Lucian, you are in your thirties. I want to see you happy."

Not that again. Who did she have in mind? And that might have been his next question, except he did not want to hear the answer at this moment.

"Why don't you try to contact Clare? I know you were fond of her, despite everything."

"Are you crazy? You think I should chase after Clare again just to stop me becoming the sad lonely and miserable old man you predicted. No chance. You forget she made it clear she was not the domestic type."

He had not thought about Clare in any capacity since he had caught a glimpse of her in Paris before Christmas. Now Luke remembered the kiss that meant nothing at the village dance and her arguments against any possible relationship between them. What was the point, he had argued in his head. She remained a lost cause.

"Excuses! You idiot! Why on earth are you frightened by the idea?" Lucy challenged him, shaking her head. Then she smiled forgivingly, kissed him and left him to sulk.

"Let me know when you change your mind." Her parting message echoed in his head. That would be a long way off, he promised himself silently.

Over the next few days Luke worked out of habit, unusually quiet and preferring his own company. He had more important matters to think about at the moment than Lucy's exaggerated attempted interference into his personal life. He was concerned about their financial future. After looking at the accounts a few days ago, it became apparent they were going to struggle over the coming year if they did not yield a good harvest. It could be difficult to support themselves. The market garden would not be established enough to supply any prospective clients. And they would have to forget the new tractor; it would have to be a second-hand one.

Luke had had a long time to think, and he found the answer to the problem lay in his own hands; he had to get that empty farmhouse into shape. He had seen other holiday let properties and the prices they charged on the internet. He was sure he could match those standards. And it had to be done sooner rather than later, because they needed that highly valuable income.

He was back in business mode. He was good at planning. It came as second nature. There were obviously regulations to comply with and certificates to obtain. He needed an expert who knew how to get things done quickly. He would need to approach the best companies to have them include the farmhouse on their books. He would need advertising, maybe their own website. Of course he had to convert the farmhouse first. Even that had to be done with the right style.

He went to Paris in his best smart casual clothes to meet with a marketing advisor Lucy had recommended. He had a profitable meeting and now he headed to the nearest coffee shop, to briefly browse through the mass of information he had been given. He wanted to get his head around some of the important facts before going home. He drank his first cup of coffee without even noticing, until he found himself drinking from an empty cup. Gathering his papers up into a neat pile to one side, he went to order another drink. On his return from the counter, he managed to knock his elbow on the chair at his table and spill the hot coffee on his leg.

"Sodding hellfire!" He swore aloud, quickly putting the cup down on the table and snatching a serviette to wipe his trousers.

"You never used to swear like that before."

He looked up and for no reason, he laughed. Of all people it had to be Clare. She smiled back. It was like seeing an old friend, one he didn't realize he had missed until he saw her again. He was genuinely pleased to see her.

"Hello."

He offered her the chair opposite for her to join him.

"Hello," she returned, before sitting down facing him.

Then they talked as if it was an everyday occurrence. Their previous awkwardness and tension had vanished, to be replaced by the mellow signs of friendship and acceptance. The time flew by.

"You are still strikingly attractive," he said, and she was. Her perky elfin face had lost none of its sparkle, her elegant slim figure and long legs were as outstanding as ever.

"And you are looking tired," Clare noted kindly.

He nodded his head. Clare ever the realist, never failed to notice the obvious.

"Are you working around here?" he asked.

"Only for another month. Then I'm going back to London."

She chatted on about how hard it had been at first and how she had struggled with the language. Normal everyday topics which drifted from one thing to another without any specific direction.

Then it clicked; she would be just the right person to help him with the conversion. Her design sense would be invaluable. He could only ask. She could only refuse.

"I'm trying to put the farmhouse into shape for the holiday market. I – I don't suppose you would do me a favour? Would you come down for a weekend to help me? I can't get my head around all these suggestions." He indicated the papers on the table.

"I am not an architect."

"I don't want one, I want a feminine eye to make the place attractive and inviting. You would be so much better than me at deciding what would look best. I'm serious. I would like your help. I can offer free board and lodging, if that will persuade you."

"Wouldn't Lucy like to be involved?"

"Heavens no! The farmhouse has nothing to do with her."

"In that case I will," she agreed cheerfully.

The arrangements were made and Clare was duly collected from the station on Friday evening. She instantly loved his grandfather's home, running her hands appreciatively over the furniture and fabrics. She smiled the whole time. She had never realized this house and the countryside around were so beautiful, she confessed happily.

Come the next morning, both she and Luke were busily engaged in poking about in the empty large stone building. Instantly they were covered in dust as they measured distances, banged the beams, tapped the walls and jumped up and down testing the floor boards. There was a long discussion over lunch about the pros and cons of various ideas. Finally they decided it was big enough to divide into two good-sized residences; they could easily rejig the rooms and put in an extra staircase. That was the first hurdle. Then Clare drew some sketches and rough plans of how it should look, together with notes on specific areas, for him to pass on to his contractor.

"I wish you were in France longer. Even when the building work is done, there is the interior to get right," he said.

The furniture, fittings and colour schemes, were just as important. Dare he ask her if she would she mind spending more time going around the numerous outlets with him on the next weekend? Just to point out small touches that would make all the difference. Again she agreed, noting how impressed she was by his serious dedication to the project. He confessed the necessity of its success to the farm.

"But it is an expensive undertaking."

He grimaced briefly, and predicted that they could soon cover the cost, once both properties were up and running. What he had not old anyone was the personal risk he was taking by putting the actual buildings up as collateral for the loan from the bank. They had demanded something substantial for such a large amount of money. But he had made the best deal he could in the circumstances. He just needed this to work.

Later, over supper in the kitchen, it was natural that they reminisced over their past.

"I have always liked you Luke, but I have been determined not to fall for your rugged good looks. I knew you would break my heart because we had such different ambitions. I did not giving us a chance. Besides, I'm sure we would have made each other miserable eventually."

He had to admit she was probably right. Being friends was much better.

"I'm sorry we didn't part well," Luke offered.

"There were so many things wrong, so many mistakes."

"About Paris. At Ben's exhibition. I didn't mean to deliberately upset you. It was a shock seeing you there."

"I admit, I did want to see you again. I regretted our last conversation. Couldn't you tell how I felt?" she asked him.

He shook his head. No, he could not, he had been in defence mode. He could not believe that had been the real reason for her coming to Paris. He could not imagine he was worth it. He had not expected her to change her mind.

"So I made a fool of myself, for nothing," she teased.

"You never made a fool of yourself. It was an awkward situation for both of us. I didn't think we had anything left to say to each other. I didn't know what you expected."

"I had not expected Lucy. She made it perfectly clear how close you two were."

He admitted they were old friends, but explained that they were definitely not romantically involved. Lucy was very strictly out of bounds.

"Surely you noticed her wedding ring? I thought you women were prone to picking up details like that."

"A wedding ring doesn't mean anything these days," Clare reminded him.

"Ah, in this case it does."

"Then what was the reason for her very deliberate performance at Ben's exhibition?"

"Believe me, I did not understand what was happening either at the time. That came as a complete surprise. I did not know what she was doing. She told me later it was meant to be a reality check."

"You heel, Luke! You deliberately let me think you two were an item. Why didn't you tell me the truth the next day?" She landed a friendly thump on his arm.

He shrugged. He could not remember much about the next day.

"Because - I was not feeling particularly kind, I guess. I didn't see the need to explain when you were not part of my life. I was still struggling with seeing you again so suddenly. What was the point of punishing ourselves? I didn't know what to say."

"So you ran away."

"It seemed the easiest thing to do."

"And in hindsight, I believe you did the best thing. Common sense won out. I made the mistake of deliberately finding a job in Paris before acknowledging the utter futility of us ever forming any romantic relationship."

"I always thought you and Ben would be the ones to pair up. It seemed natural since you are both artistic."

"Heck, I am too selfish for Ben. Or maybe for any man." She laughed.

The conversation lapsed; they were both tired. Clare disappeared to her bed and Luke managed to clear up before he fell into his bed.

The next day he took her to lunch, then for a walk around the village, before taking her back to the station for her train. They kissed each other on the cheek and parted, both declaring how they had enjoyed themselves.

"Until the next weekend."

"Until the next weekend," she smiled, waving from the train.

Luke was exhausted. It had taken three months of intensive negotiation and persistent slog to get the project complete. He had kept a sharp eye on the schedule and the actual workmanship, and the result was outstanding. The photographs of the high-spec finish, design and landscaping had already proved their worth. There were bookings for the first two months of the summer season already, from their own website and links from several other top agencies. Luke had transformed one of the small barns at the side into a dedicated reception office for the business, where he dealt with bookings, grocery orders and the laundry routine. He had arranged for the place to be cleaned and polished on the changeover days. Fresh flowers and a welcome pack were standard, and a folder of tourist leaflets and other local information, such as the village shops and opening times, awaited every guest. A great sense of achievement and satisfaction made him feel very proud of the transformation. He hoped the visitors would love the place as he did, and he intended to be there on his guests' arrival to answer any questions and help them settle in. This was going to work, he could feel it.

Indeed he never anticipated how well it would do. They were fully booked through the summer and the autumn, with repeat booking in advance for the next year from this year's guests. Some clients had left bottles of wine in appreciation at the end of their stay, or specialist cheeses, which Luke passed on to the regular shift of locals who helped keep these homes in sparkling condition. It became a different, enjoyable experience which fitted in well with the farm routine, although it meant Luke was busier than ever.

Besides the villagers who benefited from employment, the older men were equally keen to make themselves useful. Bernard liked to potter about tending the flowers and gardens in his spare time and his grandfather was on hand to take over in the office when necessary, while Luke went on errands. Naturally both of them had the right approach when chatting to the visitors; their years of experience showed and the guests seemed to love hearing their stories.

Luke had been in a heady daze for most of the time and now the season was slowing down, he began to sit back and appreciate how well they had done financially. The loan would be paid off much earlier than he had expected, thank goodness, and the farm was looking healthy. The crops had been good this year and they had in the end made a good price. At last they were getting somewhere. He could stop worrying. Tina Turner and "Simply the Best" played on the radio, one of his favourites, and he settled down with a book, put his feet up and relaxed for the evening. Such a lovely change, he sighed.

Of course there had been the Lucy element. She had popped in and out of his life as normal during the upheaval, but she had been busy with her own endeavours. There had been loads of snatched conversations. Having found a small mill by a river for her home, she was now looking for an additional building for her proposed restaurant in the same area. She had found a brilliant structure with a terrace overlooking the river. She had known it was the right place immediately and snapped it up. It was only an hour's drive from the farm, ideal for deliveries once the kitchen garden was in production. Bernard had checked the route, access and storage possibilities. Lucy told him she had been lucky to find this place on the market and that he must come and see it. And when exactly was he supposed to fit that in?

Then there was that last rather tentative conversation when Lucy had sheepishly asked Luke if was still in touch with Clare. He screwed up his face and glared at her, a warning not to bring up that old adage about his lack of romantic relationships these days.

"No, no. It is - I – her designs have made such a difference here. I really do admire her talent. Do you think she would consider helping me with the look of my restaurant? It would be a professional arrangement, I would pay the going rate."

His eyes crinkled. Well, well - who would have imagined this, Lucy asking a favour from Clare? That could be an amusing proposition after their last encounter in Paris. How would Clare react? Would she even consider it?

"I can't promise she will agree. But I'll ask her for you," he said.

The more Luke mused over the notion, the more he felt he would like to tackle this face to face, just to see Clare's expression when he broached the subject. He had time to go to London and her reaction could be interesting. Very, very interesting. He could not help smiling at the prospect. He owed Clare more than a simple thank you for all the months of phone calls he had made, pestering her over his queries, despite the fact that she always told him she did not mind. She had deserved a consultant's fee, but she had laughed that off as well. He meant to reward her somehow one day, despite any protest. This gave him the perfect opportunity, and he knew exactly what he wanted as a gift.

He caught the train to Paris the next morning, intent on scouring the busy streets and brightly-lit shops and ignoring the other superfluous attractions. He had a shortlist of individual jewellers from the internet and he was on a mission, knowing he could not leave Paris without it. It had been quite a long and frustrating day as he searched the various venues, but as he sat on the Eurostar train heading for London he beamed at his reflection in the window.

An overnight stay in a hotel and a hearty English breakfast inside him, he set out for the next stage of his impulsive plan. He realized he should have phoned her flat last night to see where she was working. He had assumed she was still in the city, but he could be wrong. Would Ben know? It would save time if he did.

"Ben, pick up the phone. Don't be out on an assignment," he challenged the ring tone. Then Ben answered, and was astonished at hearing from him. It had been ages. Luke apologized and explained he was in town, but he had no intention of holding a lengthy conversation at these call rates, they could catch up later. He quickly told Ben what he wanted to know. There was a hesitant silence at the other end before Ben informed him that he certainly knew where she was, but he had no intention of telling him.

"Why?" asked Luke.

Ben immediately listed the reasons, including the Paris exhibition fiasco, and why he had made up his mind never to become involved in any of Luke's female acquaintances again. And whatever he had in mind, he could forget it, Clare was better off without him.

"Ben! Ben, listen. We are over that awful period. Surely she told you. She helped design the farmhouse conversions. I have a proposition for her."

The phone went down, ending the one-sided conversation and leaving Luke to pull a face at the handset in retaliation. Of course, he had had the answer all the time, he was just being lazy. Clare was an exhibition designer. All he had to do was find out which exhibitions were being prepared in the city. He rang the arts editor at *The Times*. The man was very helpful and Luke was soon armed with a list of galleries in the city to investigate. It had not been that difficult. He settled down with the London A-Z to consider where to start.

Finally, in the late afternoon as he peered into the huge inner hall of the latest and next gallery on his piece of paper, he caught sight of her. She stood busy stapling a felt back cloth to a frame and was surrounded by other bits and pieces. He watched her for a little while, remembering all the things he admired about her, then he patted his pocket reassuringly and pushed the door open. She saw him approach and his attempted smile was met with a suspicious tilt of the head.

"Why are you here?" she asked quietly.

"To bring you something."

He held out his hand and slowly uncurled his fingers to show the item in the palm of his hand, to her. He had searched Paris for it, but here it was, an enamel brooch, a very modern design of a bright pink handbag. The closest thing he could get, next to the original she had given away to Emma.

"For you," he whispered, lifting his hand nearer so she could see it properly.

Clare stared at it and then up at him, without picking it up.

"I will always think of you with that awful handbag," he smirked.

She smiled weakly. He could see she looked tired. She was not in the mood for silly gestures, however well meant. She looked quite low in spirits.

"Would you like to go for a coffee?" he offered.

"No thank you. I'm busy. Can't you see?"

Not that busy. He had been watching her and had seen those moments when she glanced out of the window forlornly before turning her attention back to the job in hand without any enthusiasm. Which was most unlike her. She turned her back and continued tinkering with the metal frame, leaving Luke to slowly return the gift to his pocket, for later.

"Go away, Luke," she said.

Go where? He had just spent most of the day looking for her. He was not going anywhere.

"Please. I am having a bad day," she sniffled, unwilling to turn around. She was trembling. The unexpected vulnerability shocked him. Whatever was wrong? He carefully and slowly took everything out of her hands and put them aside, making her stop what she was doing.

"Whatever is the matter?" he coaxed soothingly, as she quickly shook her head and wiped away a tell-tale trickle, hoping he had not seen. But he had and instinctively he drew her gently into his arms and held her against him, desperate to comfort this unique female. She protested only weakly before bursting into tears into his shoulder. He did not mind tears.

"Why are you crying?" he whispered, leaning his head to rest on hers. This was obviously more than just an off day. Yet he could not imagine the cause, and he did not want to pry too much. Clare would tell him in her own time, if she wanted to. He wasn't going to expect her confidence. Yet it came naturally, without prompting.

"Oh, Luke, I have been made redundant," came her few muffled words into his chest.

This brilliant talented girl had been told she was not needed. Were they mad? How illogical were these people? She was marvellous at what she did. He felt like finding the bright spark who had instigated this and banging his head against the wall to make him see sense.

"It's the accountants. They insist the company has to make cuts," she muttered sadly.

Luke still wanted to flatten someone. He was so angry. How dare they decide that she was to be one of those they could do without. He was tempted to voice his contempt for her employer, but it did not seem the right thing to do at this precise moment. How would that help matters? Instead he stood there gently holding her for as long as she wanted, not wishing to overstep the mark as a friend. He did not know how else to console her. Gradually she pulled herself together and stood back from him.

"I'm sorry. I didn't mean to get so weepy," she said, finding a hankie and wiping her face.

"Another company is bound to snap you up," he offered encouragingly.

Clare looked around her. There was still a mountain of things to do. She still had to finish this assignment, despite everything else that had happened. The tables were littered with bits and pieces, there were the uncompleted stands and wall fixings, and there was the mountain of exhibits to be displayed, wrapped in paper and stacked in boxes along the wall. Finally she just looked at the floor, wondering how she could face plodding on with this today, when she was not in the right mood.

"I don't know if I want to be snapped up. It could easily happen again, whoever I work for. I don't know if I even want to continue," she sighed dejectedly.

"But you get the chance to travel all over the place. The prospects?" he gulped.

"Prospects? They aren't that grand. I spend days in the studio planning and then most of my time I am shut away inside a building, working all hours. Then I am chasing suppliers and deliveries, making sure nothing is damaged. I'm often too tired to see the new places I am in. There is always the battle to make the next exhibition better than the last and trying to stay one step ahead of the competition. There's the strain of knowing the next hopeful designer is there breathing over your shoulder. Someone with brighter and better ideas who would eventually replace me, it always happens. I wouldn't have lasted forever. I hope I can find other work, although with other companies making the same financial cuts there will be a lot of us in the same situation."

Luke had never heard her sound so cynical about her future. Where was the positive, feisty, modern woman he was used to? Where was the Clare he remembered? She was understandably down in the dumps and upset. Maybe this was the appropriate moment to mention what else he had come for. It might lift her spirits.

"I can find you a temporary job if you want to accept it?"

She looked at him sceptically, obviously not really believing him, concluding it was something he had said off the top of his head, in the spur of the moment, in an attempt to be kind. She guessed he intended to find something for her to do in connection with the holiday lettings, although she knew they did not need any more work. She did not need him to invent work for her, however well meaning, she told him.

"Apart from the present I brought with me, I had come with an offer of another design project in France. A proper offer. It has nothing to do with me. I represent a client who admires your ideas. But in the circumstances, I think it can wait. I don't think you're in the right frame of mind to consider it objectively at the moment."

Clare stood quietly, somewhat mesmerized at his confusing words, while he began gathering up and tidying the materials around her, folding things away, clearing the floor, pushing boxes under the tables and turning the lights off, one by one.

"I don't know why you are determined to finish this. They don't deserve your dedication. I'm going to take you for something to eat. No argument. You look pale. You need something inside you."

Clare did not protest, indeed she felt quite pleased to let him take control.

"Come on, let's go," he murmured before picking up her coat from the chair and holding it out for her to put on. She gladly left everything, put the coat on, picked up her bag, a simple canvas tote thing, and then slipped her arm into the one he offered. He was pleased to note that she did not even glance back at her unfinished project as they left the gallery.

Automatically holding her arm a little tighter, he guided her to a small quiet restaurant a few streets away, and after protesting that she was not that hungry, she found that she was. Afterwards he was pleased to see she was looking a lot better.

"How did you find me today?" she asked much later, after they had shared a dessert.

"It was easy," he lied.

In fact it had taken a lot of fancy talking and in most cases a crumpled note thrust into the hands of an attendant to even poke his head inside some of these galleries, just to see if she was there.

"I'm glad you did. I didn't realize how bad I felt. I needed a friend to lean on. Thank you."

"I'm glad I was there," Luke replied sincerely.

It had come as a welcome reassurance that she had felt content enough with his company to share her setback. He had not expected her trust concerning such personal disappointment, especially after the lack of regular contact between them lately. Apparently it made little difference to the way she regarded him these days, as a real friend. He was satisfied with that.

Luke ordered her a taxi, with instructions to the driver to take her straight to her flat. He kissed her on the cheek and guided her into the cab.

"I recommend a long, relaxing soak in the bath and some pampering. I want you to take tomorrow off and do nothing. I'll phone you tomorrow night, to see how you are."

She smiled and nodded. Not that he was going to trust

her to follow his instructions, but he had already phoned her flatmate Jane surreptitiously, while he paid for the meal, to make sure she did. His co-conspirator promised to ensure Clare took the day off tomorrow by doing so herself.

The next day he phoned the flat and spoke to Jane, who reported that Clare was sleeping in late. She moved into the kitchen with the phone, allowing them to confer further without waking Clare. Jane, who no longer worked for the same company, told him that like himself, she had been angry with them when she had heard the news. The company had insisted it was nothing personal, and that she had not done anything wrong. But Clare had been terribly upset and it had left her feeling worthless. The redundancy had dented her confidence, and she felt that she was no good enough any more. Since then she had prowled the flat at intervals during the night, then tossed and turned, to wake tired in the mornings, before doggedly dragging herself off to finish her final project for them.

On the positive side, using her insider information concerning Clare's resume, Jane had secretly begun trying to find her a new position. Sadly there were few vacancies in exhibition design at the present, just as Clare had predicted. But Jane had not given up. Other than that they did not have a definite plan to help her between them. All Luke had was the offer from Lucy.

"I wanted to discuss Lucy's suggestion properly. I'm charged with presenting her case. But it can wait until tomorrow, with any luck Clare might feel more receptive then. I will still phone her this evening."

This left Luke with a day to fill, and he found himself roaming his old haunts. They had all changed in the few years he had been away, and coffee shops and bars were under new management. Even the local public house across the road from his old flat was now an Indian restaurant. It all felt very alien and unfriendly. He knew he would be glad to go home tomorrow.

Luke was booked on the midday Eurostar back to Paris, so he met Clare for a late breakfast, over which he finally told her about Lucy's offer.

"First of all, I am not going to pressure you. I am just going to tell you the outline. I want you to take the details away and give it some serious consideration. I know you might not have forgiven Lucy after the Paris fiasco, but she really would like to employ you. She has asked specifically for you after the brilliant job you made of my holiday properties. This is a serious business proposition. She will pay you the proper fees and expenses. She is in the process of becoming a rural restaurant owner with a first-class reputation. No doubt she is aiming at attracting celebrity cliental. She wants it to look the best. Subtle and stylish is how she described it. Please consider it properly. You never know, it might lead on to other, better things."

He took a large envelope out of his pocket and gave it to her. It had all the details inside; what Lucy was after, possible schedules, her phone number and a sealed letter, no doubt pleading for Clare to agree. He had done his best for both parties, he could not do any more. His task was over.

Clare smiled softly and slipped it into her bag without comment, promising nothing. This only left him to look at her, while he finished his coffee. She was looking a lot brighter and there was a hint of the old perky grin and sparkling eyes, although the toss of the head was absent. Never mind, she was getting there, he concluded.

Still there was something else he must do before he left. He took the brooch out of his pocket again, unwrapped the tissue paper and offered it to her. This time she smiled and accepted it, gently holding it in her hands.

"You are very thoughtful. Thank you, Luke."

They parted with a kiss on the cheek as normal and he went to the station to go home. Yes, France was his home. He felt it in his bones, and the nearer to it he got, the more content he felt. A few days back in London had only proved where his heart really belonged. He could not stand the hustle and bustle, the noise, dirt and increasing crowds, any more. The rural tranquillity beckoned him on, the open spaces. The satisfaction of the farm and the familiar community which filled his days made the hard work and the odd worry of little consequence.

As kicked off his shoes, changed his clothes and padded into the kitchen for his supper, he could not help thinking about Clare and what she would do. Lucy would not wait forever. As it was, he expected a phone call within hours from Lucy to find out how it had gone. He knew she would not be impressed by his apparent lack of success when Lucy had expected a definite answer, one way or the other. But he would handle that conversation when it arose.

His grandfather had the food on the table and Luke settled back into his relaxed mode as they reflected over the year and its developments.

"You still have no female in your life."

"No, Grandfather."

"I'm surprised."

"Whatever will be, will be" Luke sighed philosophically.

He was not particularly put out by the comment and his grandfather did not push the point. There had been opportunities missed. One in particular he regretted. One he had dealt with, but the stupid mistake still niggled. He would always love Lucy deep down. As for Clare, whom he had briefly held her in his arms only recently, their chance for any serious relationship had never materialized and they had long gone past the stage of being lovers. Indeed the close indulgence of a woman's touch and the thrill it gave him remained only a pleasant memory these days.

He casually accepted his present state of affairs. It did not bother him greatly. Life was not perfect. He had never expected it to be. He still had a lot to look forward to and a lot of things he wanted to do. The utter satisfaction of domestic happiness with someone seemed unimportant today. No doubt he would think differently in the future. Today, tired from his travelling, he savoured the warm, familiar atmosphere of this old house, ran his hand over the comforting furniture, went to put his favourite CD on and stretched out on the settee, as was his habit of late. What could be better? For now, it was enough.

* * * * *

MISS IVY TREE

Victoria snuggled into a corner seat of the compartment and let out a contented sigh. She had seen Fonteyn and Nureyev dance together for the first time recently at the Royal Ballet and now she was on her way to Kent and a sleepy backwater where many inhabitants preferred the old-fashioned values of the previous decade. She always enjoyed her weekend train journeys between London and her uncle's village. The conversations she overheard on the way were a constant revelation, and today they were even more fascinating.

"Have you seen that new housekeeper? Ivy Tree! What an absurd name anyway. Mind you, I suppose it suits the woman."

"A typical spinster if ever there was one. Did you see those terrible brogues?" added the second voice.

"Such an old-fashioned, frumpy person."

Victoria bristled at the haughty, prattling voices behind

her. How grossly unkind of them, she thought, especially since she had picked Ivy, the new live-in housekeeper for her Uncle Charles, herself. The annual task of finding someone suitable to take care of the property while he left on his regular summer history lecture tour abroad had usually been easy. Victoria had never let him down yet, but this year the agencies had been surprisingly short of suitable applicants and the limited candidates she had interviewed had proved unsatisfactory. So who on earth was she going to find this year?

Her uncle was very particular as to the type of person to be entrusted with his Edwardian house. She must be a respectable, older woman, someone who would stand no nonsense from anyone.

Then Ivy had appeared, a plain Jane without a doubt, no makeup, pale skin, straight hair, wearing small glasses through which her eyes peered and squinted at people, as if she really did need them changing soon. Ivy was ideal for the purpose, and Victoria had every confidence in her, instinctively sensing she could trust this woman to manage everything.

Victoria switched off from the conversation to let her mind wander, smiling to herself. Only Victoria knew the true worth of Ivy.

***

Indeed Ivy had followed Victoria's instructions precisely, and having collected the spare keys from Victoria in London, she had duly arrived in the rural backwater. The taxi from the local station had dropped her outside the house without attracting any interest from the immediate neighbours. Ivy took a sneaky look out of the corner of her eye, and hiding a smirk she unlocked the front door, picked up her small battered case and stepped quickly inside. Then, after shuffling into the kitchen to make a cup of tea, she settled down to make herself at home. Her task was to keep this period property clean, aired, tranquil and private, and she meant to be as efficient as all her predecessors.

Ivy had been primed as to those she would encounter and warned about the nature of her possible adversaries. Victoria had provided the background on most of the community, which easily split into the 'nice' and 'not to be trusted' categories.

The next morning, exactly as predicted, a gentle tapping on the kitchen door heralded the appearance of Mr Russell the gardener, who came once a week to keep the gardens at their best.

"Just to let you know I'll be in the garden today," he informed her.

Nodding her acceptance of his presence outside, Ivy continued with her own chores and left him to his routine. Later she glanced discreetly into the garden as he worked quietly away. It was obvious that this little man loved doing what he did. No wonder Mr Russell was one of the very special 'nice' people on the list. What had been unbelievable was the fact that Mr Russell had never won the local flower and vegetable competition, despite all his excellent produce.

Apparently, after being beaten for three years in a row, he had been so disappointed and disheartened that he had decided not to bother to enter any more. Somehow Ivy hoped, in her own way and in due time, to persuade him to try once more. With any luck this year he would awarded the recognition he deserved.

***

One of Ivy's other important tasks, had been to endear herself quickly to the village community. So one morning, on the trusty old bike belonging to Victoria and borrowed from the shed, puffing and blowing a bit from the exertion, in her country tweeds, old felt hat, little leather gloves and flat laced shoes, she bustled down the lane to the collection of local shops. She knew that first impressions were important.

"It has been some time since I have been on a bike," she confessed to the locals, who could not help smiling at the image the woman presented. Then, having introduced herself to the shopkeepers, she gathered her few items and stowed them into the basket on the front of the bike. "I don't think I have the energy yet to cycle uphill," she remarked as she left.

Not that she had ever intended to. The slow amble back allowed her plenty of opportunities to pass the time of day with almost everyone she saw, with the result that it took her a whole hour to get back to the house. Indeed Ivy was quite exhausted, but she was quietly satisfied by the time she had sat down and put her feet up. Everything looked very promising indeed for her stay here.

Ivy's next encounter was with someone she had not been warned about. She had left the back door open to let some fresh air in on an unbearably hot day and was surprised to be visited by a very large, fluffy apricot-coloured cat, which casually made its way to the centre of the kitchen, sat down and looked up at her, curiously tilting its head on one side.

"Well, hello," said Ivy, slowly bending down so as not to scare it away. The cat responding by immediately curling on its back and stretching, seemingly expecting to be stroked.

"Now what do you think you are doing here?" she scolded softly as the cat purred, bending its head under her fingers.

This would not do. She could not have it make a home for itself here, however lovely a creature it was. She gently scooped the soft animal into her arms, where it contently nuzzled against her and purred louder as she carried it outside to find out who it belonged to. She strolled down the path and out of the front gate towards the first of the village cottages.

Florrie was in her front garden as usual, with the milkman's son clipping the hedges for her. Old Esme and her friend were walking slowly back with their dogs from their daily exercise on the village green. The enquiries went from one to the other as they stopped to chat, the cat still content to lay wrapped in her arms for the duration, taking no notice of the dogs.

Then Yvonne hurried out of her cottage opposite and

paused briefly to coo at the cat. "Hello Tibbie, what are you up to?" she enquired as she tickled him under the ear.

At last, someone who knew where it belonged. Having been told the owner was a Miss Collins, who ran the mobile library, and that it stopped beside the post office every Wednesday, Ivy made her way there. Inside the van she found a smiling lady rearranging the books on the shelves.

"If there are not enough people to make a fuss of him, he goes walkabout," Miss Collins explained before mildly scolding her pet, wagging her finger at him. "Here, let me take him."

Ivy immediately warmed to Miss Collins, and could not but voice her admiration for anyone who could drive this large square vehicle around the narrow twisting lanes. Miss Collins laughed, a soft comfortable laugh, explaining that it was no trouble at all, since no one argued with this very solid bus.

"I just trundle down the centre of the road and let others move out of the way. Everyone gives me plenty of room when I park, so I don't have to worry about having to fit into tight spaces either."

Ivy grinned. Yes, she liked Miss Collins a lot. So much so that she made a mental note to develop this new-found acquaintance. Ivy had the inkling of an intriguing idea forming, where she might just need the assistance of Miss Collins and her bus in due course. If she could persuade her.

Victoria had organized herself to check her own London flat for any outstanding post early every Saturday morning before heading off to the village. There her purpose was to deal with any bills and letters at her uncle's house, while allowing Ivy to enjoy her free weekends. So far Victoria had been pleased with Ivy's first foray into the village. She happily she set off to visit her two favourite locals, a couple of widows who lived in a pretty cottage around the corner. Uncle Charles had always said how dear little Mrs Plum made the most wonderful jam he had ever tasted and Mrs Driver the most delicious cakes, and he was right of course. They were a delightful pair of ladies and she returned to the house with a fine example of both cake and jam clutched eagerly in her hands.

The new vicar and his wife were doing the rounds of their new parish, and soon arrived on the doorstep. They explained that they were attempting to organise the summer fete a little differently this year. They were hoping to inject a little more fun into the event, without upsetting any of the older parishioners, and were naturally keen for any fresh suggestions.

Naturally Victoria soon had them ensconced in the kitchen, where all three of them easily devoured the newly-made cake together with cups of tea whilst they debated the possibilities.

"You must try this home-made jam as well, it's much better than the mass produced stuff," Victoria enthused the moment they had finished the cake. Thus the discussion continued, amidst more tea and buttered scones and the delicious jam, all of them enjoying the get-together, which lasted much longer than any of them had expected.

***

The weekend over, Victoria returned to London and Ivy continued her normal routine and her regular visits to the small village shops. The villagers genuinely seemed to like Ivy, with her natural, friendly disposition and a willingness to chat and pass the time of day, which was welcomed by those who were similarly inclined. Ivy simply fitted in, as was her way. It was a characteristic she had cultivated. Ivy knew she was going to enjoy her time here, including the prospect of trying to achieve the other schedule Victoria had compiled prior to her arrival here.

Ivy was looking forward to the next stage of her instructions. All she needed were her wits, and her knack of being in the right place at the right time, to achieve the right results. It was not difficult. It was only a minor incident of course, when she turned to Mrs Jones with the most innocent of remarks.

"Why Mrs Jones, I am glad I have bumped into you. I do hope that mark came off that beautiful dress you wore on Friday to the Church Benefit. If not, I might have a remedy for removing stains, if you would like me to find it."

A startled Matilda Jones felt her body tense up, and felt herself colouring slightly. She could not believe this dreadful woman had not only noticed that stain but had now drawn attention to it, in front of a shop full of people. Everyone looked at her and then turned away to hide their grins as Ivy rambled on with other trivia, apparently completely oblivious to the embarrassment she had caused.

"Do you mind telling me, which magazine was it that

had that recipe for lemon cake in it? I remember you mentioned it was one you were trying," Ivy enquired softly.

"Trying! You are trying!" Matilda snapped, unable to control herself any longer.

Ivy looked incredulously at her, clearly stunned at the outburst.

"Why my dear, I only asked, because someone else was interested," Ivy mumbled apologetically.

Mrs Jones became aware that others, including the vicar's wife, were now looking at her again. Then, sensing their disapproval of her speaking to Ivy in that manner, she hurried off as fast as she could. The unwarranted outburst had clearly only added to the locals' dislike for the woman, although Ivy herself let the moment pass, refusing to make a fuss over such a silly remark.

Ivy, always polite, naturally greeted everyone else with either a wave, a nod or a word of acknowledgement. To her even simple manners were important, and she would certainly not tolerate anything less in others. She had her own way of handling people who attempted to ignore her. Mrs Alice Hogarth, for one, had come unstuck in her attempt to shun Ivy's annoying friendliness as she left the antique shop. To her utter abhorrence, the woman found that Ivy had put her hand on her arm to catch her attention

"I said good morning, Mrs Hogarth. I don't think you heard me," Ivy said quietly.

Her action forced an insincere smile from Alice before Ivy allowed her to escape. Again, this had not gone unnoticed by others in the street.

Back at the house, Ivy felt pleased with the way things

were going. The subtle campaign had started. She thoroughly enjoyed these performances. They had been fun, and these two 'not so nice' residents were marked for more attention during the summer.

***

The following weekend Victoria had found herself in an almost empty carriage for her journey back to the village. However, seconds later, two women entered and plonked themselves into the seats behind her. Victoria instantly recognised the voices of two of the least favoured people on her list.

"What an awful woman. Whoever is responsible for employing her as a housekeeper?"

"According to Martin, it is Charles's niece."

"Well she should have had more sense than to select this one."

Victoria resisted a snigger from her concealed position.

"Martin physically cringes when she bumbles into his bank promptly every Thursday to cash her weekly cheque. She is always full of chatter, disrupting his domain."

Martin was another on Victoria's list who had come under Ivy's scrutiny. His unapproachable manner, normally enough to discourage any familiarity, had no effect on Ivy. His attitude did not bother her in the least. She was much too interested in people to be offended, as she wandered off into another topic. Unwilling to engage in conversation with a woman he really had no time for, on her last visit he had eventually stormed out of the building, bumping angrily into the new vicar as he went.

There was a pause before Victoria overheard the next rather loud complaint about Ivy, from Mrs Matilda Jones and Mrs Alice Hogarth.

"That Ivy Tree! I find her so embarrassing. She never seems to know her place," said Matilda.

"The woman is such a nuisance. She is so difficult and infuriating to deal with," Alice replied.

"Do you remember when she drew attention to that little mark on the dress I wore to the Church Benefit? Then offering to find a remedy for removing stains. Of course, I had to put her in her place."

"The woman is such a nuisance," Alice agreed.

"Then completely oblivious to the embarrassment she had already caused me, she rambled on to ask which magazine was it that had that recipe for lemon cake in it."

"Lemon cake? Oh, the one you entered into the summer fete competition last year."

"Yes, that one," Matilda huffed.

Victoria's attractive eyes crinkled, perfectly aware of the reasons for these comments. These two women had in turn fallen prey to Ivy's mild concern.

"What an awful woman. I wish she would go back to London," said Alice.

Victoria listened intensely to their renewed conversation.

"Martin would have quite happily recommended a suitable housekeeper, except that Charles told Martin quite bluntly that it was none of his business."

"How rude."

"Indeed. Martin felt quite disgruntled."

"I'm not surprised, considering Martin's position in the community."

Victoria resisted a snigger. What position? He was only the local bank manager! Nothing else, despite all his airs and graces. No wonder her uncle disliked Martin so intensely.

Uncle Charles had also mentioned how Martin and his friend Travis had caused endless upsets with the villagers in recent years. Now they were intending to stand for the parish council. What an awful prospect! Victoria could not help dwelling on this matter for a while, until she found herself listening to their conversation again.

"What about last week in the village hall, when that dreadful woman tripped and tipped the tray of juice over poor Martin?"

"Yes and all that fuss, apologising every few minutes until the poor man finally gave in and let her sponge his jacket down, just to be rid of her unwanted attention."

Dear Ivy! Her way of unsettling certain people had to be admired. Ivy was good at her various skills, and maybe that was an understatement, Victoria told herself wickedly.

***

Ivy had mulled over what to do with her days off. During the week she had mentioned to all those in the village shop that she might take herself off on the bus to explore the area a little further. Asking for suggestions, of which there were plenty, she then stopped deliberately in front of Mr Travis Longford on her way out and smiled sweetly. Ivy knew that Mr Longford, a financial advisor, was not popular amongst the locals because of his dominating attitude towards other people. Not that this would deter Ivy.

"Now Mr Longford, you must know the area well, can you recommend anywhere historically interesting to visit?" she began.

Travis Longford seemed astonished that she had the nerve to ask him such a direct question, since she barely knew him. He hadn't even drawn a breath before she continued.

"I am told Tunbridge Wells is pretty. Are the Pantiles worth seeing?"

Ivy was the only one who noticed the effect the question had on Mr Longford, as his mouth fell open for a second or two. She had obviously hit a nerve. Recovering himself, he told her that a lot of people liked the place, without committing himself as to his own preference.

Ivy smirked as she walked away, fully aware of the reason for his discomfort. Ivy had in fact already been to Tunbridge Wells and had treated herself in one of the coffee shops on the Pantiles. There amid the unhurried atmosphere of a more tranquil setting she had seen the said Travis also enjoying a leisurely meal nearby. "Oh dear," were the only words which had escaped Ivy's mouth at the time. She turned her attention back to her drink, reflecting that she had just gathered another piece of useful information to store in her memory bank. She was gradually gathering background on these far from pleasant people, all of which would help her achieve her goal by the end of the summer. She hoped.

***

Ivy's latest achievement had not been on the list at all. Having agreed to look after Jake, Esme's grandson, for a few hours, she had settled for a simple game of catch in Esme's garden. Naturally the youngster was full of energy and Ivy could see she would soon be in trouble as he eagerly threw the ball back and forth. The obvious solution stood a few feet away, since Florrie's granddaughter Susan was watching them from over the fence. Ivy suggested to Jake that he should ask Susan to play as well, but he stubbornly shook his head. Maybe he felt awkward with girls. Never mind, she would work on it. It was not long before Ivy deliberately threw the ball so erratically that it bounced on top of the fence to drop down on the other side, at Susan's feet.

"Goodness, how clumsy," Ivy puffed as a little face peered at the gate, the ball in her hand.

"Hello dear," Ivy cooed, smiling to the child.

The little girl tossed the ball back across the garden, her chin remaining on the gate, watching them but not speaking. What a shy child, Ivy observed. What a pair!

A few throws later, the ball hit the fence again and

dropped the other side. The girl eagerly scampered after it and returned to the gate with it, where she stood hesitantly, obviously wanting to join in. Ivy paused and let out a deep sigh.

"Thank you, dear. I am not very good at this am I? I don't suppose you would you like to take my place, so that I can have a rest?" she pleaded softly.

Susan's eyes lit up. A smile beamed back and within a moment, the child had hurried through the gate and up the path to where Ivy stood. Ivy handed the ball to the little girl and left them to get acquainted. At first there was a tentative silence between the children as they bounced the ball slowly to each other, but she soon heard them giggling at the missed catches. The game progressed with deliberate quick returns, as they called to each other. Half an hour later, when she returned with a drink for them, she found them sitting on the step reading a book together. Ivy smiled at the pair of them. They had easily become friends, just as she had originally suspected they would. They had just needed a helping hand.

If only it was that easy to get Mr Russell to win the vegetable and flower section, and likewise to arrange for Mrs Plum and Mrs Diver to win the jam and cakes sections at the summer fete this year. Ivy pondered. She still had quite a bit to do.

***

Victoria knew that Ivy had purposely made every effort

to become accepted in the village. In passing from the butcher's to the bank, the post office and then the general store, she was able to keep up to date with the latest gossip and happenings without any prompting. Ivy never complained and never gossiped; she was not one to bemoan her lot or burden others. She had won the locals to her side without even realising there were sides in this game. And what was wrong with that?

"You are always on the go, don't you ever take a rest Ivy?" the butcher's wife observed one day to her.

"I don't think I would know how. It's a way of life," she said. She laughed softly. "I enjoy my work."

And she did, although many a time she paused to consider her situation, as she dusted the large gilt frames around the house. She often sighed and glanced at herself in the mirror as she passed, checking the tell-tale signs of age creeping across her face and noticing the dullness of her dated hairstyle before tidying those loose strands into place. Regretfully there was nothing she could do to improve her appearance; she had accepted that she would always be plain and unattractive a long time ago.

Shrugging, she turned back to work. She could not afford time for self-pity, for she had more than enough here to keep her mind occupied and her hands busy.

Then, climbing the stairs again, she would stop to smooth the creases from her skirt and push the wrinkles down over her hips. She knew she had slowed down of late, but there were moments when it was hard to remember that she was in her fifties.

***

As the day of the local parish meeting arrived, Ivy wondered if she had done enough to influence events. She could only wait and see. The prospective candidates for the Parish Council had to submit their signed declarations in person today, between one and two in the afternoon. Then they were expected to elaborate on the campaign issues they wanted to fight for to the assembled hall and answer questions. After which the vote would be taken and the election would be over by teatime.

Travis had been in his office all morning when Calum phoned him concerning a lorryload of building supplies awaiting payment at Travis's home. The arrangement had been cash on delivery and Calum had no intention of sending the lorry back with its load still intact. After a lot of moaning, Travis finally agreed to return to his house with his chequebook. His arrival and subsequent begrudging payment to the delivery driver coincided with his wife receiving a phone call from a restaurant in Tunbridge Wells. Apparently a young lady there had enquired if they were interested in attending a themed dining event taking place next month. As one of the regular customers, the couple were entitled to this special offer before it was put into the press. The very helpful caller, having mentioned that their normal booking, the day of the week and time, would fit in perfectly with the proposed event, found that the call was ended abruptly. Travis's wife was outraged at the discovery of her husband's clandestine dining arrangements with another woman. If she had not been so furious, she might have given the actual call a little more thought; she might have wondered how the restaurant would have had their phone number in the first place. For one thing, Travis would not have been stupid enough to give them the number because of the repercussions, and secondly, even if he paid by credit card, there would be no reference to address or phone number then either. Then maybe she would have realised the call might not have been from the restaurant after all.

Still, the damage was done, and World War Three soon broke out between the husband and wife. Calum discreetly left them to it, smirking to himself all the way back home. When Ivy had hinted that changing the delivery day might influence the outcome of the village elections, he had not believed it. How did she know what would happen? He could not wait to tell her of the development at the house. It was clear that the last thing on Travis's mind today would be the parish elections, as he had a more serious problem to deal with. His marriage was at stake, and Travis was quick to see he could easily lose everything.

Victoria slowly put the phone down, thankful for the day Ivy had witnessed Travis in Tunbridge Wells with the leggy brunette. Victoria had promised to behave while she visited her uncle's large home in the country village. And she fully meant to, well almost, but it was so tempting to be just a little naughty, and she knew that aided and abetted by her co-conspirator Ivy, the subtle campaign she had planned for some time was achievable. Although she had her fingers crossed today, being unsure if matters which they seemingly had no control over would work out in their favour.

At midday Martin, the bank manager, had wanted to pop home as usual for lunch, before heading off to the village hall, but within minutes he hurried back into the office, announcing that his car had been stolen. That he was angry was an understatement. He fumed and growled all kinds of threats, pacing the office floor. He could not understand how this could have happened. This was a quiet little village, not one of those densely-populated suburbs where such things were commonplace.

Ivy was one of many witnesses to his the ranting and raving, but she was the only one to receive a thunderous glare as he headed back outside. Still unable to believe it, Martin walked back to the spot, just to make sure the car had really gone, before phoning the police station. This time his car was back in its usual place, with his wife sitting in it. Martin went ballistic, although his wife failed to understand the state he was in, since she had merely borrowed it for a few errands of her own after catching the bus.

"For goodness sake Martin, the car is back here in time for you to use, why are you so angry?" she said.

"Because you have just made me look a complete fool at work!" he shouted.

"Well that's not my fault. And you're the one who's making a scene in public!" his wife told him, with equal volume.

After dropping his wife at home, Martin drove back towards the village. He knew he still had time to attend the election meeting that afternoon. Unfortunately, he should have known better than to assume any such thing. Today there were other forces at work. The mobile library had just swung into the entrance of the narrow lane which led to and past his house. Martin found himself facing the large slow trundling van filling most of the width of the track as it came towards him. Impatient to return to the main road, he flashed his lights, banged the car horn and waved the driver to back up. Miss Collins just looked at him in astonishment. She had no intention of reversing backwards into a main road; it was much too dangerous. He should have known that, and his irritated use of the horn only made her more indignant and stubborn. She flashed her headlights back, almost blinding him, and kept coming, nearer and nearer to his precious car.

Martin did not understand why this woman was being so difficult. Didn't she understand he was in a hurry? With no other way to the village and with no passing places either, he was forced to reverse back up to his own driveway and wait until the vehicle finally crawled passed his entrance towards the cottages and the turning point at the far end. Then he revved his engine in anticipation, desperate to finally to put his foot down, only to have the engine stall and then refuse to start. He swore under his breath as he tried it again and again, until he gave up. Slamming the car door, he dashed inside to phone Travis for a lift, hoping he had not left yet, but there was no reply.

After that he reluctantly he tried the local taxi office, but the answering machine told him that all services were suspended that afternoon. If he had used his common sense he would have realised that everyone local would be at the village hall. He now had to accept that he would never get there in time.

Miss Collins smiled to see his car still there as she returned past his house a little later. She had played her part exactly as Ivy had asked, and she had been very willing to do so. She had never liked Martin in any case, and him missing the very parish meeting he was trying to get to was a bonus. She nearly cheered aloud.

Everyone knew the specific rules which applied to this particular election; unless the candidates were on hand in person at the beginning of the meeting, they were not allowed to stand. Absentee nominations were null and void. Martin and his friend Travis had just lost out.

Not that anyone in the village hall minded that neither of them had put in an appearance. Most of them were immensely relieved. There were plenty of local people willing to protect local matters. Who would have suspected the men's absence been deliberately arranged? Ivy smiled that little smile of hers. Indeed she could not have hoped for anything better today. The additional help had been in a good cause. There had been no need to worry after all.

***

Her next task, the Summer Fete, just needed a little more tweaking and Ivy began the next part of their scheme.

Ivy had called unexpectedly on Mrs Jennings, a previous jam and preserve winner, under the pretext of asking for some advice about setting the jam she was making. Mrs Jennings was naturally surprised she had been consulted, but had remarked that Ivy had left it a little too late to enter any jam for this summer's competition. At which Ivy reassured her that the jam was for her personal use only. Besides, she would never dream of entering any competition, since there were so many experienced jam-makers in the village. She then continued by asking what other event her host intended to enter, since the entry conditions for all the categories had been changed this year, including the jam competition. Mrs Jennings looked more than puzzled at the news, forcing Ivy to relay the new rules to her.

"Apparently any previous winners who have won more than twice in a row are to be excluded from entering the same categories again this year, to give others a chance," she explained.

"Are you sure?"

"Oh yes. The vicar told me himself."

Her host looked utterly aghast, stuttering that she had made already made various varieties of jam for the competition.

"Oh dear me. What a shame you did not see the posters. They were in every shop in the village. But no doubt, you can sell them on one of the stalls, I am sure people will love to buy them, you have such a fine reputation with jam," said Ivy sympathetically.

"How dare the vicar do this! I must I have a few words with him. He needs to be told what I think of his new rules."

"There is no reason to get so upset, Mrs Jennings. It is

much fairer this way."

"Rubbish, he can't change things just as he pleases."

"I think you will find he can," was all Ivy managed to contribute before the woman went to vent her displeasure at the vicar on the phone. Ivy left her to her ranting and quietly slipped out of the front door.

As the vicar firmly told Mrs Jennings, he could do exactly what he wanted, since the fete was held in the vicarage grounds. As it was church property, he and his wife were in overall charge of the whole event. Their prime aim had been to ensure it was for the benefit and enjoyment of all their parishioners. They wanted it to be a success for everyone, not just the same few every time, and this year the fete indeed looked very promising in achieving that very aim, he concluded.

The actual day of the Summer Fete began really quite pleasantly. The sun was shining and bunting was fluttering against a blue sky, and the stalls and tents, erected satisfactorily, had encouraged a good turnout. After the vicar opened the afternoon with the obligatory welcome speech, the tannoy system crackled its announcements and the local band struck up its foot-tapping tunes to entertain the bustling crowds. The vicarage grounds were full of people wandering about amongst the many attractions. All the old favourites had reappeared. The usual white elephant stall, the hoopla and guessing the number of beans in the jar, the home-made jams and cakes stand, the lucky dip, the coconut shy, the candy floss stand and ice cream van, the tea tent, all had their many devotees. The children's fancy dress was followed by the sack races and the parent's three-legged races, but it was a hilarious version of musical chairs, involving people grabbing hats from a circle instead of sitting on chairs, which brought the loudest cheers. The smiles around the place proved everyone was really entering into the spirit and enjoying themselves. It was a good day, and Ivy felt very satisfied.

Uncle Charles had always said how unfair he thought the some of the judging was in some of the competitions. Not this year. The judging committee had been completely changed for every section. There had been fresh, impartial people brought in. Some of them were minor radio celebrities from London, whom Victoria had secretly suggested to the vicar.

Some of the marquees were set aside for the various classes of produce, and people passed in and out during the intervals to see what their friends and neighbours had exhibited. Ivy, like many of the others, was viewing the selection of cakes laid out on the judging table, with the interested parties who had entered their efforts waiting impatiently around at a discreet distance. As the judges were beginning their scrutiny, Ivy could not help remarking in quite a loud whisper how the lemon cake looked identical to the one in the specialist bakers' in Tunbridge Wells. Florrie, a little way away, muttered her agreement equally loudly, adding that she had thought the same last year about some of the entries. Other people nearby also began to stare at the cake in question. The rumour soon reached the judges' ears and their doubt concerning its authenticity began to show on their faces.

Meanwhile there were other remarks being aired about other cakes; goodness knows why, since this time they came from the youngsters, who knew very little about baking.

"What do you think of that one?" Susan asked of her new friend Jake.

"Yuk! It looks like the one she gave Aunt Lucy. It was horrible. Even the birds wouldn't eat the crumbs. It ended up in the bin."

"Darling children, you should be outside." Alice Hogarth smiled very sweetly, trying to elbow them out of the way, or at least away from her offering. Not that it was really her offering. She had entered the cake Matilda Jones had made, since Matilda could not enter herself under the new rules. She could not afford their remarks being heard by the approaching judges.

The two of them left willingly, winking mischievously at Ivy, who was smiling back, before she lifted her finger to her lips to indicate that their collusion was still a secret. They had promised to keep silent about their part in this and she did not doubt their word, as they were good children. They had been primed as to what they had to say and they had been thrilled to be trusted to help; it had been fun. No doubt Ivy would reward them later with an ice cream. She was always kind to them. They liked Ivy.

And as for Alice Hogarth, she did not win anything this year, nor did Matilda Jones with her quilting, which received similar dubious comments from the locals. Thus the day progressed. It was surprising how many of the 'not so nice' people were disappointed at their efforts this year. These new judges were hard to please, and no one knew of Victoria's own good influence on matters, having encouraged the vicar and his wife to invite her actor friends to the fete.

It was wonderful that without any outside help, Mrs Plum and Mrs Driver won their respective classes this year purely on merit. They were cheered and clapped loudly in appreciation of their efforts by all the spectators as they both collected their well-deserved cups and certificates. Utter pleasure shone in their faces. It was well worth seeing and their neighbours and friends were truly delighted for them.

Likewise Mr Russell won a cup for his garden produce and another for the cut flowers. And at the instigation of the Vicar, he was presented with surprise gift and framed certificate in recognition for all he had done to keep the village looking so colourful and lovely over the years. Again the applause was overwhelming and heartily meant. Lovely Mr Russell was near to tears with all the praise heaped upon him and he was quite glad to escape to his own little potting shed afterwards. He had never had such a wonderful day.

Dear Ivy had worked her magic, ensuring that the Summer Fete would be the success Victoria wanted, most of it thanks to her many friends who had all played their parts so beautifully.

***

Victoria was eager to hear the opinion of the two women who provided her weekend train journeys with amusement.

"The villagers were besotted with the woman. Look what happened at the summer fete," said one woman.

"Even the vicar fell under her spell, asking her to judge the children's fancy dress," replied the other.

"And her iced buns were a great favourite on the cake stall."

"Frank saw Travis at the golf club last night, he thought he looked pale. I wonder if he's ill."

"Maybe that was why he didn't offer to stand for the council," her companion pondered.

Not at all. Ivy and Victoria both knew what was wrong. The man was living on an emotional knife edge. His wife was making him suffer any way she could. Not that he wanted his personal life made public, because it would ruin his image in the community.

***

The summer was nearly over and Victoria knew Ivy would soon have to return to London. Yes, she really was going to miss Ivy about the place. Dear Ivy, she had a quick eye for detail and an excellent memory. She was good at her various skills, and she had pieced together so many interesting facts which contributed to everything slowly falling into place.

***

A few days later, Victoria stepped out through the village, refreshed and energetic. Her eyes were bright with secret pleasure and relished the satisfaction she felt. Everything had been tidied up.

Boarding the train, she positioned her relaxed, lithe and beautiful body comfortably back in the seat, eagerly anticipating the gossip of her regular fellow passengers. Indeed they soon arrived and sat with in hearing distance, allowing her to enjoy the idle chatter. For once she would be delighted at every unfair criticism they uttered, because it would prove how little they knew about Ivy.

"Such an ineffectual woman."

Ineffectual! They would have been surprised at all Ivy had achieved, including chasing after and catching the young Tommy after he had been scrumping in the orchard. Just as her sharp words had been enough to stop him or his friends from raiding the orchard again.

"I'm glad that woman has finally gone back to London," Mrs Jones sighed, nearby.

"Yes, thank goodness. Ivy Tree, a ridiculous name, ridiculous person."

Victoria smiled, bemused at their ignorance. Victoria had not thought her name so ridiculous, although she was biased. Admittedly it was a name which had that unmistakably mundane quality, but that had been the whole idea from the start. It had been important that Ivy had blended in with the other inhabitants.

"Miss Tree, Miss Ivy Tree." was how she had first introduced herself, except maybe if people had really listened carefully they might have realised how 'Miss Tree' would have sounded like 'Mystery', if it had been emphasised slightly differently. Then they would have realised that everything was not as it seemed. "Ivy Tree, ridiculous name, ridiculous person," they had repeated.

Ivy was never ridiculous. They really had no idea about Ivy, what she was or who she was.

Ivy had been a gem of an invention. At the time Victoria had been stumped for a name, but a last-minute inspiration, always relied on in a crisis, had proved its worth again. It had been a gift of a part, and Victoria loved it. Who was Ivy Tree anyway? She did not exist, well not really; she had been a construction of parts. Her clothes and hair were back in the theatrical box, her makeup washed away and all her characteristics vanished.

A wide smile of appreciation spread across Victoria's face and her eyes twinkled. Ivy certainly gave the right impression. Dressed in less-than-fashionable clothes and the obligatory sensible shoes, she could easily have been one of those mild, inoffensive ladies in an Agatha Christie story. Every one of the villagers considered her to be a sweet, unpretentious, perfectly ordinary middle-aged lady, with a natural friendly disposition, a warm heart and good intentions. But then that had been the whole idea.

In fact Victoria was proud of herself. As Ivy, she had kept perfectly in character. Her actions in the village had been carefully designed to achieve the result which best benefited her uncle and his friends.

***

The train slowed into the London terminal, and Victoria stretched to lift her hand luggage down as the two ladies bustled past her along the compartment. Apparently they still failed to recognise her as Charles's niece from the village, and their continued ignorance amused her. No doubt they were too preoccupied in their own lives to notice anything unusual. They certainly hadn't so far this summer.

The doors banged and thumped, windows rattled and scurrying footsteps heralded the rush of various travellers as they descended into the station. All except Victoria, the very picture of casual elegance, immaculately groomed and attractively dressed in the soft, expensively-cut clothes, as she ambled confidently along the concourse. She admitted that she felt good, and today she did not mind being noticed, being fully aware of the admiring glances which followed her to the other platform. Her face and figure had provided plenty of lucrative photographic modelling work when necessary, but she loved the theatre more.

***

Victoria's Uncle Charles returned home to find a much more contented village, and his gardener, Mr Russell, could not wait to relate how the village fete had been a cracker this summer. The old man still had an inner glow of satisfaction about him as he continued his gardening, and was often heard chuckling happily to himself. Charles did not understand what had been happening in his absence, but he suspected this was all down to this latest housekeeper, since nearly everyone he spoke to had a good word for her.

He had often wondered about the housekeepers his niece Victoria had engaged over the years, but he had always been happy to trust her judgment. In the past they had all sounded just like the professional no-nonsense people he would have approved of, but this latest one, besides keeping his home in pristine order, had also left a lasting impression on the local people.

Charles rang his niece to try to clarify this unusual situation, suspicion immediately surfacing as he remembered that special gleam in her eyes when she had met him at the station in London.

"All right Victoria," her uncle began quite sternly, his tone indicating the trouble she was in. "I have only been away a couple of months. Just what have you and your latest protégé been up to?"

"I don't know what you mean," she replied in exaggerated innocence. "I kept my promise to behave."

"Hmm. Then what about this paragon of virtue you hired? I don't believe in fairy godmothers."

Victoria giggled. "Really?"

"What have you done, Victoria?"

There was a pause.

"Come on Victoria. Give."

"Nothing much, really. We just gave matters a little helping hand, to put a few things right. You're not cross are you?"

How could he be, having learnt about this year's other winners at the Summer Fete? His favourite neighbours had finally received the recognition of their wonderful skills which they deserved.

"And how did you persuade the housekeeper to go along with all this?"

"Ivy? It wasn't difficult. I... sort of invented her," she whispered confidentially. "She was me."

"You wicked, wicked child!" Uncle Charles scolded, suddenly realising what she had been up to. "That repertory company has a lot to answer for!"

Indeed Victoria felt quite satisfied with herself. The months of acting had been a worthwhile experience.

"If you wouldn't mind still keeping my bike in your shed, I can use it when I come down on my visits," she said.

"I really don't know about that, Victoria. Haven't you confused the locals enough? Are there any other housekeepers in the future who might need it?" he teased. "And by the way, I have another query. Why do I suddenly find myself belonging to the mobile library when I really have no need for any more books in my life?"

Victoria avoided answering that one, and he began to get a nagging feeling that it was not the books Victoria had in mind. His niece had always told him that all those objects cluttering up the house were no substitute for the company of the right woman. Miss Collins had clearly been selected as the right woman. This niece of his had a lot to answer for.

"I'm off to see father in Portugal tomorrow," she interrupted, changing the subject.

"How is the old devil? Still one step ahead of the law, I hope."

"Of course." Her answer was based more on hope than expectation.

"I don't know how the scoundrel deserves a lovely daughter like you."

Victoria's life had never been dull while she was growing up, with her father around. He had never been the perfect role model, but she had learnt to adjust and make allowances for his imperfections. She had even learnt a few tricks of her own, none of which were exactly on the right side of the law.

"I expect he has another project in mind by now, he is always full of ideas," she teased.

"I think it's safer if I don't know any more, Victoria," Charles butted in quickly.

Indeed, she agreed, it was much, much better that dear uncle Charles did not know anything concerning her father's present lifestyle. He had retired to a pleasant little farmhouse in the hills of Monchique, where he spent his time quietly renovating and painting his canvases, safe from prying eyes. For a very good reason. They provided an illicit income.

"Talk to you soon," she cheerfully finished.

"Bye for now."

***

She gave a wistful sigh. Victoria was looking forward to seeing her father, seeing those mischievous features and enjoying being together again for a while. They would talk and laugh and share confidences, although the details of her months working in a country village would require discretion on her part. It would only give the old rogue more outrageous ideas. She could almost hear him suggesting a tantalisingly similar scheme with an ingenious alternative scenario. Another village, with a private art collector the target and another nondescript domestic help. A housekeeper, maybe, who would deliberately keep attention diverted from the art restorer as he worked quietly away to replace the valuable originals with his copies. He would love that! Oh yes, she could well imagine the whole plan.

Victoria screwed up her face. She could not deny that she still relished a great feeling of satisfaction concerning her recent escapade. Maybe she was her father's daughter after all, because the feeling of success was infectious.

They would make a perfect team, but she was never ever going to let it happen. Victoria shook her head. No, no, no! Ivy would never have approved. She had to preserve all the values Ivy had come to represent. Dear Ivy was that prick of the conscience which would keep her on the straight and narrow. Bless her cotton socks!

* * * * *

KAY LA LA, KAY LAY LAY

CHAPTER 1

'Kay la la, Kay lay lay!' The island parrots echoed their call through the vast dense vegetation of San Maron where the three young children played.

"Here I come, ready or not!" Jacqueline shouted to her companions, spinning around quickly, hoping to catch one of them moving. Her laughter pealed out into the familiar tropical greenery as Simon, her brother, and Hillary, otherwise known as Hicky, their best friend, darted from one rock to another, from rock to tree, trying to outguess her. Their own giggles were hard to stifle or control in their energetic scramble.

A little while later, with the game over, they had sat content in this untamed corner of wilderness. Here in their own private domain, they repeated the old childhood ritual of their allegiance. They painted each other's palms with the red pulp they had just made and although the symbols trickled out of shape and smudged, their hands met over the centre of the circle of stones. The words were spoken, the deed done, and they lay back in the sun to enjoy its wonderful warmth. They shared a grin between them, knowing by the length of the shadows creeping across the ground that they would soon have to return home.

Home: a magical, safe, happy place, where they had spent all their charmed, idyllic lives engulfed in comforting affection. There they were indulged there by the housekeeper, Hillary's mother, or their father Daniel gathering all three of them at his knee. Even in this the last decade of the twentieth century, their remote isolated island in the Caribbean remained untouched by the influences of the wider world. Such was their contentment, such was their world. They could hardly imagine their days would ever be any different.

The day had started just like any other, with the three of them racing about the place, revelling in the freedom the summer and the school holidays allowed. Jacqueline eagerly waited for her father to call her to him, because today it was her turn, her day, her chance to find her own set of the coloured markers he would have hidden around the farm. As she was eight now, a year older than both Simon and Hicky, her father had made the clues a little more puzzling each time for her. But she was always determined to solve them. The three of them thrived on his ingenious challenges and were always eager for the next game, because of the hugs of delight they were rewarded with as he enthusiastically praised them for finding the right answers.

So where was he? She was impatient to start, and disappointed at the delay. There was no excuse, no reason for this failure to keep to the plan. What was he doing? Why wasn't he here? It was not at all like her father to break with the routine he had so lovingly set every week for each of them in turn, for their enjoyment. He had never let her or the others down before.

She returned indoors to search for him, but found no sign of him. Now she was puzzled enough to seek out Ernestine, the housekeeper, to see if she knew where he was. It appeared that Ernestine had no idea of his whereabouts either. Apparently she had not seen him since breakfast. She had not even seen him leave the house, and he certainly had not mentioned he was going out anywhere today. Nor had he left any messages for anyone to indicate where he had gone. It was not like him to just disappear.

Maybe he would not be gone too long, Jac hoped, as she went out onto the veranda to watch for his return. But as the time dragged by she became increasingly disappointed and then very annoyed at her father. She would certainly not forgive him easily for spoiling her day, and was ready to give him one of her peeved, tight-lipped faces on his return. When he returned. Just how long was he going to be? It was approaching midday. If he did not return soon, there would not be enough time left to play the game. She sulked.

Jac could hear the distant riotous sounds of her brother

and Hicky playing down on the beach as she restlessly paced up and down. It was not fair, what was keeping him? He could not be too far away. Maybe there had been a problem on the farm. This was no good; she had no choice but to set out to look for him herself. So she walked from field to field, asking the itinerant workers from the village she came across if they had seen him. Every response was negative. The occasional sight of someone in the distance on one of the various public footpaths bordering around the property had given her hope, only to be dashed when on closer inspection she could see it was not him. So where was her father? Where had he gone after breakfast?

She trudged back to the house. She had missed lunch, but she did not care. There she kicked her feet on the porch, unable to find anything to take her mind off her nagging concern for his absence.

Jac was still waiting there when a note addressed to her father was hand-delivered by one of the couriers from the hotel in town. Ernestine thanked the boy and put it on the hall table, neither of them thinking it was of much importance, since it was in an unsealed envelope. Then Ernestine wondered if it might have needed an answer and opened it quickly to scan the contents.

"Oh dear. I should have stopped the courier before he left," she loudly exclaimed.

"What's the matter?"

"There are two men from the hotel coming here this afternoon, in a few hours, expecting to see your father."

Visitors, strangers were coming here uninvited! Jac was

incensed. Most people on the island would have had the manners to wait for a suitable response before arriving at someone's door.

"What are we to do? There is no way to stop them before they make a wasted journey."

Maybe her father would be back in time, but neither of them thought that likely, the way things looked at the moment.

"Your father has never failed to let me know where he would be. I shall have to send one of the men to see if they can find him," Ernestine complained.

"I have already been around the farm looking for him. He is not here," Jacqueline informed her.

"Goodness, then where is he? I don't understand it," Ernestine sighed.

Meanwhile Jac had instantly seen something important and more worrying in her father's disappearance. With him not here, these strangers would find the house empty except for one other adult, Ernestine. She did not like that idea at all. Their precious home would be undefended and unprotected! She would have to do something.

She needed Simon and Hicky to be here immediately to help her mount a defence, and she rushed to the beach to find them. However, although they had been there that morning, they had naturally wandered off elsewhere since. By instinct she knew where they would have gone. She would have to run like mad to reach them if she was to get them back to the house in time.

"Kay la la!" The shrill cry of the parakeet broke through the normal jungle sounds, so shrill it made the two younger children instantly stop their play, turn and run back towards the call. Jac ran as fast as she could, willing her legs to go faster, until she stumbled to a halt and they all met on the pathway. Severely out of breath, and almost bent double grabbing in great gulps of air, all she could tell them was that they should get back to the house as quickly as possible. Without question they immediately obeyed, following her lead as she dragged them with her, ducking low along the edges of the fields to avoid their strange behaviour being seen, not daring to stop until they reached home. Thankfully, after darting around the last of the outbuildings, Jac realised with relief that they had arrived before their visitors.

By then she had a plan. It was not brilliant, but anything was better than nothing. Hurriedly she sent Hicky off home to keep watch on the road, before she explained her idea to her brother.

"We must not allow strangers into the house while father is not here," she said.

"And how do we do that?" Simon asked.

"We must position ourselves on the front porch to prevent them entering the house and convince them that there is no point in them waiting around. That father is not expected back today."

"And they're going to believe us? What children tell them? I don't think so!" her brother argued.

"They will, because we're going to pretend we are perfect

little angels. Innocent, sweet and very good, well dressed and on our best behaviour. That butter would not melt in our mouths. With us being so young and naïve, why would they imagine we had any reason to lie to them?"

Simon did not mind playing charades, they were fun, but he did not like the bit about having to look their best. "Yuk!" he remarked, putting his finger in his mouth and gesturing that the idea made him want to be sick.

"We have to give them a false impression, best behaviour remember," she warned.

Simon could not believe what she expected of him. He was horrified when he looked in the mirror to see his mop of blond hair brushed almost flat, in clean clothes and wearing sandals. They were both used to running about the place barefoot, especially indoors. Likewise Jac had similarly dragged out one of her cotton dresses reserved for special outings, pulled her hair into bunches and tied them with too pretty a ribbon bow at each side. A little deception would not hurt, if it provided a fitting distraction, she had decided. And their father would be bound to approve and see the funny side of their performance when he came home.

They did not have time to reflect on their uncommon appearance, since a "Kay la la!" burst into the air, warning them that the two strangers were coming up the driveway. She dragged a reluctant brother down the stairs and into position. A little nervously, she watched them come closer and closer, wondering if they could pull this off. It all depended on what type of people they were, but Jac was prepared to do her best.

As the men continued their approach, it became obvious which of them was the more important by the manner of his walk. The taller one seemed more confident in his slow amble towards the house, as if registering everything around him and smiling too confidently to himself. Jac instantly resented his manner. Taking a deep breath, she bounced out of the front door, pulling her almost unrecognisable brother behind her, to skip cheerfully along the veranda and jump deliberately to a halt in the centre of the top step, coming face to face the strangers and clearly blocking their way.

"Hello. Who are you?" she asked directly, smiling brightly, without any sign of shyness.

"Good afternoon children. If you are Jacqueline and Simon Liscombe, and I presume you are, then I am your uncle, Maurice Collmann," he explained calmly.

Jacqueline felt her body tense up at this unexpected revelation. She could not help being cautious.

"Really?"

He nodded and smiled, too much for her liking.

"Yes. I am your late mother's brother."

She noticed that he was a little hesitant for a moment, no doubt unsure of their reaction at mentioning their mother to them. It obviously worried him. Little did he know that her memory was still an everyday part of their lives. She screwed up her eyes and deliberately frowned at him. How dare he suddenly turn up like this? He had never even bothered to write to their dear mother or keep in touch before. She decided she did not like this brother.

"Are you? You look more like father," she countered, smiling innocently and tilting her head to him, her big bright brown eyes staring into his own dark features.

Simon, who stood beside his sister, looked at her sideways, up at the stranger and back to his sister, frowning deeply, but remaining silent. Having heeded the instructions earlier, he was content to let her take the lead.

"I'm sure father was not expecting you. You should have written to let him know you were coming," she continued, a thoughtful expression indicating her doubts, whilst she still stood her ground making it clear of her reluctant to allow him into the property.

"I did." The edge of annoyance was just detectable in his tone.

"There have been no overseas letters for a long time. We would know because we always save the stamps for our collection," Simon mumbled, glad to play his part.

"We don't allow strangers into the house," Jac warned.

"I am not a stranger. I am your uncle. Family."

"You are a stranger to me."

"Where is your father?" he asked, trying not to sound agitated and looking at the open door behind her, as if expecting him to be in the house.

"I don't know exactly. He could be anywhere, especially if he wasn't expecting you," she sighed, shrugging and absently running her fingers along the wooden balustrade, without attempting to move.

The standoff continued. Smiling, Jac turned her back briefly before settling into the large rocking chair which dominated the porch, where she sat happily rocking it to and fro, to study this man again. Utterly relaxed, she hoped to indicate that such absences were commonplace and that neither of them were ever intimidated by visitors. Meanwhile Simon, appearing to look decidedly bored by events, remembered to position himself on the floor right in front of the doorway, to block any entrance. Then he crossed his legs, leaned his head on his arms and stared at the men, quietly sceptical of everything.

The tall man hesitated, uncertain of the steady scrutiny he seemed to be under. He was obviously still considering his next move when Jac made hers. She did not know what type of person he was or if he was really their relation.

"Are you the uncle from Africa?" she suddenly challenged him enthusiastically.

"Err, yes," he replied, thrown a little by her unexpected knowledge of his past.

She saw the other man snigger and saw the glare from their supposed uncle which swiftly stopped it. A sign which encouraged her to continue. Now, what else did she remember from all she had been told over the years?

"From the diamond mines?" she gushed, leaning forward, her eyes widening in anticipation.

"Er, well that was a long time ago. I have travelled a lot since then," he explained.

"Are you rich?" piped in her brother, the idea grabbing his attention.

"Unfortunately not," Maurice shrugged.

"Oh." Simon sighed, pulling a face, disappointed and resting on his arms again.

"Now then, I do need to see your father. I have come a long way to see him," he stated, looking over their heads, hoping that someone in authority would appear, having been stirred into life by all this conversation.

Then, as if to satisfy his unspoken request, their housekeeper Ernestine appeared on the front step, wiping her hands on her apron.

"Good day sir, the master is out at present. Are you the gentleman who sent the note from the hotel earlier?" she asked.

"Yes. I am his brother-in-law, Maurice Collmann, and this is my colleague, my business associate Brian Nevison," the man repeated for her benefit.

"Oh dear, I am really sorry. He is not here. I've sent someone out to look for him. Did he have any idea you were coming to see him?"

"Apparently not, although the letter announcing my visit to the island should have arrived last week. I suppose it might have travelled on the same slow supply boat in which I came and is in the sorting office here, awaiting delivery even as we speak," he purred placidly.

Jac could not help cringing. His artificially soft, kind tones annoyed her. She disliked this man.

"I'm sure he would have been here to welcome me, if he had received it," Maurice added.

"I expect he would. Goodness me. I don't understand. Never mind, you had better come in and wait in the cool for him, sir," Ernestine clucked merrily.

What? No no no! Jac exchanged a look of horror with

Simon. This plan was not working. They did not want these men in the house! She pulled an expression of disgust at the men's backs as they stepped over Simon, who had been made to move, and followed Ernestine towards the interior. There seemed nothing she could do to prevent it.

An instant later she smartly darted in behind them and pushing in in front of them, trying to delay every step they took as they gently eased their way on into her home. Her efforts were to no avail, because these men were being made welcome by the housekeeper, who ushered them into the cool interior of the house. She stopped on her way to fetch their guests' refreshment to give the children one of her intense glances, letting them know she was fully aware they were up to some mischief.

"I don't know what you two are up to or why you're dressed up like that, but don't you dare get those good clothes dirty," she whispered. Then in a louder voice she instructed Jac to play the host in her father's absence.

In the lounge, Jac reluctantly bade them sit; she had no other choice. Her objective now was to keep them contained and occupied, to keep them from wandering wherever they wanted all over the house. Silence would give them time to think, to plan, to manoeuvre matters their way. There was only one answer. Once they were seated, she began.

"What was it like in Africa? I bet you had lots of adventures. Father didn't mention you much. What do you do now?"

Jac was full of questions and could not keep still for a minute, staggering her uncle by her interest as he struggled to answer one question before the next was fired at him. She wanted to know everything and was not shy about asking, refusing to be daunted by their dull replies. Simon, meanwhile, just stood in the doorway and stared at them for all of five minutes before wandering off. With Jac in full flow, he knew he could not think quickly enough to be of much use to her. Besides, as far as he was concerned his sister's scheme had failed and he was totally bored by her attempts to continue the whole uninteresting game. With the result that Jac was left to fend for herself. Brothers were no help at all she seethed.

After a time, she ran out of steam and began to fidget, unsure of what to do next. She had hoped that this visit was just a casual call, merely to renew family acquaintances, and it would not be that important. Which hopefully meant they might not stay long. Except that Maurice and his friend had now taken off their jackets and were sitting enjoying the refreshing coffee and biscuits. How was she to stop them making themselves too much at home? She pointed out the box from India on the table and the wooden camel from Arabia, and then every other precious object of interest on the walls, items brought by their parents. They nodded and smiled just that little too benevolently at her chatter, but they were not really listening any more, only gazing out of the windows regularly in the expectation of seeing her father.

Eventually her uncle went to find the housekeeper to enquire if anyone had found Daniel, or why he was not home yet. Ernestine admitted that such prolonged absences were normally connected to going fishing. If the fish were biting he had the habit of staying out at sea longer. Theirs was a routine which seemingly had no routine, she joked. Her explanation accepted, the guests were obviously unsure what to do next in the circumstances, and were wondering how long to wait before returning to the hotel in town. Then, to Jac's utter dismay, the housekeeper suggested they could stay overnight; to her it seemed the natural thing. Being a relation, her master would have expected nothing less, she added persuasively. Jac almost froze, knowing they would hardly refuse.

"I am afraid you will have to settle for us all eating together in the kitchen as usual," the housekeeper warned as she hurried off to make up the beds in the spare rooms and then prepared extra food for the evening meal.

Ernestine called out across the yard to her daughter in the small cottage next door and Hicky appeared instantly, her little face eager for supper. Yet the atmosphere at the meal was decidedly different from usual, the younger ones looking at Jac for guidance, unwilling to engage in their normal merry banter and even devouring their food less swiftly than normal. Between them and the visiting grown-ups expelling great sighs quite regularly, the meal time became decidedly awkward.

"I don't expect there's anything to worry about," Ernestine repeated, trying to ease the concern.

Having shuffled off to their beds whilst the adults remained talking quietly downstairs, the children exchanged a quick conversation at the foot of the stairs before Hicky went back to her own home.

"Where is father?" asked Simon quietly, once they were alone.

Jac wished she knew, really, really wished. Her initial disappointment from this morning when she had tried unsuccessfully to find him had now changed into a growing pang of anxiety. He had failed to answer the whistle signal with his own in the way they used to locate each other. It was most unlike him. How could she not worry? And more importantly, how could she hide her worst fears from her brother?

"It was your turn, your day for the game with him," Hicky murmured.

"That is why I don't understand. He never misses our games. He would have told us if he had to postpone it. He would not have just gone away like that," said Jac.

"Do you think he went fishing?" Simon queried.

"Maybe," she shrugged, trying to sound more cheerful than she felt.

Except Jac knew that her father would never have gone fishing without telling either them or Ernestine first. It made her wonder why the little lie Ernestine had told Maurice to hide the truth had been really necessary. Maybe it was because she could not think of the real reason for his disappearance either; maybe she was actually as worried about her father's unusual absence as Jac now was, but had not wanted to show it.

That night Jac could not sleep. She tossed and turned and looked at the sky through their window. The arrival of these two men had cast a shadow on the house, and for the first time in her life, Jac made sure they both locked their bedroom doors for the night. She felt a vulnerability she had never sensed before. It frightened her.

***

At first light Jac and Simon were up and dressed, listening for any sounds of their guests on the landing. They paused at their visitors' doors before creeping downstairs and running across the back yard. The little bird from the other cottage, calling to them from the top window as they passed, comforted and reassured them. Climbing over the wall, they hurried on and rushing down the flight of stone steps to the rocky beach, and stopped in their tracks at the last bend.

They stared at each other. There was no boat at their little jetty.

"So father went fishing after all!" Simon whispered, although there had been no need to whisper, as there was no one else around.

Slowly they continued down the rest of the steps, wandering to the end of the jetty and back and gazing out to sea. The early morning sun shone, reflecting the dazzling brightness on the rippling water, but there was no sign of a boat anywhere. Jac checked the mooring ropes idly tossed on the decking. Everything looked perfectly normal, nothing seemed out of place. Had the boat been there yesterday, when she came in search of Simon and Hicky? She could not remember. In truth, Jac felt cold inside. She even shivered in the warm morning sun before deciding to go back to the house.

"We don't tell anyone about the boat being gone," she instructed her brother.

"But it might be important."

"It might be more important not to, if father took the boat secretly for some reason."

Simon did not really understand, but he sensed that his sister considered there might be more to this whole occurrence than anyone imagined. As usual he was content to go along with her plan. He automatically trusted her judgement.

On their return to the house they were met by the sight of their unwanted relation making himself too much at home. Maurice was lazily stretched out in the old steamer chair with coffee already at his fingertips and a plate of half-eaten toast on the small table on the back terrace.

Jac fumed internally. Maybe she was being over-sensitive, but this was their home and no one else's. She did not want either of them there, but she would remain patient. Once father was home, they would leave.

"Are you staying long?" she asked him, without hesitation.

"Until I have seen your father. I have a business proposition I wanted to discuss," came his equally frank answer. Her curiosity apparently satisfied, she nodded and dragged her brother off by his hand, pulling him gently towards the kitchen for their breakfast.

Not that she allowed Simon the opportunity to eat, until she had torn upstairs to the attic window, from where she could see nearly every outbuilding and ruin on the farm, all the hedgerows and ditches, the Wilson property next door and their own private jungle. Frustratingly, there was no unusual activity. The few workers were in the fields as normal, and everything was exactly the same as every other day. No one seemed to be looking for their father. Jac shook her head and then leaned out over the attic window sill, waving urgently to Hicky and signalling for her to come over.

At first the children sat on the back terrace, fidgeting about, attempting to play and watching the path from the beach, in case their father appeared from that direction. They refused to risk leaving the house, all of them determined to be the first to see him, to run to him and welcome him home. For Jac, her only spark of relief came when Nevison, their uncle's associate, decided to go back to the hotel in the town. She was glad he had gone, as having one less stranger in her precious home pleased her immensely.

So the morning dragged on, until Jac could not stand it any longer. They had to do something. No one seemed to realise the seriousness of their father's disappearance.

Ernestine had been bombarded with reasons for their proposed venture. All of them were eager to do their part, although she was reluctant to let them go.

"He might be lying hurt somewhere!" had been the final

persuasive argument. Therefore, with sandwiches reluctantly supplied by Ernestine, the three children headed out to make their own combined search for Daniel and the boat.

They headed to the cliffs first, where many rocky, dangerous edges dropped straight to the sea and the dense prickly shrubs and the untidy crop of wild bushes stuck out at every angle. They looked impossible to climb, except that these three knew that the inhospitable vegetation hid a series of tiny, narrow ledges, almost like secret tunnels, from which they could reach either the very top of the cliffs or the bottom completely unseen. Thus arriving at the base of the cliffs they eagerly searched for any piece of wreckage caught in the crevices, anything to show if their father had gone to sea or if the boat might have been damaged. They continued searching until they had scoured the whole of the bay on their side of the island. Simon kept diving repeatedly, deep and long into the various cave entrances concealed well below the water line, looking for any jetsam. Meanwhile Jac and Hicky had splashed through every rocky pool at the base of the cliffs and checked inside every hidden grotto. Nothing.

After scrutinizing the fields, they split up and scampered up and down every path and raced along and trampled through every inch of thicket, everywhere they could think of. They were extra diligent around the scattered ruins and various sheds, but with no success. They found no sign of their father, or any clue which might tell them where he had gone.

Disappointed, dirty and dishevelled, they met up as

arranged and sat in silence munching their food. Even the island parrots usually so vocal, were quiet, as if sensing their mood. Jac had to think. If he was not at sea and not on the farm, then where, where was their father? What had happened to him? He had never, ever stayed away without telling them of his plans.

Leaving the exhausted Simon and Hicky to rest, Jac ran up to the headland point, from where she could see the most of the coastline and beyond. How often had she raced up here to watch her father clear the reef and round the several large rocks that jutted out to sea, when he had gone fishing. How often had she waved, and by instinct he had turned his head and waved back. Her eyes scanned the sea, determined not to miss anything, the pattern of the waves, the movement of the birds, yet everything was the same, normal. There was no sign of wreckage, no floating pieces of wood, no boat. Indeed why should there be? The weather had been good and he knew these waters, knew the sea. Her eyes ached, she had stared so long. How could she give up hope of seeing something she was so desperate to find? Her heart was thumping, and it wasn't because of the exertion of her running; it was because of a sudden inner fear, a sensation. An instinct that something was terribly wrong. Eventually she turned away, her eyes tearful at the horrid thought of what all this actually meant.

There was one last thing they could do; they could resort to the spirits for help. So the three of them sat in their jungle clearing, cast their hands over the circle of stones and stared into the sky, each silently reciting the message to be carried high into the atmosphere, each concentrating on the person it was meant for.

Finally the three children trudged reluctantly home, dirty, scratched and bruised, to be gathered into Ernestine's comforting arms. For while she had guessed it would be a fruitless task, she had not had the heart to stop them from trying; besides, it saved her temporarily from the questions which were bound to come. Questions with no answers.

The evening meal was silent and the conversation stilted. The adults were obviously trying to pretend everything was all right for the sake of the children, although the looks exchanged were far from encouraging. No one, it seemed, was willing to voice their concern.

"He would never have gone anywhere without telling one of us, you know that," Jac said to Ernestine.

Ernestine admitted she was right, she had never known Daniel to be lapse in his routine. The room fell silent again and an exasperated Jac followed the housekeeper into the kitchen and tugged at her sleeve as she began the washing up.

"He has been gone so long, it's not like him. We have to go to the authorities," she pleaded. She suddenly did not care if the whole farm was invaded, battered and flattened by hordes of big feet. She wanted to know where her father was.

A sad Ernestine admitted that it had already been decided that she and her uncle were going into town first thing tomorrow to report their father's disappearance to the police. Ernestine took her hand in hers. She wanted Jac to promise that the children would wait at home and not wander off on another search while they were away. She wanted to know they were not going to do anything silly. Jac could not understand why they needed to be confined to the house. For Ernestine, for her, Jac would do as she was asked, but not for anyone else.

The children were sent off to bed as usual, although how they expected them to sleep with all this uncertainty surrounding them, wasn't clear. Simon eventually dozed off, but Jac's fears kept her awake. The questions she had asked herself all during the day returned. Something was terribly wrong.

**

The next day a subdued Ernestine fussed about, making sure they ate their breakfast before getting ready to leave. The children had heard the postman knock and heard their uncle answer the door to him. When the man had gone, Maurice stood in the kitchen doorway and tried to beckon the housekeeper out of the room without his silent signal being noticed. But Jac did notice, and within seconds she tore after them into the lounge.

Maurice held an official-looking envelope, which he handed to Ernestine. She nervously tore it open, and gave a slight gasp as she read the contents. She handed it to their uncle, who in turn read it, then stared back at her and handed it back.

"This makes no sense," she muttered.

The housekeeper sank into an armchair in a daze, while her uncle headed off past Jac, not really noticing her, murmuring he was going to get fetch a glass of water for Ernestine.

"How do I prepare the children?" she whispered into her lap, her hands clenched together.

Jac knew in that instant that it must be really bad news. Her father - what had happened to him?

"What is it?" she screamed, running towards Ernestine. Her voice alerted the others in the kitchen, and they burst past their returning uncle, nearly knocking him over in their haste to see what was wrong. Ernestine swallowed hard, clutching at the children gathering around her lap, her face strained and sad, whilst they clamoured for information.

"Oh, my dears. This is from your father's solicitor in town. Apparently your father has instructed him to draw up some important documents concerning your future. He requests that we should go to his office as soon as possible, so that he can explain the details."

What documents, Jacqueline wondered? She did not understand.

"I would prefer to wait for father's return. It would be much easier if he explained matters, rather than some legal person," said Jac.

"We have no choice. According to the solicitor, your father has left the island and gone away indefinitely."

"What?" the three children mouthed in unison.

"I am sorry children, but Daniel has told him it is unlikely he will return."

It must be a mistake. The children stood unable to believe her words; they could not take it in. They looked in horror at the paper she held, stunned and silenced. She was forced to read it aloud again to them. Their father had gone, just like that, his departure left to someone else to put in a letter. Why hadn't he taken them aside and told them himself?

Jac shook her head fervently. No, no, no! It was a lie, there was no reason for him to leave them. He would never have gone off like that. So suddenly, so quickly, so secretively, without a word of warning. Her jaw set, she rushed upstairs. Her father's room looked just as tidy as it always did. She flung open the wardrobes and drawers in a frantic search, checking all his clothes. There were some missing, only a couple of things, barely enough for an overnight stay, but they could also be in the wash. She raced down to the laundry room, desperate to convince herself that nothing was really missing, that he had not really left, but she could not find his clothes or anyone else's. Ernestine had done the washing and the ironing at the beginning of the week, and everything would have been put away, everything in its place, tidy in their own rooms.

Gulping, she tore back upstairs to his room and stood there, trying to think. She looked around the room again. Everything seemed normal; the pens and papers on his desk, the photographs and other items on the mantel, sat there undisturbed.

He would have had to take something to carry his clothes in, yet all the cases were still there on top of the wardrobe, even the smallest, untouched and covered in a thin layer of dust. None of them had ever been used as long as she could remember, because he never went away. He could not have gone.

She checked his shoes, not that he had many. The only ones that were not there were those he had been wearing that day. As she was rummaging through the bottom of the wardrobe, she sat back on the floor with a jolt. His old rucksack, the one he used all the time for family picnics and their Sunday afternoon hikes, was not there. She searched and searched, but it had gone. He had taken it with him.

There was one other important item he would also have taken. Reluctantly and slowly she opened the top drawer of his desk, knowing where it normally lay. Although it must have been out of date, his passport had gone. He would have had to send it away to be renewed, but he could have done that without them knowing.

This final piece of proof, the lack of his passport, merely supported the words in that dreadful letter that had been read to them downstairs. She stood ashen faced, unable to believe the evidence. How could their father have left them? How could he do that? This could not be right. This could not be happening.

Slowly, still in denial, she retreated back down the stairs, where she could hear the other two shocked children, who had evidently found their voices, persistently demanding suitable answers to all their questions. What did it mean? Their father could not be gone forever. Surely he was coming back? No one wanted to believe they would never see him again. That was an impossible thing to grasp.

All they could do was go into town to see the family lawyer, to find out more. The solemn group trooped into the lawyer's office, where he related the incident of a few days before. Their father had rushed into the office to make certain detailed legal arrangements. His only urgent task was the immediate care of his children. For that he had arranged that Ernestine would continue to look after the domestic side, while their uncle would deal with the financial requirements and also become their legal guardian.

"Then he must have received my original letter, to know I would be here. So I could do this," Maurice commented, interrupting everyone's thoughts.

Jac glared at her uncle. As if that stupid letter was important any more. Although if Maurice hadn't written at all, then maybe their father would not have been able to make these arrangements and in turn he would not have gone off anywhere. Father, what have you done?

"When did he come into the office?" Maurice asked.

"On Monday."

"The day before he disappeared," Ernestine commented, summing up everyone else's conclusion.

"Isn't there anything more you can tell us about his plans? What was he going to do?"

"Daniel refused to give any indication of where he was going or why this was so suddenly necessary. He withdrew only a few funds to get him by for a few days. He closed his bank account and signed the necessary papers transferring control over to you both."

Ernestine and Maurice were each given letters written and left by Daniel to explain his wishes. There was also one for the children, which they tore open instantly, hoping for some satisfactory explanation. But it gave none. It was brief. So brief that at first they could not believe he had written it, except they had to admit it was his handwriting.

Dearest children

I have had to leave urgently, for reasons I can never explain to you. I am sorry I have had to do this. I know it will be difficult for you. I expect you to be brave, study hard and listen to Ernestine and your uncle. I know they will do their best for you. I regret I shall never see you again. How I wish I could have seen you grow, but it was not to be. Please do not think too harshly of me for the hurt I know I have caused you. I shall always love you.

Father

They did not know what to say to each other. They still could not believe this was happening. The room was held in a hushed spell, while the world outside was unreal and distant.

"Is there no way we can get in touch with him?" Maurice asked.

The solicitor shook his head. There was none. Daniel

had obviously not contemplated the necessity for any contact from anyone.

"Sadly, I get the distinct impression that none of us are likely to see or hear from him again. For some unknown reason, he has cut himself off from all he knows, quite deliberately. There will be little chance to trace him. It must be something really serious to make him abandon his children and his home, overnight like this."

The lawyer could not give them any more information. He knew as little as they did.

The rest of the day passed in a blur. They all returned home and the children, still stunned, just sat, lost in Ernestine's comforting arms. She held them tight, her heart full of love for these unhappy precious children, until slowly they found their own quiet places to try to come to terms with the news, in their own way.

Jacqueline shut herself in the attic, where she stared blankly about her, her mind in such turmoil that it began to ache. She tried to deny the utter despair and misery she felt. She loved her father, and missed him. She stubbornly refused to believe he would have abandoned them so easily in this manner. Her dearest father would never have been so cruel. This behaviour was not like him at all. He would not just disappear. This was rubbish! None of it made any sense.

She tried to think logically, but emotion was clouding her reasoning. She sat concentrating on one point in front of her, focusing on the sound of her breathing to calm herself. Now her brain was working properly. Never to accept anything or anyone at face value, she had been taught.

So what bothered her about all this? Firstly, there were three words missing from the letter, three words he always used for her. Had that been a clue in itself, because they were not there? Was he in trouble of some sort? Although at this moment she could not imagine anything bad enough to make him take such drastic measures. That he could be in danger from something or someone also seemed impossible. He did nothing unusual. They were a perfectly ordinary family, living a perfectly ordinary life in this remote Caribbean island. It was very, very strange.

Yet there was the manner of his departure, so furtive, so secret, so strange and so suspicious. She wanted to know how he had left the San Maron and when exactly he had gone. There were no ferries until the weekend and the main cargo boat, the only other way off the island, had left the very day their uncle arrived. Had anyone checked if their father's name was on the passenger list for the cargo ship that day? Of course he might have used a different name, but he had taken his passport. Someone might have seen him in town that morning, but was anyone even going to enquire?

Then there was the question of the missing boat. If father had taken their small boat and left after breakfast, it would have been at the wrong stage of the tide. It was not something her father would normally do. Although the boat's small engine would cope around the coastal currents, it would struggle further out at sea. Had he been that desperate to risk such a trip, and where would he have headed for?

Jac pulled out some of the local maps from the trunk, scattering them on the floor to study them. In favourable circumstances, it would have been possible to reach the larger island of Port Saunt, although few would have risked it. Not that Port Saunt would have been much use, since it was not on a direct ferry route to anywhere in particular. There were no small airports anywhere close to help him cross to any of the larger main islands where direct flights linked them to the outside world, and where else would he go?

Her over-active brain was bursting with a mass of important questions. Why did no one else seem concerned? How dare they simply accept this, she demanded, beating her small fists into the papers. Why did no one care how he had gone or why?

Over the following days Jacqueline pleaded and begged Ernestine, at every opportunity, to make enquiries anywhere, to find anyone who had seen him leave. Someone might have noticed him, she insisted.

"Oh, my darling girl, you can't go on like this," she replied. "It's no good tormenting yourself. Although I disapprove of his actions, leaving us without any warning, your father has made it clear he intended to vanish from our lives. We must just get on with things. That's what he would have expected." The housekeeper tried to console her, hugging her once more in those precious warm arms.

"Our boat's missing," Jac suddenly blurted out; she could

not help herself. She had not meant to, but it had to be aired, in case it was relevant.

Ernestine took a step back and seemed genuinely surprised.

"I had no idea. When did that happen? We shall have to ask your uncle if he will replace it."

Jacqueline wasn't interested in replacements. She wanted Ernestine to see the other possibility it presented. The connection to his departure.

"You don't think Father might have used it to leave that day?" she whispered softly.

But the housekeeper refused to consider the suggestion, and their uncle, once informed of its disappearance, put it down to a simple mistake in the mooring knots. He readily accepted that such things happened, that it could have drifted out to sea, rather than considering anything else. Mistake in the mooring! Jac scowled at the pair of them. Ernestine should know this family better than to go along with that suggestion. Her father would never make that mistake. As children, they had always been taught the importance of double-checking ropes.

Whilst she was naturally sympathetic to the children's sense of loss, it was Ernestine who had to comfort and cajole them every day. It was Ernestine who had to force them to be realistic.

"Jacqueline. You must stop this. There is no point in these endless questions as to how or why. It does not matter or make any difference to the harsh facts. For his own reasons, Daniel did what he thought was the best for him.

Your father left us all, he made that decision. He planned this in such a manner that we could not trace or contact him. I know it is hard to take in and accept, especially for you, being the oldest and closest to him. But it is done. He has gone from our lives. We will all have to help each other to adjust."

But adjusting was what Jac found the hardest. Only a few days ago their lives had been normal, well normal for them. Now it was upside down, full of doubts and uncertainty.

Over the days that followed Jac prayed for word from their father, but none came. There were moments when she was angry, really angry, with her father for leaving them. She struggled to deal with his departure. How were they to get through this? Her pained expression was evident as she, like the other two, pushed her food around their plates at most meal times, instead of devouring it swiftly as usual.

She looked at this other adult, this unknown uncle, this stranger. Jac resented the idea of Maurice being in their home. His everyday presence niggled her. He did not belong here. How were they supposed to accept this man into their lives? How could he ever compare to their father? She wanted her father back, no one else.

"I'm going to talk to mother," Jac suddenly told the other two very firmly.

In other words she did not want them with her, and diplomatically they let her walk alone into the village. It had never been a daunting prospect visiting the village graveyard for any of them; it did not upset or bother them.

They were never sad, and were in the habit of sitting quite happily telling Hannah everything and sometimes singing one of her favourite songs to her. She might be asleep, but they knew she was listening. And today Jacqueline had a lot to share with her mother. So many private thoughts and fears needed to be expressed.

Hours later Ernestine came to collect her from the graveyard. Jacqueline had told Hannah everything, and was sitting trying to make a daisy chain out of the surrounding wild flowers.

"What do you think mother would have said?" Jac asked.

Ernestine paused thoughtfully before replying.

"I think she would have asked you to give her brother a chance. A chance to become part of the family and share your home. For her sake I think you should allow him that."

Of course, that made sense. Maurice was Hannah's brother and her mother, being the kind woman she was, would have forgiven any past mistakes and welcomed him back into her heart immediately. Likewise she would have expected the same understanding from her children.

Jac nodded her head, accepting the advice, but it was going to be difficult.

She had tried to keep herself busy, to stop herself thinking too much. She had tried not to cry.

"Where is father?" Simon had asked repeatedly of his sister, expecting she might secretly know. The plausible excuses for his absence were running thin, yet she tried to boost his flagging spirits by reminding him that in all good story books there is always a happy ending, the hero always survives and eventually returns. It was obvious he was safe and all they had to do was to wait until some miracle restored him to them. Surely they were capable of waiting for that? She for one would wait, in the hope that he would eventually return, she promised.

Later as she held her brother's hand, both of them sitting on the window seat looking out into that night, she reminded him that their dearest father loved them and that they must believe he was somewhere, thinking about them at this moment, just as they thought about him. For now, she sadly admitted the truth.

"I don't think Father is coming back for a long, long time," Jac confided quietly.

CHAPTER 2

Like it or not, Maurice Collmann, this distant relation, soon became part of their lives, and moved into one of the spare rooms in the house. On advice from Ernestine, he made no changes and allowed their normal routine to continue without interference.

Maurice had been grateful to Daniel for his suggestion that this was the ideal location to build and develop his shipping empire, because in this fast-changing world, these islands would not be isolated for long. This new start was important to him; this was the chance to make something of himself. Hard business he could deal with, men he could deal with, but he had never expected these extra responsibilities imposed on him. Daniel's previous schemes had never included family. What had Daniel done to him? What did he know about children? Nothing. They were foreign to his nature.

He looked around this warm family home, feeling out of place and wondering how he would manage. He had no experience with children. He only hoped that if he kept his distance they would not become too much of a problem.

Initially Jac was pleased that he kept his distance, but she soon noticed that as time passed he made no real attempt to become involved with them or get to know them. He did not talk to them much or ask questions about their interests and hobbies. He still knew precisely nothing about them. They were used to interaction, conversation, exciting bedtime stories and games. It was not the same trying to amuse themselves, and this was not good enough. If this uncle was going to live there with them and be part of their lives, he had a lot to learn about them and what it meant to belong to this family. He would have to change.

Cautiously she started by asking him the odd question at meal times, nothing important, just curious things that came to mind. He showed no sign of being put out by her attention and encouraged, Jac would follow him into the sitting room afterwards and sit smiling at him. This did not seem to faze him either, so she began asking questions about the exciting places he must have seen in all his travels.

His answers were not exactly enthralling; in fact she knew more about these places from her books than he could tell her. He did not have anything that interesting to say; not that she would give up this easily. Did he have any photos or mementos he could show her? Then, before he could answer, as if struck by the obvious, she leapt up to rush towards him, bright-eyed and excited, and pushed her face right up into his.

"Do you have any photos of mother?"

She should have thought about this before.

"Er - no. Certainly not with me," Maurice stuttered,

"What about any photos of your home?"

"Which home? I have moved around a lot."

"No no, the one where you grew up with mother. Do you have any photos of you as children, any of mother as a young girl?"

"There might be some back in England, somewhere. I imagine your other relations will have some in their albums."

"Would you ask them, please? We don't have many of either of our parents."

She suddenly felt so happy. This grumpy adult wasn't as bad as she thought. It had never hurt to talk about her mother, it never upset her. It would be wonderful to know more about her. He must know lots of stories, stories to be gently prised from him, little by little. Now she expected him to be more open with them, and as a sign of her new understanding she was going to show him some of her most precious objects.

Here in her room, she introduced her uncle to her especially favourite toys, the row of teddy bears and the one rag doll from her mother. She was most particular and precise in telling him their names as she replaced them in order on the window box, hoping he would appreciate and be pleased by the carefully-chosen family names they had. He smiled a little too weakly and she was disappointed that he made little comment on her collection of sentimental toys. He soon disappeared, and Jac scowled, decidedly put out by his lack of response to her interesting items. She felt even more determined to make him realise his responsibility in this house. This time she was not going to be so subtle.

Jac, Simon and Hicky were singing outside in the garden; it was the weekend.

"There's a hole in my bucket, dear Lisa, dear Lisa."

"Then mend it, dear Henry, dear Henry, mend it."

They all stopped and put their heads together before approaching the open French windows. Rattling their fingers on the glass to attract his attention, they made their entrance, all stepping inside to smile at Maurice. Did he know if it was 'mended with straw', they asked in unison?

He looked up from the papers he had been concentrating on, enquiring what on earth they were talking about. So they repeated the song and the question, at which he grimaced. Couldn't they see he was busy, he mumbled, before he firmly told them to go and play elsewhere. They flounced out of the door and down the garden, complaining loudly so he could hear that their father had always spared the time to talk to them.

Maurice huffed and stood up. He had made mistakes already, small ones, but mistakes nevertheless. He had let his guard down. The girl had drawn him in. How was he supposed to contact their family? That was not possible. Even Daniel himself had deliberately kept out of touch with them. He would have to find excuses for the lack of replies. He walked to the doorway and watched them for a while, content to leave them alone and acknowledging that at least their unrestricted freedom would exhaust their energy and allow him peace for a few more hours. Then he returned to his papers. He could only hope their return to school soon would keep them busy and at a distance.

"Hickory Dickory Dock, the mouse ran up the clock," Jacqueline sang, crossing the yard. Hicky instantly appeared from the cottage to join them for their walk to school. The two girls skipped happily down the drive with Simon following dragging his schoolbag, scuffing his shoes and then being scolded for it by his older sister. He was not in a good mood, he hated mornings, they were not the same any more, he complained. Their father had always sent them off with a smile and a riddle to solve, it had been such fun.

Maurice made it a routine to conclude his business dealings every day in time to be reading his newspaper as they came home from school. He did not know what being a guardian meant; just being there, he hoped, was enough. Ernestine seemed to handle everything else. He had been as amiable as possible and patient, out of respect for their father. What more did they expect?

Inevitably they disturbed his relaxed composure. Like most children, they could be good or bad. Today Simon dropped his satchel deliberately heavily on the floor as the two of them began their new habit of deliberately taunting each other.

"Simple Simon met a pie man, Going to the fair," Jac yelled mockingly at her brother.

"Jac be nimble, Jac be quick,

Jac jumped over the candlestick," Simon retaliated. She pulled a face at him and he responded by poking out his tongue, so Jac threw her gym bag at him, which landed with a very heavy thump on the floor. After which she chased him down the garden, ignoring the instruction of their guardian to behave.

Out of sight, they headed for their old haunt, where gulping, they threw themselves down on to the soft pile of leaves. The smirk and wink exchanged between indicating that they were pleased with the results of their tactics.

Hicky soon joined them, after being made to change out of her school uniform by her mother before she went to play. Unlike the two of them, who were bound to be in trouble from Ernestine for doing the opposite. Their clothes were creased and dirty, and would have to be worn tomorrow to school. A quick brush down would be all they could manage, once they went back to the house. They would not get away unpunished by Ernestine for this careless behaviour, not that it mattered.

"He is nothing like father. Father would have joined in the fun immediately," Simon commented.

They could not help compare him to their father on every occasion. He was so different from what they were used to.

"After all our efforts, what does he know about us? He has not asked if we were doing well at school. He doesn't even know what class we are in," Jac complained.

"No doubt Ernestine keeps him up to date with the important things," Simon offered.

"Well, that's not good enough, Simon. Now the school term has started, he will find a big difference," Jac smiled.

Jac had another plan to force Maurice to interact with them. Their homework would allow them the opportunity to badger their uncle with any amount of questions. He could hardly refuse to help them, she insisted.

Simon did not see the point. Why bother? This was not much of a game, he argued uselessly. So they soon settled into the habit of pestering him in the evenings, and it was surprising how, by pretending to be incredibly ignorant, the pair of them could take up so much of his time. Did he know much about history? Which book would tell them about geography and literature? Was he any good at maths? Goodness, she could hardly wait until they had to learn lines for the school plays, she grinned to herself.

Jac was contentedly humming to herself while she used the coloured crayons on the pages of her colouring book, ignoring the annoying thump of the ball her brother was bouncing on the steps in front of her.

"Hey diddle, diddle, the cat and the fiddle, The cow jumped over the moon, the little dog laughed to see such fun, And the dish ran away with the spoon," he recited in time with each regular beat of the ball against the wooden floor.

A short time later Simon had left the house and was to be found sitting under the large old tree by the dilapidated woodshed. After a decent interval his sister wandered along to join him, having approached from a different angle.

"What's wrong?" she asked.

"I'm fed up. Do we have to keep this up much longer? You know we're smarter than he is. It's hard to continually come up with dumb questions," he sighed, leaning forward to rest his head on his arms.

Indeed she had to admit that for a brilliant businessman and entrepreneur, their uncle had soon proved his basic general knowledge was greatly lacking. Maybe they had almost pushed this game to the limit, although she was unwilling to give in too quickly.

"This isn't fun. I liked having proper fun, like we all enjoyed before. When father was here," he sighed.

Jac was constantly surprised at the ease with which Simon would refer to their father, while she found it so difficult. There was still an emptiness in her heart, a dreadful ache for her father to come back. She didn't care what trouble he was in, what he had done wrong or why he had left. He was simply her father, and she wanted him back.

"If we antagonise him too much, he might curb our freedom," Simon pointed out.

Jac confessed that she was surprised at their uncle's apparent ability to tolerate their unusually endless noise and games. He rarely raised his voice to them, whereas Ernestine always kept them in line and told them off immediately when needed. They knew the difference between right and wrong, they knew when they had gone too far. And they had deliberately been naughty over these past weeks.

"There must be some way we can use this to our advantage," said Jac.

Simon nodded, willing to accept her explanation, and then wandered off to the pond, where he had seen Hicky earlier. Jac meanwhile worked her way up the tree. It had split into two separate trunks from ground level and by bracing ones feet against one side and ones back against the other, it was easy to lever yourself up into the canopy of branches and leaves. There alone she could concentrate her mind on a whole host of things.

Once more curiosity encouraged Jacqueline to test their uncle's lack of response by reciting another rhyme.

"One, two, buckle my shoe,
Three, four, knock at the door,
Five, six, pick up sticks,
De dum, de dum."

She heard him close the door to shut out the sound of her voice. Jac did not like being ignored. It made her more determined to annoy him, as a punishment.

Later that evening Maurice sat with his cigar, gently puffing and enjoying the moment, stretched out on the deep upholstered chair, his feet resting on the footstool and with a glass of brandy on the table by his side. There were few sounds to disturb him; everyone had gone to bed and the wireless was off, yet it hummed strangely. Closing his eyes, he imagined it was making a little tune, and concentrating harder he tried to make it out. Once or twice the soft, muffled sounds fell into a rhythm, the pattern of a children's rhyme, he thought. It finished and repeated itself, but he still could not make out the words or recognise it. He took another drink. Obviously the constant nursery rhymes plaguing his days were beginning to have an effect. How could those children remember so many?

He looked in on them on his way to bed. The children were sound asleep in their own rooms, safely tucked up and dreaming their own pleasant innocent dreams, their thoughts far away. The simple smiles on their faces were the only indication of the memories they carried in their hearts. Jacqueline lay with a doll and a teddy bear wrapped in her arms, her little fingers relaxed around them and her pretty ribbons cast on the box by the open window. Simon in the next room lay with one arm dangling towards the floor, where another soft toy had fallen from his hand as he slept. Above each of them on the shelf stood a photograph of their parents, Daniel and Hannah Liscombe, silently protecting them from harm. Maurice crept away, unwilling to come under the unsettling influence he felt every time he saw their photographs about this house.

The strange incident of the radio was soon forgotten as Maurice settled down on the porch the next day, glad of the peace and quiet whilst the children were at school. He took a drink, let out a long sigh and closed his eyes, reflecting on his recent luck. He had already set up a trading venture of his own in the capital. He needed to go into town tomorrow, to see the bank. There was a possibility of investing in another warehouse, and he could not let that opportunity slip by.

Maurice thrived in the ruthless manipulations of business schemes. Men he could deal with, manoeuvre, cajole, put pressure on. Men he knew; he hadn't realised just how different handling children could be. One minute they were as docile and as nice as could be, the next they were at loggerheads with each other, sulking and bickering, often driving him to distraction, noisy, boisterous and running wild in the garden. Ernestine was the only adult who controlled them properly. He did not have the knack. In retrospect, he found it quietly amusing that they did not seem actually afraid of him at all, but then of course they didn't know of his former reputation.

***

Hicky raced up the drive after being diverted on her way home from school, but she stopped as she reached the buildings and calmly went inside her cottage as if nothing was a miss.

"Curr-rootu, curr-rootu!" came the bird call from her window.

Within half an hour all three of them were in their jungle hideaway. Hicky was fidgeting and jumping up and down, hardly containing herself as they gathered. She was bursting to tell them about what she had read in one of the old newspapers in the village library. There had been an article on a clairvoyant who had found a missing person just by holding an item belonging to them. What did they think?

"We might be able to find out if your father is still alive after all this time or not. We would be mad not to give it a try," Hicky surmised.

They had all heard rumours about so-called mediums, but this had more substance to it. The idea fascinated Jac. The chance to at least know where their father was seemed beyond her dreams. To know if he was safe - dare they hope? How long had it been? Was there a medium on the island?

Ernestine was taking them to the capital next week for new school uniforms; if they could buy a local newspaper, they might find an advertisement. Although it was a desperate idea, they suddenly had a glimmer of hope. If they could take something of their father's for the clairvoyant to look at, it might just help them know where he was or what had happened to him. After all this time, good or bad, they would have an answer.

The children were full of smiles for the rest of the week and behaved perfectly on their trip into town and back. They had acquired a newspaper, smuggled it home and eagerly spent the rest of the afternoon scouring the back pages in their room. There were two such people advertised in the small ads, but their prices per session came as an awful shock. It would take ages to save up their pocket money.

Even so, they slowly built up their funds by sacrificing treats and refusing to buy anything on any of their excursions. They put their money into a tin box hidden in the window seat in Simon's bedroom. Another month and they would have enough. Jac grinned to herself as she sat sewing another dress for her rag doll.

"Summer time, when the living is easy, summer time, when the cotton is high," Jac crooned contentedly. The song her parents sang added to the small glimmer of happiness she felt. There were moments when she imagined everything was still as it had been, with the pair of them sitting on the porch of an evening. Her mother's brilliant blue eyes and her soft laugh as she lay against their father's shoulder. Memories she would keep forever.

They would soon have to find something of their father's they could take to town, but it would have to be something small, because of smuggling it out of the house and keeping it hidden during their bus ride to town. Yet they had no idea what would be suitable.

The next time their housekeeper went into the village for supplies, they had their opportunity. Jacqueline hadn't entered their father's room since the day she had found his clothes and rucksack gone, despite the fact that the door always remained open. They had seen Ernestine in and out of there all the time, as she dusted and aired the room regularly, but it felt odd, as it did not belong to them any more. He was not in there.

Simon refused to go in, but Jac, once having entered, completely forgot what she was there for and slowly wandered about the room lovingly running her fingers over every surface. Each one a memory she treasured. She opened the chest of drawers and the wardrobe, touched his clothes gently with affection and sighed. Everything was here ready for his return.

"Hurry up," Simon hissed in the hallowed quietness.

What could they take? She stopped by the table in the bay window where their father always set their puzzles, his scribbling and draft ideas for their riddles and crosswords, stuffed in the top drawer, with pencils and sheets of blank paper and his favourite pencil sharpener. She wondered if the pretty wooden pencil sharpener, in the shape of a clown, would be personal enough; no one else would have handled it. Yet she could not bear to take it from its resting place. It did not seem right to borrow anything.

On top of the table nearest to the curtain sat the familiar old worn wooden box, containing the little wooden markers he used to plant in the grounds for their treasure hunts. Her clue markers were red, Simon's were blue and Hicky's, because he never left her out, were green. Sadly she lifted the lid. She had often wondered if he had taken any of them with him as a reminder, a keepsake, to prove he would not forget them. She found she had to touch them, just to hold them in her hands again, wanting to feel his closeness. She picked up a red one, then another, and then slowly picked out all the rest and laid them out on the desk to count. They were all there. All four of each colour. He had not taken even one. Another of her secret hopes lay destroyed.

Jac threw the markers back into the box, closed the lid quickly and ran from the room. Simon, startled by her behaviour, was soon in hot pursuit.

"What's wrong?" he called after her.

Down the stairs, out through the kitchen she fled, ignoring the astonished Ernestine and Hicky in the driveway. She outran her brother in minutes as she headed across the fields. She had to be on her own.

Her father had never set her puzzle that day - because he knew in advance he was leaving them. It hurt to think he had chosen that day to leave. Her day. But had he any choice? Her over-active mind suddenly reopened all those vague doubts she had previously pushed aside. Over and over again, she went back to the events of the disappearance and the last letter their father had written to them. Those three missing words. She was not satisfied.

"Kay lay lay!" The sound recalled her to their glade in the jungle, where the two youngsters sat impatiently waiting.

"Why didn't you get something?" Hicky demanded.

"I couldn't. I just could not," Jac declared quietly, her eyes cast to the ground.

Simon and Hicky exchanged glum glances. They had never seen their leader in such low spirits. Since neither of them had had the courage even to go into the room, they could hardly rebuke her for her failure to bring anything out of it. Sympathetically they let the matter drop. The experience of going back into Father's room had obviously upset her deeply.

"Are we ever going to see that clairvoyant?" Hicky whispered.

Jac nodded, knowing they had to. They could not waste this opportunity after they had deliberately sacrificed everyday treats for so long in order to save up for this. She would have to go back into her father's room.

A few days later, with Ernestine gone to the village, Jacqueline ventured inside the room again. There she stared at the contents, not sure what would be suitable. She had to find something. The silver pen on the desktop seemed the easiest thing to take. Trying not to touch it, in case it made a difference, she wrapped it in some tissue paper and put it in her pocket. Silver? Pocket? The thought of her father's silver whistle sprang into her mind. He always carried it with him. Quickly she searched every piece of his remaining clothing with a pocket. It was not there.

She sat down and smiled, a wide beautiful smile, her spirits suddenly full of happiness. He had taken it with him. It was a sure sign that he would not forget them or the home where he belonged. He would come back some time. She trusted him to do that.

***

With no one asking what they were up to, the next weekend found them standing for quite a while outside one of the wooden terraces, just off the main street in town. Staring at the door in front of them, Jac clutched the silver pen tightly in her hands. It was protectively wrapped in layers of tissue inside a handkerchief.

She looked at the other two again. "Well, are we going to or not?" she asked them.

Simon took the money out of his pocket, counted it once more and nodded.

They knocked twice and waited nervously; there seemed no sound from inside. They knocked again, still with no response. Maybe she was not here. They were about to leave when the door was suddenly thrown open and they found themselves confronted by a tall woman silhouetted against the light behind her. Scowling, she stared down at them, then, stepping forward, she pushed her face into each of theirs in turn, making them all take a step back. She was nothing like they expected. She was dressed in an array of bright silk flowing robes. With endless beads hung about her neck and a mass of wild hair tumbling about her shoulders, she looked like... well, they weren't quite sure what. They had never seen anyone like her before. They were speechless.

"Well, what do you want?" she demanded.

"Are you the clairvoyant? We, er... want you to find our father," Simon burst out jerkily.

The lady leaned back and laughed, a deep raucous laugh. Then she leaned forward.

"Go away! I don't have time to pander to any stupid childish games!" she snapped.

"No, please miss. We want your help. We have brought this," said Jac, thrusting the bundle of tissue forward.

The woman stood there, weighing them up for a moment, obviously suspicious and unwilling to take them seriously.

"Children are always up to mischief," she grumbled.

"It has taken us ages to save the money," Jac pleaded, pulling Simon closer to show her their savings.

Eventually the woman allowed them inside, ushering them into the dingy front parlour. The room was like nothing they had ever seen before. It was full of old faded furniture, musty stuffed animals, metal ornaments, dark portraits in heavy gilt frames and large potted plants which they kept knocking into as they tried to avoid touching anything. It smelt and felt very creepy, thought Simon, but not as creepy as the back room she showed them into next. It was bare by comparison, with only a table and a few chairs. The dusty fringed mantelshelf over an empty grate, and the moth-eaten nets, were hardly visible in the darkness, which became darker as she closed the heavy curtains to shut out the daylight.

It was obvious she would not proceed any further without a little information about them. After a short silence, the children reluctantly mumbled their names and the name of their home, in an effort to persuade her they were genuine. To be honest they were worried that she would contact their uncle or Ernestine and their secret appointment would be exposed. But she seemed satisfied enough, and asked nothing else.

A little lamp on the table was the only light in the dark room as she bade them sit. They were warned that she could not guarantee anything, and that the money was not returnable. Reluctantly Simon handed over the money and they were told to place the object they had brought in front of her. Jac carefully unwrapped the silver pen and placed it on the table. Rubbing her hands in the air and then holding them poised above it, the woman closed her eyes to concentrate.

The silence was intimidating as they waited, no one hardly daring to breath, let alone move.

"Is he alive?" Simon asked rather bravely, startled into life by the chiming clock from the hall.

The woman nodded.

"Is he safe? Not in any danger?" Jac asked. She was desperate for any information.

"There is no indication of such things," said the woman, her eyes still closed.

"Where is he? Can you tell?" Jac whispered.

"I see a town, with old buildings, some brick, some stone. A cobbled square."

"Where is it?"

"It is nothing like anywhere in the islands or on the immediate mainland. It must be a long way away from here. I cannot identify the place or country."

She did not say any more and the silence continued for a long time, until she opened her eyes and pushed the silver pen back towards them. The session was over, and she rose to pull the heavy curtains open again.

"Is that all?" demanded Jac, feeling cheated.

"What did you expect?"

"To find him."

"I told you, nothing is guaranteed," the woman replied.

They all stared back at her. They had hoped for so much.

The confused children were ushered out. Jacqueline stomped angrily down the street, the others in tow behind her.

"What a very expensive waste of time. She was no help whatsoever. She told us precisely nothing," Jac complained, once they were out of earshot of the house.

"We know he is alive," prompted Hicky, trying to find something positive in this disappointing event.

But Jac already knew that. She had never ever thought any differently.

All their efforts, all the money they had saved, and for what? Hicky felt awful, because she had been responsible for suggesting the idea. It was her fault they had no funds left, she moaned all the way home. Jac gave her a cuddle and kept hold of her hand, and reminded her several times that they had all agreed to do this, they had all been keen to come today. No one was to blame; this setback did not make any difference, Jac insisted, and Hicky eventually smiled at them both. Especially after Simon gallantly gave her his hankie to wipe away her tears.

"Goodness, we can't have your mother seeing your face like that. She'll ask questions. She'll be bound to get the truth out of us and we'll be in trouble," he joked.

Jac wondered if they would ever know where their father was. This idea had given her so much hope; it was such a shame it hadn't worked. She refused to give up this easily and as she sat staring vaguely out of the window at the patches of lush jungle, she found she was already considering another slightly more unusual option. Jac knew she could do better than that clairvoyant and she did not mind resorting to other unorthodox methods.

The three of them sat over the fire, in their secret place where the overgrown jungle protected them from unwanted observation.

"Are you sure you want to do this?" Hicky asked, already worried.

"I don't think you should. We don't know enough. It could be dangerous," Simon added, grabbing her hand, to prevent this going any further.

Jac shook him off, refusing to be persuaded by either of them. In fact she had wondered if she could actually do this, because her hand was shaking, but yes she could, she convinced herself. She had to see her father's face, his eyes and that smile again. She had to know where he was.

As was their habit, they had always read everything they could. Their father had encouraged them to expand their knowledge in any way. Naturally many of the books had not been for children, but Jac did not mind looking up the big words she did not understand. She was fascinated by some of the old local folklore and some very strange customs connected to superstitious witchcraft and spells. She had to believe her idea would work.

She had gathered the various herbs fresh that day and now dropped them into the boiling water. Slowly she stirred it until the water changed into a strong green colour.

"We don't know what effects it might have," Simon argued.

"I have to try it. I will only sip it."

Jac had come this far, and she wasn't about to back out now. It had to work. Letting the liquid cool, she tasted it. It did not taste that bad. She sat there, her eyes fixed on the blurred flames, which formed a distant halo. She wondered how long it would be before she saw what she wanted.

Simon and Hicky continued to watch nervously, exchanging worried glances. They did not want to be here any more, nor did they think Jac should have risked such a stupid idea.

Jac found the strange liquid did not take long to make an impact. She soon felt dizzy and flames hissed loudly at her. It was hard to concentrate, her tummy felt unsettled, and she sat bolt upright with her mouth wide open, sucking in air to cool the heat in her throat. Then she scrambled up and dived into the nearest vegetation. She needed to be sick. Several times.

Having recovered enough to speak, she admitted she had not seen anything in the flames, no picture had come to her. She couldn't tell them anything. She had failed, yet as children, maybe they should not have expected anything different. Had it been worth it? Actually, no.

She continued to be sick on and off for the next few days, which concerned Ernestine, who dosed her every morning and night with a concoction which tasted worse than the one she had drunk in their private jungle. She would not make that mistake again, she vowed. For the moment they would be children, enjoying their games and happily tormenting Maurice whenever they had a mind to and not being too clever to draw attention to themselves. It was obvious they must wait.

***

Six months later, having put the clairvoyant and their own drastic attempt with supernatural forces well out of their minds, they were startled by a most curious announcement at home.

"Some relation of your father has arrived and booked into the hotel," Maurice informed them as they ate their breakfast. "Make sure you don't dawdle home from school today. I have arranged for him to be here when you get home. He no doubt wants to spend some private time with you. Even if only to check that I am looking after you both properly," he added sarcastically on his way out of the kitchen.

On the way home they discussed the situation. Thanks to their Uncle Maurice, the regular schedule of vessels, trade and cargoes which came to the island had gradually increased. Therefore it was just possible that one of their relations might come, although there was no reason for a visit. They had never had any family visitors as such before; they had lived here in perfect, happy isolation, the whole of their lives. So why anyone had come all this way after all this time did not seem to matter to them. They could not really decide if it was a good or a bad thing. They weren't excited by meeting another stranger.

Unless he had some photos! Jac suddenly remembered her request to her uncle, a request which had never achieved any reply from England.

Once more dressed in their best, they came to greet their visitor.

"Hello children. I had better introduce myself. I am Stephen Liscombe, a distant cousin to your father," he said.

This scenario sounded so familiar, Jac concluded cynically, before smiling in the same friendly manner at their guest, exactly as she had done the last time an unknown relation, their uncle, had appeared on their doorstep.

"Now children, how are you both?"

"We are well, thank you," Jac answered politely.

"Behaving properly, as your father would have expected?" he teased gently.

Jac nodded in an exaggerated manner. Such familiarity! How dare he presume he could share the same kind of relationship they had with their father. She could feel her jaw set, but did her best to play the part.

"Of course. We would not do anything to disgrace him. Neither do we ever forget him," Jac stated very firmly, having precisely chosen her words for effect.

"No, no. Of course not. The lawyer had informed us of the situation," the man mumbled sympathetically, although he was obviously unsettled by her reply.

He changed tack, expressing his delight that they were being cared for properly and foolishly asking if there was anything they wanted. The two of them glanced at each other, both thinking the same. They still wanted answers. They wanted to know when he was coming back. That was what they wanted most of all.

"Do you know where father is?" they asked together.

"Oh children, I wish I did," he replied.

Exactly as they expected. He was no use, why had he bothered to come? He hadn't brought anything with him, not even any photos to show them, nothing, no postcards, no mementos from the family. Not even any messages or letters from the other relations who meant nothing to them. They were used to being on their own, depending upon each other, why change things? Even Maurice had let them down. He had not turned out as they had hoped.

They were not inclined to volunteer anything of themselves to this adult. Instead they sat down facing him, because it was time for them to play the inquisitor before they could be interrupted.

"Did you go to the same boarding school with father? Which one was it?" Jac tested him.

Startled by her attack on his memory, he pretended to reflect.

"No, I didn't. We did not live in the same part of the country. Goodness, Let me think. I can't actually remember which one it was. We only played together when we visited an uncle in the holidays."

"Oh, was that his Uncle Chester? I have a bear named after him," Jac chirped in.

"Er, yes," the stranger agreed.

"He lived by the sea. Father used to tell us about the ruined monument, an old fort surrounded by the long stretch of shingle and the sheltered inlet where he learnt to sail."

"Yes, that's right, although I was never a good sailor. We worked together in London for a while before going our separate ways. We should have kept in touch, but we each had our different lives to lead."

They all shared the tea and cakes Ernestine had brought in from the kitchen and kept up the courteous conversation, until, looking at the clock, their visitor stood up to go.

"I must get back to the hotel. It was lovely to meet you both," he purred, shaking their hands in turn. They hated it when people purred at them, hated insincerity and false sympathy.

"Could I send you anything?" he asked. They all shook their heads instantly without considering it for a second. They did not need to be bought off with useless gifts or trinkets. Not now, not ever.

"Thank you for coming. Please give our love to everyone," Jac heard herself saying automatically. They waved their new-found relation off, smiling sweetly until he was out of sight.

"What was all that waffle about Chester and the old fort? You made most of it up," Simon exclaimed as they ran upstairs to change.

"I was trying to find out how much he really knew about father and us."

"And?"

"He gave all the wrong answers. He is not one of the family. He is a fraud," Jac scoffed. She knew enough about their distant family from their father to know certain details which others did not.

"So who was he? Why pretend to be our relation? It doesn't make sense."

"I agree."

At that point Maurice returned home and casually asked how they had got on with their relation.

"All right, I suppose." Jac shrugged and went on with her sewing, while Simon did not even raise his head from the book he was engrossed in.

"I thought you would be pleased to see him," said their uncle, puzzled by their lack of interest.

"He was very dull," muttered Simon.

"Nothing like father," Jac added ambiguously.

It was time for another gathering in the hollow. Simon fiddled with the remnants of a piece of string he had in his pocket, until, bored, he tossed it away out of the kitchen door. Hicky picked up the string from the grass outside and idly untied the knot, absently wandering back across the yard to the cottage. The sign had been understood.

"Kay lay lay!" the parakeet shrilled.

"Kay la la, da da, de dum," another replied.

The children sat in their private grove, their heads together, trying to find an answer.

"Everything has a meaning - the problem is discovering what," Jac said, quoting their father.

This visit had no purpose, so why had he come? Why suddenly now? It was not as if he was trying to find out anything. Whatever this little act was in aid of, all it had achieved was to make her suddenly suspicious of everything. "Never trust anything or anyone at face value" had been one of her father's instructions.

Should they check this Stephen out? But how? They could not ask Maurice. It was doubtful he knew the man either. He had just accepted him at face value and trusted him to be who he said he was when the letter arrived. Did they dare to write to any of the family? Their father had written and received letters from England in the past, not regularly and not very often. It was worth a try.

The three of them huddled together, once more focusing on their next project. They just had to find their father's address book first.

The next time the place was empty, Jac immediately took

the opportunity to look in her father's desk again. It was the obvious place. Flipping through the assortment of papers in the drawers, she came across the odd old birthday card and Christmas card. Everything was muddled up, a chaos of bills, orders and farm accounts, together with their puzzles and old drawings and scribbling they had done themselves. Alas, no address book or letters from England came readily to hand.

As if expecting some miracle, she checked the drawers again. She had been sure she had seen a seen a small collection of letters scattered in his desk, all in different inks and different handwriting. Old letters from the family, each one a keepsake, a piece of history their father had been saving for them. A source of information. Where were they? They had been here in one of the drawers on the day she had taken the silver pen.

She could not help being suspicious again. A book and letters don't just disappear. Had they deliberately been removed? By Maurice? Who else, but why would he hide them away? No, he had probably only borrowed them, to write to their relations, she tried to persuade herself. Although Maurice had certainly been vague about any response to his request for photos and they hadn't been given any foreign stamps for their collection from any return mail. Now, after all the excuses he gave for their lack of replies, she wondered if Maurice had actually written. Indeed, there was never any way to check the truth of anything he had told them.

Slowly during the next few days, the hunt got under way

to find their father's address book. He must have had one, although Jac could not remember exactly what it looked like, whether it was big or small or what colour it was. Whenever they had the house to themselves, they were checking cupboards and all the bookshelves, in case it had been casually placed between other books. They continued searching, a little area at a time, to include most of the house, cellar and attic.

That only left Maurice's room. The idea made Jac nervous. Did they dare invade? She stood outside his door. Then unexpectedly a yell from Simon had Hicky and herself both running along the landing to his room. He stood there waving a letter in his hand. Here in one of their own rooms, the only two other places they hadn't considered, Simon had found an old letter tucked away inside an even older book of fairy tales. It was from their grandfather Oscar Liscombe in England, still in its envelope, with an address on the back. At last they had somewhere they could write to. They could hardly contain their excitement.

Later they tried to compose a very nice letter between them, often scribbling bits in the margins and crossing out words, always changing their minds as to the contents. This first letter was important to get right. It took several days before Jac had copied their words in her best handwriting and addressed the envelope. They could only hope their grandfather still lived at the same address.

They decided against taking it to the village post office, where they would easily be remembered, preferring to post it in town. Once it was done they smiled all the way home, more than content with their secret achievement. All they had to do now was to wait for however long it took, and they were well used waiting - for everything.

CHAPTER 3

Of course the prospect of resuming the search for their father's address book in their uncle's room still existed, although it did not seem so urgent now. But it would have to be done at some time.

So what excuse was Jacqueline going to find to allow them to invade his room?

"Have you borrowed father's silver pen?" she asked her uncle one evening in front of everyone at the table.

"Er, no. I didn't know he had one," Maurice replied, a little taken aback by her question, unaware that it was more of a subtle accusation.

"I haven't seen it for ages," Jac continued.

"And why should you? The silver pen has always been on his desk, in his room," interrupted Ernestine firmly, daring them to argue with her.

"I thought I saw it on the mantelpiece last week," Simon chipped in, taking the lead from his sister.

"Then you are wrong, since I'm the one who cleans this house from top to bottom regularly. I think I would remember if I had seen it there," the housekeeper corrected him.

"I remember he used to leave it in the sitting room sometimes," Jac insisted brightly, giving everyone a smile.

They could both see that Ernestine was beginning to get annoyed with them. "How many months have I kept this place tidy since your father left?"

They were beaten into silence. This wasn't going to work. They pulled sullen faces at each other.

Then, out of the blue, they were given another chance.

"If it means so much to the children, I suppose we could look for it tomorrow," their uncle sighed, unaware of the repercussions of his careless words.

"Oh no! I will not allow it," Ernestine stated, standing up to make her point. "Do you realise the mayhem these children can cause? It would give them the perfect excuse to turn everything upside down. Yes it would be great fun for them, but I'm the one who would have to sort out the mess they left."

"I didn't think," Maurice mumbled, also put in his place.

"If there's any looking to be done I will do it in the peace and quiet, when you are all out," she concluded, and that was the end of the matter.

The three of them trudged home after another day at school. Jac kicked the ground, still disappointed that the only excuse she had invented to rifle Maurice's room had been ruined by Ernestine.

"Trust mother," said Hicky.

"He must have the book. We have looked everywhere else," Jac insisted indignantly to them.

"And if he does have it? What does that mean?" said Hicky.

"He might have borrowed it to write to our family and just left it in his room, rather than putting it back where it belonged," Simon suggested logically.

"You hoped he would ask them for some photos, remember," Hicky added.

Jac looked at them both. What was it with these two lately? They seemed perfectly content and determined to make sense of everything.

The next day Jac impatiently sat through the maths and the dreaded English literature lesson, awaiting the mid-morning break. She had an idea, and quickly sought out the games mistress, who luckily was on playground duty. She carefully put her case to the teacher concerning her plea to go home at lunchtime, promising to run both ways, so as not to miss any lessons.

"And miss your lunch altogether? I think not. You children need your meals at proper times. I don't want you coming back exhausted and unable to give your best in the afternoon's sports session."

Jac sulked. Admittedly she had intended to bunk off the first lesson anyway, to give herself more time for her search. It would be worth the repercussions, lectures and scolding, even a detention. Jac would have happily endured anything to achieve her aim, including the harsh words from Ernestine which would naturally follow.

Instead she endured the rest of the day and joined the other two on their journey home as usual. Simon was tapping the football from side to side of the path, concentrating on his control, while Hicky had been happily humming the new song she had been asked to learn.

"I deliberately forgot my running shoes today, hoping I would be sent home during the lunch break to fetch them. With Ernestine gone to the dentist, I hoped to have a sneaky look in Maurice's room," Jac moaned despondently.

"So, what went wrong?" asked Hicky, grinning.

"That idiot teacher lent me a spare pair of trainers from the sports cupboard."

Simon stopped and smirked.

"Which hampered your ability to outrun the rest of the class as normal?"

She nodded. She could have easily beaten them barefoot if she had wanted to, as well the others knew. They lapsed into their own thoughts again, Simon and Hicky considering their homework, while Jac could only think about her latest uncompleted task. It seemed that everyone was out to scupper the plan completely. When were they going to get another chance?

In fact it came the very next day. Their uncle announced that he would be absent because he was going to inspect the new warehouse and might stay in town overnight, whilst dear darling Ernestine would be elsewhere helping a friend prepare large amounts of food for a church function. Luckily it was a weekend, and both adults had been quite content to leave the youngsters at home to safely amuse themselves.

Maurice had taken the room next to their father's, not daring to seem heavy handed; besides it seemed the most practical. Jac had never felt the urge to enter it before, as it had never interested her before. Maurice's apparent unconcern at their intended invasion from last week indicated that he had nothing to hide, nothing they knew of, but that wasn't going to stop her. Unpleasant as it might seem, she really wanted to search Maurice's room thoroughly, without the other two knowing that it wasn't only the address book she was interested in.

Would searching his room allow her to find out more about him? She was not afraid to invade it, nor nervous of what she might find. She was only nervous of being discovered in the process. Ernestine would be furious and her punishment severe.

Thus, while Simon and Hicky became the lookouts, Jac began her quest. Still sparsely furnished, the room remained regimentally tidy. Surprisingly he had very few personal possessions; just his shaving bag and toiletries, and some cuff links. No family mementos or photographs, no diary, no old letters or cards from his family or friends. Nothing from his travels, not even a picture, map or tickets, nothing to indicate the character or history of the man. It was weird.

It took ages, but she had emptied every shoe, unrolled every sock, felt in every pocket, unfolded every piece of clothing and shook out every piece of linen, before replacing it exactly as it had been. Nothing had been hidden in between. There was not a cupboard or drawer she had not inspected.

"Curr-rootu, curr-rootu," came the bird call from a distance.

Some minutes later Simon bounded into the house, after he and Hicky had rushed to meet Ernestine from the bus stop. He sat down in a chair to pull his shoes off and smiled at his sister and the embroidery silks she had left scattered on the kitchen table, indicating she had been sewing. Yes, everything appeared normal.

That evening Jac admitted she had not found the book. She was forced to concede that she could not suggest any alternative for its disappearance. If only she could think like her father.

***

The echoes of the parrot calls resounded frequently as they returned to their old haunts and beloved jungle, although Jac wished she was clever enough to ensure they spent their days more productively, as their father would have wished. Simon had been staying behind at school for extra coaching because the boys were in training for a cricket competition at the weekend. Now the weekend had come and Jac felt no compulsion to go into town and witness the sporting prowess of the school. Simon was not even keen on cricket. He didn't need her to show her support, so she was going to make the most of her time to read.

The moment Simon returned from the capital, she could see that his agitated expression had nothing to do with the result of the tournament. His healthy colour was marred by his wide eyes, and his cheeks were sucked in. She knew something was wrong. He sat silently in the kitchen, warding off questions about the game, waiting for the chance to speak to her alone, while she in turn hurried the task she was sharing with Ernestine. Then, grabbing her arm the instant she had finished, he hurried her outside, desperate to let out his discovery.

"I saw that man Stephen outside the hotel talking to Uncle Maurice."

"What? I thought he had already left!"

"They were laughing and joking together like old friends," he declared as they rushed down to the old tree, away from the house.

Simon had been with his classmates. They had all been treated in a café to a lemonade and a sandwich after winning, he gushed, as if that was important. That was when he had seen them. They hadn't seen him.

"Get on with it!" Jac snapped.

"They headed off towards the dockside and parted shaking hands. A few freighters are departing today, so I guess he's leaving on one of them now."

"I don't understand," Jac mumbled. And she really did not. She could not think of a reason which would have kept him here.

"Do you think uncle Maurice knew him before?" Simon was beginning to think like his sister.

Even if he had, why would Maurice have needed Stephen to pretend to be a relation? It hadn't been necessary. And nothing had been gained by the performance. He hadn't come to find out anything, even indirectly. It had been a totally useless exercise. Very, very strange! She just hoped a letter would come from England soon to help resolve the mystery.

As they sat deliberating, Jac suddenly found inspiration. Her eyes sparkling and with the broadest of grins, she grabbed her brother's arm excitedly.

"The address book and the missing letters could be in the shipping office," she said. "They could have been used to supply background information for this man. They could still be there. How can we get into the office?"

Simon looked at his sister and groaned, instinct warning him of her intentions. Heavens, not another search! It was all they had done recently. It was becoming a habit, one he was not keen on. Important as it might seem playing detective, this time they could be caught out.

"Don't be such a sook. The warehouse is busiest on a Saturday, we can easily slip through the side door to the office," she said.

As if he had any choice.

The next weekend, Ernestine was taking Hicky into the capital, looking for a new dress for her. As a soloist in their end-of-term concert, she wanted to look special. Naturally Jac and Simon asked if they could tag along, promising not to stray too far, while they were in the shops.

Arriving at the shipping office, Simon was still reluctant to go ahead with this.

"And if the book and letters are there? What are you going to do?" he asked his sister.

"Nothing."

"Then let's not bother. He might return them anyway to the house if he has finished with them."

"I want to know if he has them."

"You always want to know!" Simon moaned.

Once inside, they darted between the rows of shelves, stacks of crates and pallets of boxes, dodging the men loading and unloading. They kept to the shadows, creeping towards the internal door from the warehouse to the office. The door opened sharply, causing them to duck behind the nearest set of boxes. They heard two sets of feet on the metal steps and although they hadn't been able to see who the men were, they soon recognised the voices. It was Maurice and Nevison.

"Are you going to keep the book and letters here?" said Nevison.

"No, I'll take them back when I get the chance. I don't think they have been missed," replied Maurice.

The children, huddled tightly in their small space, squeezed each other's hands happily. They had their answer. Their items would soon be returned to where they belonged. And as soon as Maurice and Nevison had gone out of earshot, they scuttled out of their hiding place and escaped from the warehouse. Both were relieved that their mission was no longer necessary.

Maurice sat in his office, glad that he had taken on everything Cleo, the clairvoyant, had advised. Any relation would be better than a real one; he still could not afford the risk of that happening. And luckily the children had given up asking about the photos for a while.

"I saw John got off all right. He wouldn't take any payment for his trouble," he said.

"So what was the conclusion of his performance?" Nevison muttered, checking a shipping list in his hand.

"He was convinced that they simply missed their father, nothing more."

"Which was exactly what Cleo told you. Wasn't it? You worried over nothing. They are children."

"Children who go to a clairvoyant. I don't like it."

"They thought she could help them. You can't blame them for wanting to know," scoffed Nevison.

"Well, I suppose they don't suspect anything," Maurice retorted.

Jac challenged her brother on the way back to the shops to join Ernestine and Hicky. "Why do you think Uncle Maurice would have gone to so much trouble to bring someone here?"

"I don't believe he meant any harm. It was probably all he could think of to stop us worrying about father," Simon argued plausibly.

"Mmm. Then why didn't he ask a real relation to come?"

"Maybe no one wanted to come all this way. You're always looking for a mystery. Give it a rest Jac," Simon moaned.

But she wasn't going to give it a rest. Jac's perception was on a different level from her brother's. Besides, after studying Maurice's room, she had felt there was something very odd about it. Which sort of category did their uncle really come into? He was hard to sum up. Observation was information, or would have been. Except the room had been too empty. She did not remember any documents or papers to connect him to either their father's family or their mother's. In fact nothing to connect him with anyone, anywhere. That was suspicious in itself.

The weekend had been relaxed, the afternoon was mellow, the occupants of the house, each comfortable and at peace, idly enjoying their own thoughts. Simon was reading a book upstairs and Maurice stretched comfortably in an armchair. Jac had been wandering around the place, looking at all the keepsakes her parents had. For some odd reason she took the box from the hall table and presented it to Maurice.

"Do you think this really comes from India?" she asked thoughtfully, running her fingers over the decoration and concentrating on the lid.

"I don't know. I am not an expert," her uncle grinned in a kindly manner.

"Hmm. What do you think about the wooden camel? That is quite pretty, isn't it?" Jac sighed wistfully.

"Yes it is. You have some lovely things in the house."

Jac wondered away in a happy dream and returned the box to its normal place in the hall.

That was that then. Their uncle had proved his ignorance again. He really should have remembered both where the box came from and the significance of the camel. She was quietly satisfied with her conclusions about Uncle

Maurice. It was about time to share her thoughts with Simon and Hicky.

The sound of "Kay la la!" had brought them to their special meeting place. No sooner than they had sat down than Jac began expounding her theory.

"How do we know Maurice is who he says he is?"

"Why does the slightest thing set you off again? You are just unable to let things go," Simon complained.

"If Stephen was a fraud, then Uncle Maurice, who knows him better than we think, could be as well. Has anyone in authority really bothered to check? Why has everyone automatically accepted him as being who he said he is?"

"For goodness sake, Jac. Father must have known he is our uncle. He anticipated Maurice's arrival, otherwise he wouldn't have left instructions with the lawyer concerning him before he left. It must have been prearranged between them. Father must have known Maurice could be trusted, otherwise he wouldn't have made him our guardian."

"Why do you suddenly think he isn't your uncle?" Hicky asked wearily, yawning in the sun.

"Don't you think bringing Stephen here seems highly suspicious? There are a lot of little things. They all add up. The items mother brought with her from her childhood home. The box in the hall, her brother gave her as a present. He failed to recognised it, even when I deliberately asked him about where it came from. He didn't recognise mother's favourite song, when we sang it the other day. You both saw that."

Simon and Hicky exchanged glances and shrugged, both looked unconvinced.

"He failed to realise the significance of the important names of our bears, which family members they were named after, or to recognise mother's rag doll. He should have," Jac continued.

It was Hicky who pointed out the obvious. "Old people forget things. How long is it since he saw any of those things? Years. He's been in Africa, suffered sunstroke, illness and disease in those remote parts, what do you expect?"

Simon agreed, anyone could forget things, look at the trouble he had with the school lessons. Both of them were unwilling to concede, insisting this was very flimsy evidence. Jac could not believe it.

"They are only little things, they are not important to him. He's concentrating on his business," Simon added.

"If he was not your uncle, why would he look after you as he has? No one but a relation would be tolerant enough to put up with the way we behave," Hicky declared.

Jac didn't have an answer. She look at them both, realising she wasn't going to win them over, and walked off in disgust.

***

Jac was Daniel's daughter, the eldest, and that was half the problem. She was too much like him. Peeved at their lack of trust in her judgement, she deliberately began an annoying rhyme outside the open door where Maurice was working.

"*One, two, buckle my shoe,*

Three, four, knock at the door,
Five, six, pick up sticks,
De dum, de dum.
Seven, eight, lay them straight,
Nine, ten, a big fat hen."

'Eleven , twelve, dig and delve' never crossed her lips, since it was too obvious a clue to her intentions.

"You're wrong about him," Simon said in a low growl.

"No I am not." Jac grimaced at him.

"How can you be so sure?"

Jac set off across the cliff tops and flung herself down with a frustrating sigh. To her, her reasoning made perfect sense. She could not understand why the other two were being so stubborn. She stared at the beautiful sea, the sun glinting on its surface, as the faint reflections of her father's face drifted into her mind and she remembered with a jolt, sitting upright suddenly, her father's voice advising her to deal with any trouble cautiously and with wisdom, not immediate aggression, one thing at a time.

Brushing herself down, she headed smartly back to the house, ready to do exactly that, to be met by Hicky who had come to find her. Hicky hated being at odds with her, but she did have her own theories.

"I'm sure Stephen's appearance was your uncle's way of trying to reassure you that you were being thought of, rather than admit the reluctance of your distant family to write to you or send photos. In a way that is kind of sweet, that he took that much trouble."

Jac huffed and puffed, snorting at the idea.

"At least he provides some semblance of being a guardian," Hicky went on. "Look how he has treated us to the funfair when it came, sent us on school outings, and even donated a few small prizes for sports day. The situation is not perfect, but Jac, don't spoil everything."

Jac listened attentively to her young friend, confounded that Hicky, a good year younger than herself, had displayed such profound logic so often of late.

"Isn't it time you stopped trying to look for problems that might not exist?" Hicky concluded.

Maybe Hicky was right, she thought.

The three of them sat enjoying the afternoon sun on the stone steps of the jetty, paddling their feet in the warm blue water, each of them content to wallow in their own private thoughts. Jac was reconsidering her whole strategy. Had she been that stupid? Had she jumped to too many conclusions? The evidence did not exist. Should she stop playing 'the game', as her father taught her? Did it matter? Maurice wasn't doing them any harm. He was too preoccupied with building up his trading company, his one obvious real motive for coming here. And true to his word, he had put the letters and address book back into her father's desk, which had alleviated the fear of being isolated from their distant family. The necessity to contact them had receded and even the lack of a reply from the one letter they had sent did not bother them. She just needed to know her father was safe and coming back. Then she would be happy.

Jac stared at one small piece of stone in the jetty until

her head ached, concentrating as never before on that one area in her vision, aware of nothing else around her. She was trying her best to blot out the everyday things, even her awareness of breathing, to find that trance-like state she needed to see where her father was.

"I never thought Uncle Maurice would get us a new boat. And with an outboard motor," Simon said, breaking into her silence and shattering her attempt.

Yes, their benevolent Uncle Maurice had had no qualms about letting them have a boat, his only stipulation being that it was tied up properly every time. And thanks to him, periods of pure enjoyment had returned. Life was returning to normal, as all three of them explored those inaccessible coves once more, jumping from the boat onto the shallow shingle shores, running and shouting for the pure pleasure of it, while Simon could dive into those deep underground caverns and swim beyond the calm water of their little sheltered bay.

Maurice was also enjoying life and slept well, thanks to his habit of taking a drink or two in the evening, but in the early hours he dreamt of that children's tune again and woke with it persistently playing in his head. It had been months ago that it had first slipped into his awareness. It had not cropped up since. Now here it was afresh in his mind.

"There was a dum de dum, and he dum de dum de dum, he found a de dum de dum."

The rest of the song remained inaudible and confusingly irritating. He kept his eyes closed, convinced it would soon drift away. It did not. He sighed and dragged himself from the bed. There was only one cure, and he plodded downstairs for another drink or two to help obliterate its presence.

The next day he had forgotten all about it as his busy day had kept it from his mind, yet come the night after retiring, having drunk his normal several glasses of wine, he dreamt it again. Just the same and still unrecognisable.

"There was a dum de dum, and he dum de dum de dum,
He found a de dum de dum."

He did not like this. Why should this stupid childish tune bother him, why couldn't he shake it out of his head? What were the missing words?

After several nights, the recurrence was becoming almost routine, and he began to wonder if he would ever be allowed to sleep properly again. It began to annoy him, yet still he could not pinpoint what had been responsible. The children were asleep in their rooms, safely tucked up and dreaming their own pleasant innocent dreams, so he could not blame them. Surely the ghosts of the past were not about to interfere in his life at this late stage? He did not have that much of a conscience.

Luckily for him, the cure came easily and quickly enough. On one occasion, unable to acquire the usual local red wine, he tried a more expensive known brand which pleased his palate better. He found his dreams stopped.

Jac had gone into the capital early, to collect a book she had ordered from the town library. She had wanted to read a translation of the Russian poem 'Wait for me.' It was something her father had heard and remembered, because the words had touched him so much. Which was why he had used the three words as their private code.

As she sat alone reading it, she understood the emotion of the poem, and it made her want to cry. It had a simple message; even when you think it is impossible, beyond hope, 'wait for me', the soldier asks. She felt cold. How long would she, could she, wait? It was hard.

***

As she waited and waited, the months passed into years. The children's childish games and annoying nursery rhymes had been abandoned, and Maurice was left in peace. Their days had settled into a routine of either enjoying the fun and imagination of their secret jungle haunts or studying hard at school. There Hicky excelled at her singing talents and flourished in the school choir, while the other two maintained their misleading practice of not drawing attention to themselves by not excelling at anything in particular. Hadn't their father always advised it was important to keep their real strengths from people they did not know? It was a strategy she was content to follow at the moment, although it was a routine that Jac was not always happy with herself.

"Why can't we be ourselves?" Simon kept asking. He was finding it hard to contain his enthusiasm for everything.

Indeed there were moments when Jac longed for the satisfaction of displaying her knowledge and being recognised for excelling in a difficult subject. But she resisted the temptation. So she continued to expand her knowledge in secret. She had enjoyed learning even the obscure topics. Recently she had returned to studying the herbs and potions used in local folklore, determined to achieve a good understanding of the core of this subject, after the previous experience had been way so far over her head.

But this new understanding presented a new challenge. It filled her with a nagging desire to repeat her earlier experiment, one she could not ignore. Should she risk it? It had not been that harmful when she had experimented before. Yes, she decided, she was going to do it.

Simon screamed at her as soon as she began to tell him of her plan. She could not to be so stupid! He wouldn't let her. "Look what happened last time," he pointed out.

Hicky just shook her head. She could not believe it either, how could Jac be that stupid? Ernestine had been a firm believer in the herbal remedies which had seen them through all the usual childhood illnesses. She had taught them a lot, little things which were important to their health, but Jac had sourced ingredients which were not for native remedies. This time she knew more, she had learnt a lot more about the subject. This time she was older.

"It's only hallucinogenic, nothing else," she said.

Carefully she mixed the improved concoction and made the spell. After a quick glance at the others she slipped the liquid into her mouth and swallowed hard. Yuk! It tasted horrid. Nothing like before. They sat in a circle holding hands tightly, while Jac closed her eyes and kept perfectly still, waiting for the concoction to take effect.

She seemed to sleep, and knew that the others had let her lie down; she heard the sea and the wind in the trees. The little sparkles of tiny lights remained in her vision as she began to slip into semi-darkness. Strange hallucinations in which objects were distorted floated silently about. The shapes of people exploded like fireworks into hundreds of pieces. A nightmare of dark, unknown places tumbled together, all falling down in slow motion on top of her. She was terrified and screaming; she felt unable to move. This was bad. She had to get back, she told herself, out of this place and back into the daylight.

She began to hear a soft methodical whisper, over and over again. At first she imagined it was her father coming to help her and she smiled, but it became more urgent, more pleading, and she was aware of being shaken. Back in the real world she found her brother bent over her, his face pale and concerned.

"Come on Jac, please come out of this!" he cried, he was almost in tears.

She sat up slowly. She felt exhausted and sick.

"You look terrible," Hicky told her, looking as distraught as her brother.

"You frightened me. You were shaking all over. Don't you dare do that again," Simon complained.

She smiled weakly. She felt so awful and drained of energy that she promised she wouldn't.

"You said that before. You don't keep your promises!" he shouted.

They helped her to her feet, but she was so wobbly on her legs that they had to support her on either side during the lengthy walk home. As they hobbled together across the fields towards the house, it was clear that there was no disguising her condition. Ernestine would be suspicious the moment she saw her; they had to come up with some plausible reason for the state she was in.

Jac didn't feel much like talking. She was afraid her tongue would just run away with her and she would end up mumbling a lot of rubbish. She picked up a stone and swiped it down her leg, drawing blood. The rest was up to them. She just wanted to lie down.

Simon kicked the kitchen door open, yelling for Ernestine, declaring to anyone within earshot that Jac had had a fall and had cut her leg on the rocks. Ernestine was there in a second to take control of the invalid and patch her up. Cuddled into those lovely arms, fussed over, swept upstairs and made to drink horrid sweet tea for shock, Jac soon found herself tucked up in her lovely soft bed, to be left to rest.

Simon crept in a little later to check on her, warning her that Ernestine was playing the protective housekeeper, which meant she would probably insist Jac should be kept in bed for a while. Jac squeezed his hand and nodded, lay back and closed her eyes again. She really didn't mind that idea at all. She just wanted to sleep, anything to get rid of all those frustrating images in her head.

Jac remained in bed for the next few days, wishing she had never tried the experiment again. It had not helped, and it certainly had not been a success. She had achieved nothing except making herself ill. All she had gained was escaping the routine of having to go with the others to church this Sunday morning. Instead she lay lazily in her bed, savouring the peace and quiet of the house. Determined to make the most of it, she snuggled down again between the sheets, comfortable and cosy, until she was disturbed by voices from downstairs. It could not be the others back so soon, because Simon would be thundering up those stairs to get changed the minute they returned.

She listened; no, it wasn't them. There was nothing for it; she would have to investigate. She quietly crept along the wooden landing to look down through the banisters towards the front door.

"What on earth are you doing here on a Sunday?" Maurice demanded in hushed tones.

"Something has happened, it's urgent," said Nevison. "I waited until the children went off to church."

"Quietly then, my niece is still upstairs recovering from some accident."

Maurice ushered Nevison in towards the main sitting room and closed the door.

Jac's whole body tingled with expectation as she crept down the stairs, making hardly a sound, to listen at the keyhole. She could hear every word.

"So what's so important?" Maurice asked.

"A visitor from England arrived at the shipping office asking after you."

Maurice failed to see the problem. He had visitors from everywhere, dealt with all types of customers.

"If we have someone from England interested in our company, then we must be doing something right."

Nevison indicated this was nothing to do with their business, because the man had informed him it was a purely personal matter. Also that he would remain in the town and would wait there indefinitely until Maurice had agreed to see him.

"He can come to the office any time," said Maurice.

"He did not want to do that. He was most insistent on having a private meeting with you."

Maurice was thoughtful and paced the room slowly.

"Then he had better come here."

"I don't like the sound of it. There was something about him. It could mean trouble," Nevison continued.

"What trouble? I'm sure it's nothing to worry about."

"He doesn't appear the sort to be foolish enough to put himself at risk."

This was intriguing. Jac's toes wriggled excitedly. Didn't she just love a mystery? But eager as she was to discover what was going to happen, her uncle said he required longer to consider this situation and instructed Nevison that he would be in touch in a few days.

"I suppose I had better see him, but I want to find out more about him before I do," said Maurice.

Bother, bother, bother! Jac retraced her steps back to her room, realising this meeting might actually pass by without her knowing anything about its content.

Their island was not as isolated as before and visitors had started to call, but to come from England to speak personally to her uncle seemed extreme. Unless it was very, very important. Who was this man? Jac wanted to know what this was all about. But if Maurice intended to meet him here, how could they manage to be around at the same time? It was something interesting to consider, but how was she to coerce the others into thinking the same way?

Jacqueline and Simon were more pleased with themselves about their performances at the school's sports competitions today. Jac, who could run like the wind at home, had deliberately paced herself to come a poor third in the first race and then fourth in the combined classes races. Likewise in the swimming gala, Simon, who could swim like a fish in the sea, never reached the final heats. They had both continued to pretend to be less athletic than they were and today it was for a very good reason. Not needed in the afternoon finals, they were allowed to go home early, where they quietly hid themselves around the place, in case of this man's arrival. Simon was stationed up in the big tree, watching out over the front, while Jac had picked the view from the attic window.

The "Curroo, Curroo", indicated that Simon had seen them first and she dashed downstairs to witness their uncle pulling on his coat and hurrying out to meet the stranger at the top of their wide drive. Nevison, having providing a discreet escort, bade farewell to his companion and left them to return to town, as Maurice led the way indoors to the apparently empty house. Jac had slipped unseen out through the kitchen, urgently waving at her brother to join her. Then, when he had caught his breath, they made their way around to the back terrace and tiptoed closer to the open doors of the sitting room. They had obviously missed the beginning of the conversation, but the long silence indicated that both men were both being cautious.

"You have not given me your name," said Maurice.

"You do not need to know it," replied the newcomer. "Let's say it's Jones, since that is what I used on my ticket and in the hotel register. Both of which your associate Nevison has clearly inspected and reported back, together with my activities so far."

"And why are you here exactly?" Maurice asked.

"To see if you can help me."

"Help you? I don't know you. You say it had nothing to do with business."

"Correct. My arrival here on the island has nothing at all to do with your shipping business. I only require some information from you."

"What sort of information?"

There was another unhealthy silence, causing Jac and Simon to look sceptical. What was this about?

"I have made a few enquiries during my few days here," the man replied at length. "You have a successful business here. You have some standing in the community. I admire anyone who can shake off his old life and begin a new one."

"Get to the point," instructed Maurice.

"You and Daniel have a history together from way back."

Maurice was not inclined to defend or elucidate his personal history, and a silence returned briefly.

"He arranged for you to come here. Yet he left suddenly," said Jones.

"You have come all this way to ask after Daniel?"

"Yes."

"Who are you?" Maurice demanded.

"Was that all part of the plan? Did you meet him earlier that morning? Did you help him by supplying false papers for his new life?"

"For heaven's sake, I'm a business man. What are you implying?"

"That your close connection with Daniel in the past has involved you both in some rather illegal transactions."

"All ancient history. It is no longer of any importance and despite what you may think, it is of no present relevance," Maurice stated firmly.

Both the children gasped and stared at each other. What had their father been involved in? Meanwhile the voices were getting louder and louder, their argument more hostile by the second. Jac gulped. She did not like this confrontation with her uncle. What would it lead to? The pair of them needed time to think and digest what was being suggested.

"What do we do?" Simon mouthed silently. They had to stop this, end this meeting and somehow make this man leave. They had to create a diversion, something which would grab Maurice's full attention. Jac jerked her head towards the front of the house and they both crept away; it was time for a little more acting. She grabbed Simon's arm, gave him instructions and then without hesitation, they both burst noisily through the front door, resorting to the familiar nonsense they had not used for ages.

"Simple Simon met a pie man, going to the fair."

"Handy Spandy, Jac-a-Dandy,

Loves plum cake and sugar candy."

Jac threw herself at one of the small tables, deliberately sending everything crashing to the floor.

"You can't run for toffee. Your class came last in the relay. You're useless!" Simon yelled.

"So are you. I hate you!" she shouted at the top of her voice.

"I hate you as well," Simon yelled back and stomped his feet, before running out of the front door again and slamming the front door behind him so hard it shook.

Maurice swung the door of the sitting room open wide to bellow at them both, to find Jac rolling on the floor at the bottom of the stairs, holding her leg and howling. He then opened the front door and yelled at the top of his voice after Simon, ordering him to come back. Not that her brother listened; he disappeared out of sight, as instructed.

Jac remained in the hall, blaming her brother for kicking her and for the destruction around her as Maurice finally gave up and closed the front door again. The stranger remained unmoved by the situation and impatiently fidgeted at the door of the sitting room, waiting to continue. "Why won't he go?" she cursed silently.

Maurice wasn't exactly a hands on person, he usually left everything domestic to Ernestine, but with no one else around he knelt down beside her, trying to comfort her.

"We haven't finished our conversation," the stranger interrupted, suddenly closer to them.

"It will have to wait. Can't you see the children are home early?" her uncle snapped.

"I want some answers," came the terse reply.

Goodness, why didn't he take the hint? This stranger was proving stubborn. How was she supposed to get him to leave? All she could do was sit down on the bottom step and burst into loud sobs, hoping that might work.

"Not now! You are upsetting her. You had better go," Maurice shouted at him.

After a loud, purposeful huff, the man begrudgingly conceded and reluctantly walked towards the front door. However his departing glance met her eyes meaningfully, and in that second he read her too well. The slight nod of his head indicated that he knew exactly what she was doing.

CHAPTER 4

Why did she wake with a start in the middle of the night, still demanding answers she could not find? This time she had more to consider - her lack of knowledge concerning her father's former employment. She had always assumed he had always been exactly the person she knew and loved. But that brief conversation indicated something quite different, something she really did not want to know about. She did not want the image of her father spoilt in any way. That her father and Maurice had been old friends was never in doubt. Yet what they had been involved in hinted at something darker.

But why had their father vanished the very day Uncle Maurice and his friend arrived, and why did the coincidence now make her uneasy? Memory is a dangerous thing, often too selective and inaccurate, but she did remember two men that morning on one of the footpaths near their farm fence. Two strangers. Even if Maurice had met their father earlier that morning, what difference did it make? And if he had, why pretend otherwise, unless Daniel had wanted it that way for some reason? Possibly to give him time to get off the island, before anyone knew he was leaving.

It always came back to his leaving. Her father had no business on the mainland or even back in England. So why had his departure been so secret? Had he been in danger from anyone in the past? No, that was ridiculous. They had lived here too long in this peaceful idyll without any sign of outside influences. Goodness, she had played this game too long.

They had long ago begun to realise that nothing was ever that straightforward. There were too many questions and not enough explanations raging in her head. This man from England had definitely unsettled her; he had given nothing away about himself. Who was he? What was he? What did he know, and how? He had been very clever with his words. He hadn't actually revealed anything specific, although he had certainly hinted. What was he after? Was he about to expose some dark secret? God help them! She could not believe this was happening now.

The man arrived again the next day, unexpectedly, striding out across the farm track to where Maurice was overseeing the itinerant workers. Hicky, the only one to see him pass the garden, ran like a tornado to the beach to fetch Jac and they both ducked and dived their way back along the hedges and ditches to reach the old mill site, where Maurice and the young stranger now stood. The workers had slowly drifted away across the fields well out of earshot before they began talking.

"Well, well. Back again, Mr Jones."

"I said we had not finished. At least here we won't be upsetting the children".

"Very considerate," mumbled Maurice sarcastically.

"You are not exactly the person everyone thinks you are, are you?"

"Meaning?"

"I have information concerning your former associates and your previous and varied business endeavours."

"What difference does that make to anything?"

"Your new business is conveniently based far away from your old haunts."

"Where is the relevance in all this idle speculation? Get to the point, Mr Jones."

· Jac felt Hicky's fingers dig tight into her palm as they held their breath, waiting, not daring to move.

"You know why I am really here, Magnus," came a soft reply.

Maurice did not correct the name. He simply ignored it. Magnus? Who was Magnus? Maurice's middle name? Jac had never heard it used before. Nevison had never called him that. This was fascinating.

"Not really. At the moment all I can hear is some vague threat to ruin my reputation or attempt a little blackmail. Even if I were all you think or worse, I am not harming or cheating anyone here. You can do your worst."

"It was all very convenient, this arrangement with Daniel."

Just where was this conversation leading, Jac wondered?

'I am responsible for looking after Daniel's children. What difference does that make?"

"I am surprised he chose you, especially when he knew who and what you were Magnus."

Jac pulled a rueful expression. Maurice's dilemma was none of their concern really, although as Hicky had pointed out before, they could be worse off without him. Would this man care? Jac had matured in her thinking; nothing was ever black and white, good or bad. She did not even mind if their uncle had a dubious history, she had dealt with all her previous doubts and suspicions.

"But he did!" Maurice raged. "I was the one he trusted to provide for them and protect them. And I am not about to fail in that obligation."

An awkward pause developed before Jones continued. "Daniel must have great faith in you."

"Hmm. I appreciate you sharing your theory with me, but where is this going?"

"I am here to find out about Daniel. Your loyalty to him. Did you help him leave? And where is he?" demanded the stranger.

"Daniel did not confide his plans to me."

"I think you are lying."

"I have no reason to."

"The whole scheme must have been prearranged for some time for you to arrive exactly on the right day. He would have to make sure you were here before he risked going. I believe you must have seen each other before he left, considering the safety of the children was his main concern."

Maurice made no comment, although Mr Jones waited. Then, realising he was getting nowhere, Mr Jones continued.

"I do wonder. If Daniel suddenly wanted to change his mind at the last minute, how would that have affected your business plans?"

"It wouldn't have made any difference."

"I'm not so convinced of that. You're not the type of man to let anyone ruin your plans. Did your valuable investment here depend on you being accepted here because you would be the children's guardian? Did you argue about it?"

"What?" Maurice bellowed.

What? Oh, what was this man suggesting now? Jac could not imagine. She did not want to imagine. She did not want any more dire thoughts returning to haunt her. She wanted this man to go back where he came from, to leave them all alone.

"Did you come to blows?" taunted the other man.

"I don't like what you are hinting," said Maurice, clearly shocked at the suggestion.

"They are only my own suspicions. No doubt I am wrong, Magnus." The young man paused, "But until I find Daniel and talk to him, I won't know what happened."

"Why is Daniel so important to you?"

If Maurice hoped to get an answer, he was disappointed. The stranger merely smirked. He left Maurice to think and wandered off back towards the main road, promising to be in touch soon.

Not if I have my way, Jac fumed. She would not tolerate

someone else interfering and upsetting their lives. She wasn't sure exactly what she was going to do yet, but something had to be done to stop this man. Maurice had not admitted anything, yet the man indicated that he had not given up either. While any actual threat or attempt to expose their uncle's shady past might not have materialized so far, this stranger was a threat in himself. Instinctively Jac sensed him to be more shrewd, more difficult to assess, more of a danger than Maurice had ever been. He played the game to perfection. She would have to be careful.

Simon crept back into the house very late that night, and avoiding detection, he made his way to Jac's room, where he reported what he had discovered about their visitor. It seemed Mr Jones had arrived on the passage steamer bringing the occasional visitors and other European migrants. He had booked into the hotel in the capital indefinitely, and made no secret of whom he had come to see and the meetings he had already had. Why was he so interested in Daniel, after all this time? What did he want to know? Who was he?

"Somehow we have to talk to him," Jac sighed, not looking forward to the prospect.

"If he will let us!"

"We can only try," Simon confirmed.

The three of them were up early the next morning and went on the bus into town. There they hurried to the hotel and sat quietly in the lobby waiting for Mr Jones to appear after his breakfast, desperate not to miss him. He had ambled to the reception desk and handed in his key, picked up a newspaper and headed slowly towards the outside, when the three of them nervously rushed forward.

"Mr Jones. May we speak to you. I am…"

"Yes Jacqueline. The actress from the other day. I know who you are," he smiled mischievously.

Simon and Hicky were anxiously glancing around the whole time, not really knowing what they were worried about.

"Can we talk in private? Please," Jac whispered.

"Shall we adjourn to somewhere less public, say the coffee shop around the corner? I usually pop in there."

They nodded and the little group followed him. Settled with cold drinks while he supped his hot coffee, perfectly relaxed, the children felt a little less awkward.

"Now what is this all about?" he began, looking from one to the other.

"We, er, want to know why you were asking uncle Maurice about our father."

He shook his head, bemused.

"I presume he doesn't know you are here?"

"Heavens no!" they all responded instantly in unison, absolutely horrified at the idea.

"My dealings with your uncle have nothing to do with you. You have nothing to worry about," he reassured them kindly, still smiling benevolently at them.

"That is not how it sounded yesterday," Jac challenged.

"So you overheard. I'm sorry about that."

"Why are you here?" Hicky asked, before the others could.

"I don't think I should tell you. Not yet." Jones sighed thoughtfully.

"If it has something to do with father, we have a right to know," Jac hissed at him.

He did not blink, he did not give anything away. Like Maurice, he did not confirm or deny anything.

"I promise I will talk to you before I leave," was the only concession he would make.

"But I want you to leave our island, now!" Jac yelled.

He stood up, his expression changed to one of complete indifference. "I can't do that," he told them and left abruptly.

They could tell it had gone wrong. They slumped silently in their chairs and slowly finished their soft drinks. With the rest of the morning to fill, they headed off to the park by the post office, to treat themselves to an ice cream before they went home.

"Look, there is that clairvoyant," said Simon, nudging Jac.

"And there is Uncle Maurice," added Hicky, hardly a second later.

On the far side of the park, they could see their uncle greet the wild-haired clairvoyant in a most friendly manner. The fact that they were more than acquaintances was evident from the affectionate kiss and hug they exchanged. Then Maurice took her arm in his with all the familiarity of a long relationship and they walked away in the sunshine.

The three of them stood there open-mouthed, eyes agog

and in state of shock, before they pulled themselves together to shuffle off in the opposite direction.

"Would you believe that?" Hicky uttered.

Simon shook his head.

Jac felt so annoyed. She narrowed her eyes and screwed up her face. There was no doubt that this clairvoyant was a very close friend of their uncle's, and had been for some considerable time. She must have reported their visit straight back to him. With Maurice made aware of their interest in finding their father, she guessed that he had been responsible for arranging that imposter Stephen's appearance. Their own mistake in visiting this particular clairvoyant had caused this. How were they to know? Talk about bad luck! Well, at least this explained why the unusual random visit had happened. She had always thought it had to be connected to something, but they had never been able to guess before.

If they started talking about father again, would Maurice be concerned enough for this Stephen make another appearance? Unfortunately this theory would have to wait to be tested; they had to deal with Jones first. But how? How could they get him to abandon his diligent quest? How could they watch his every move or follow him every time? They could not; it was impossible. No, Jones had the upper hand.

***

Then, as if to help them curb Jones's movements, nature

took a hand. Any activity on anyone's part was held up by one of the seasonal gales which swept across the island, restricting everyone's movements as they kept themselves inside, safe from the storm. The children hated being cooped up, but the moment it let up, they were outside again, dashing down to the jetty to make sure the new boat had survived another battering. It had, and relieved, they retraced their steps back over the soggy grass.

Simon suddenly jerked Jac's arm and pulled her behind a very wet bush, putting his fingers to her mouth to stop her complaint and pointing across the fields. There were two men in the distance engaged in a prolonged discussion. Then they slipped under the fencing back onto the road, where they brushed themselves down and headed off out towards the road to town.

Of course this required investigation. Because of the damp, it was easy to follow the path the men had just taken. It led back past the edge of their fields through the scrub towards the cliff edge. There was a lot of bent foliage, as if they had been searching for something and then given up, since the steps retraced back the way they had come.

A fall of rocks sliding down the nearby cliff edge caught their attention and peering over, they saw Jones gripping onto the loose rocks. He looked up and saw them.

"Help me!" he shouted.

Jac shook her head and turned away to leave him to his fate, but the next thing she knew Simon had leapt onto the ledge next to him and given Jones his hand to help haul him up to the top. Once there, Jones thanked her brother and quickly strode after her.

"Did you want me to fall?"

She shrugged, looked him up and down, and shrugged again.

"You weren't in any real danger. You wouldn't have fallen far. Besides, you are nothing but trouble. We don't want you here."

"Look, I wanted to speak to you both, in any case."

"Why? Haven't you said enough to Maurice?"

"I am not your enemy."

She laughed at his feeble attempt to ingratiate himself.

"You're trying to blackmail him."

"No I'm not. I'm trying to find out what happened to your father. I am here to find out what Maurice knows."

"After all this time? Why?"

"You really should have to come up with a better story than that," Simon scoffed.

"Go back to the hotel and go home," Jac added.

"You don't trust me."

"No."

He looked around, to make sure there was no one else to hear.

"You wrote to your grandfather. I am his reply. I came on his instruction."

Jac shook her head and then just started at him in utter disbelief. Well that was a good one! She did not trust him. Their grandfather would never have sent a stranger to contact them without some means of absolute proof. Did he think them that gullible? She remembered Stephen, the previous fake relation, set up by their uncle. So this was someone else who was able to construct a very plausible ruse, based on a lucky guess. Well, whatever game he was playing, it wasn't going to work. If he was trying to find out if they had ever written to anyone, it was not going to work. The best defence was no defence; in this case, just silence.

"Look, I'm not the villain in this. Meet me later. We must talk," Jones insisted.

She shook her head.

"Jacqueline, Simon. This evening, by the old mill. Please."

Then he was gone, before she could tell him not to bother. He had a habit of doing that. How on earth were they to persuade Jones to keep his suspicions to himself, make him leave and promise to stay away? Although the niggling comment that he had been sent by their grandfather did bother her. A trick? But what if it was not? It could be dangerous to meet him again.

Even so, later that evening, Jac and Simon locked their bedroom doors and climbed down the trellis outside without being detected, to meet the mysterious Mr Jones. Simon promised to stand lookout while Jac carefully tiptoed through the overgrown stone ruins, motioning the young man to be silent as he sighted her. There in the safe darkness, he smiled, seemingly relaxed and confident. He leaned forward.

"You are Poppy, aren't you?" he whispered.

Jac gasped, unable to hide her surprise, and stared at him. It was a lifetime ago she had been called that. No one in the world knew of her parents' other name for her, not even her brother. The soft sound of it had died with her father's disappearance. And to be reminded of it so suddenly hit her so hard that she had to turn away to control the emotion it brought her. She shivered.

"You are Poppy? Yes?"

She did not answer, but turned slowly, eyeing him cautiously, not daring to give anything away.

"You are, aren't you?" he repeated more eagerly.

She still gave no answer. Inside her stomach was churning. How could he know?

Maybe he understood the effect he had caused, because he gently went on to explain.

"In fairly simple terms, the truth is that my father told me the story. He was a close friend to your family, your grandparents and your parents before they came to live out here. Your grandfather insisted on referring to you as Poppy as soon as he received the news that you were expected. He kept calling you that at home, long after you were christened differently. It was his bit of silliness, a bit of fun to tease your parents with. He loved you all so much."

Jac could not breathe. Her whole body clenched against this enormous sensation, to be reminded of the story, her grandfather's love, of her parents' tenderness and devotion, all her childhood happiness locked inside for so long.

"Who are you?" she heard herself ask unwittingly.

"Edward. A friend who will help you."

"We haven't asked for any help," she muttered, her mind still in a whirl.

"The letter to your grandfather suggests differently. You wanted to know who Stephen was."

"Do you know how long we waited expecting a reply? We gave up. We thought no one cared."

"Quite the opposite. It went to the wrong address. Your grandfather was intrigued. Having learnt from Daniel's solicitor that you were being cared for properly, he was prepared to leave matters alone, until he received your letter."

"But…"

"He did not like the idea that this Stephen, however harmless, was pretending to be a relation, for no apparent reason. We needed time to investigate all the facts, but we had to research Maurice first. That turned out to be difficult. There are details about him which are well and truly hidden. There are gaps in his past which made us curious about everything else."

Jac's mind was in overdrive. So not only had she made a serious mistake about consulting the clairvoyant a while ago, but now she had compounded that mistake with another. Her letter to their grandfather had resulted in this latest predicament. Bringing this man here was all her fault! How could she or any of them have known this would happen?

"Anyway, I have been finding out more about Maurice's past. There is another side to him."

"Stop stop! Enough! I don't want to know!" she told him angrily.

"You do know he is no uncle of yours, don't you?"

It was obvious now that her father already knew about this Magnus taking on Maurice's identity. If he did not mind, why should they?

"What I know and choose to believe is my concern," she replied. "Father arranged for Maurice to be our guardian before he left. Whether he is a real uncle or not, our father trusted him and he has been kind enough to provide for us. We have a comfortable home, he encourages our education and he's looking after our needs. How can any of that be bad?"

"Why is it no one anywhere has heard from your father since that day? And I mean no one."

"That was what he wanted. We regret that he felt it necessary to leave us."

"You don't understand what I'm saying. There is no record of his actually leaving this island."

"He might have used a false name or some disguise, to prevent anyone tracing him," she argued. Jac smiled to herself. Her father would have been clever enough to do that, if he had to. Not that he had to go to those lengths. She had her own theory; Daniel had escaped in their boat. Jones could think what he liked.

"There were no passengers, no one left on the ferry on that day," he said. "It sailed with its normal crew, no stowaways and no extra personnel."

"You know that for certain?"

"Yes."

"How?"

"It is my business to find things out. I am good at my job."

So Edward had managed to check the passenger list, which was more than anyone else had bothered to do at the time. How clever was he?

"But you have not found our father."

"No. There have been no sightings, no communication and no money transfers from funds he could have used in England. That is why I suspect he might not have left the island. What if Daniel had met Magnus, sorry Maurice, that morning? What if there had been an accident?"

Jac did not like where this was heading, but she could not stop it.

"What if somehow, your father... died?"

She punched him violently in the chest, repeating her blows with such ferocity that he had to grab her arms and push her away.

"How dare you say that!" she spat at him, "There is no evidence he is dead."

"There is no evidence he is alive, Jacqueline."

But Jac knew there was. That information about the exact day their boat had gone had made a difference. It would protect and keep Daniel safe. She refused to be tricked into divulging anything, however small. She would not say anything to help him find her father. Edward could torment her all he wanted. How she hated this man for being so cruel. God, she wished he had never come.

"I am here to find out what happened to Daniel," he said. "I want to know if Daniel is safe. Your grandfather wants to know."

He did not mention the fact that there were others interested in Daniel, people who had accepted his disappearance, until he had reopened the inquiry.

"There is no trace of his movements. I thought by

looking around the place I might to get some idea of what could have happened," he whispered softly.

"After all this time, what do you think you can find? Don't you think we, his children, didn't look over every inch of the surroundings thoroughly when he left? We spent all the hours there were trying to find out any clue to his disappearance. There were no signs of anything which indicated foul play. You only have suspicions, no facts, no evidence."

"Which is why I hoped to fluster Maurice by poking my nose around," he confessed.

"What if Maurice is innocent? What if he actually didn't do anything? What if you are wasting your time and upsetting our lives for no reason?"

Edward was genuinely flabbergasted. He realised her tone had changed from that of a young, innocent girl to that of an adversary. A determined foe who had indicated that she had the intelligence and education to combat his arguments.

"I am asking you to stop this investigation," she said. "You will ruin everything, Maurice has set up the trust funds for Hicky to go to the music conservatory, Simon wants to study as a pilot and I want to go to university to study law. They are things father would have done for us if he had been here. Maurice is doing his best for us."

All right, so she was making most of this up, thinking on her feet, anything to persuade him to leave matters alone. His continued presence here posed more of a threat to her than the man they accepted as their uncle. He was very determined, so somehow she must be the same.

"Yes, we were hurt when father left, but we have grown up a lot since then," she went on. "We have our own plans. We have nothing to fear from Uncle Maurice. Go away. Go back to Grandfather. Please."

She could see by his expression that he couldn't believe she meant her request.

"But your grandfather is worried. After all this time he had expected to hear something from Daniel, even a card with no address. Just to prove he was alive."

"If our father does not want to be found, it is his choice. He must have his reasons. You will just have to accept it as we have had to. I am asking you stop. To go back to England. I'm sure grandfather would understand our point of view."

"You expect me to give it up just like that?"

She nodded. In fairness he could not ignore her logical judgement on the situation and he reluctantly agreed to take the next boat from the island, without contacting their uncle again.

"Magnus won't believe his luck," Edward sighed.

***

How Jacqueline wished Edward had never come, never put these horrid thoughts into her mind. Her father was still alive, all her senses told her that. Or at least he had been when he had left the island. Their small boat had gone missing exactly on that day, and they had become more and more convinced that their father must have taken it somewhere.

His assumed method of escape was the one important thing the children had kept to themselves over the years. In a small way they felt it helped keep him safe, even from Edward and their grandfather. No, she had not let this Edward into that confidence, however sincere he seemed. It was evident that Daniel had no intention of being found, even by them.

And what about the boat? The boat had never been found; there had never been any wreckage. Despite the tide being against him, he had cleared the reefs and sailed away to one of the other islands, to get a larger boat to Port Saunt. Just as Jac had speculated when she first looked at the maps in the attic.

He was alive and safe. The clairvoyant had seen him at their session ages ago. Now they had discovered she was a friend of their uncle's, she had begun to worry that she might have misled them, although she could think of no reason why she should. What difference would it make to either her or Maurice, to tell them he was alive? None.

Even if, and it was big if, Edward was right, there had been an accident that day, it still did not explain the boat's disappearance. No wreckage and no body had been found, which would have been the obvious cover-up. No. Maurice, for all his faults, had had no part in any accident that day. She felt sure of that. In any case, if it ever transpired that anyone had had some part in an accident to their father, then they would deal with it themselves. Then it would be their choice, in their time and at their hand, without anyone's interference. That she could promise.

Meanwhile, now Edward had gone, they had that other theory to clear up first. They had little doubt that the clairvoyant had influenced their uncle into providing Stephen as a relation. But, had it simply been to stop them worrying generally or had it been to stop them concerning themselves with anything more serious? Whichever it was, they would begin by finding out if he would repeat the ploy.

They began their attack slowly, casually talking across the table, voicing their ideas concerning their father's lack of correspondence. Hicky was certain he had gone to India, to work for some wealthy Indian prince. Simon agreed, suggesting he was riding elephants in the jungle and shooting tigers. No, Jac argued, she did not think either of them was right, explaining it must have been really urgent for him to have gone so quickly. She imagined he had been sent to some disaster area, with little communication to help in the rescue and recovery. She liked the idea that he had been some kind of hero. They were cheerful and were looking forward to the stories he would have to tell, as they bounced out of the kitchen, their normal noisy selves.

Their father became their main topic of conversation from then on. It was as if they were expecting him to walk in through the door at any minute.

"I wonder when father will come back," Jac pondered aloud over the next meal. "Do you think he is ever coming back?" she asked Maurice.

"I certainly hope so."

"I hope he brings us all some presents," Simon added.

"I just want him to play games again," Hicky sighed.

Maurice made no other comment and continued reading his paper without looking up. The children all watched him, wondering if and when Maurice would indeed react to their less than subtle undercurrent.

They did not have to wait long. A week later a letter arrived for them. It was from Stephen himself, announcing he hoped to be back in their locality soon and could manage another visit, if they wished. How convenient! Yes it seemed Maurice was simply repeating his previous attempt to keep them happy. There was certainly nothing to indicate anything more sinister in his plan at this stage.

"Can't we put Stephen off coming? He is so awkward to talk to. It is obvious the rest of the family aren't interested in us," Jac moaned.

"You don't want him here?" Maurice was surprised. "Then I will certainly write to him for you and cancel his visit."

They didn't need more deception, more lies.

Maurice had been delighted that Stephen's reappearance had not been necessary and he was quietly satisfied with the present situation. He could put up with them talking about Daniel, all their teasing and noise. Maybe it was the memory of Daniel which made him soft towards them. Maybe they were his one weakness. Maybe Jones had been susceptible too, since he had left without any fuss rather than turn their world upside down. Life really was getting better.

The shipping company was almost running itself.

Nevison only needed a few hours there most days and Maurice had more time to wine and dine other business acquaintances. He would have to find other investment opportunities for his money; it was accumulating too fast and he began to consider the advantages of buying his own property in the capital. It would also allow him more time with Cleo, dear Cleo, who had the knack of soothing away his worries and always offered the most sensible solution to his concerns. She was kind, soft and comforting and undemanding of him. He did not deserve the affection which remained constant over the years, despite his insistence that they kept their liaison discrete.

* * *

Alone in the house, since Ernestine had taken all the children to the village concert, Maurice had more time to ponder his future. He emptied the contents of his glass, relaxed and closed his eyes. The wireless hummed somewhere in the background, the breeze stirred the curtains and a sigh, which must have been his own, drifted into the room.

Slowly the audible hum from the wireless changed, to become that familiar *de dum, de dum* pattern of the children's chants which had tormented him a while ago. As he strained his hearing he recognised and understood every syllable for the first time.

"There was a crooked man, and he walked a crooked mile,

he found a crooked sixpence against a crooked stile,
He bought a crooked cat, which caught a crooked mouse,
and they all lived together in a little crooked house."

Maurice sat up. At last he knew the words. They were quite clear and deliberate, yet he did not associate the topic with anything specific. He went to the radio, to switch it off, and discovered it wasn't even on.

So where had the words come from? He looked about the room and walked into the hall; the front door was firmly closed. He knew there was no one else in the house. He walked up a few stairs, glancing to top of the landing thoughtfully before shaking his head and returning to the bottom.

"There was a crooked man, and he walked a crooked mile,
He found a crooked sixpence against a crooked stile,
He bought a crooked cat, which caught a crooked mouse,
And they all lived together in a little crooked house."

The words returned, whispering in the hall around him.

This was ridiculous. Where had it come from? He went to check the kitchen and upstairs, the house was definitely empty. He sat down again in his favourite chair, the house now perfectly calm, allowing him to dismiss the incident. He concluded, as he had before, that he had drunk too much. He refused to read too much into the relevance of the words. Why would anyone here think him crooked? It was just a rhyme.

***

The young conspirators sat huddled around the fire in their jungle hideaway, no longer quite sure of their previous assumptions concerning their father's safety. Maurice and Nevison were the only two suspects Jac could think of. They had arrived on the island that morning. The boat would have docked early as it always did, so they would have been able to reach their property the same morning. They could have met their father then, either by accident or by arrangement. The children had no choice but to try to eliminate one possibility at a time.

"If we ever discovered Maurice was responsible for harming our father in any way, then I am not sure what I would be capable of," Jac admitted, kicking the dust into the fire and making it spark.

This was all Edward's fault, for suggesting the possibility of something worse. There was nothing to prove what had happened. How were they supposed to find out if their uncle was involved? Their latest attempts to unsettle Maurice or ruin his composure had failed. Their uncle never gave any indication of being seriously troubled by any their actions. Nothing seemed to make a difference to him.

Jacqueline wished she knew what to do for the best. As the eldest it was her responsibility to sort this out. The pattern of the flames hypnotised her as she tried to evaluate all the ways to achieve a conclusive answer.

Maurice had felt tired lately; he was not his usual buoyant self. He had always thought himself lucky, having connived, bamboozled and generally bullied his way through early life.

These last few years had been particularly beneficial, as he had established a flourishing business empire, but recently his sleep had been broken by strange apparitions. Then he would wake feeling very hot and gulp a glass of cool water before splashing his face from the pitcher, complaining aloud how these tropical nights had never been so humid. Whatever he imagined in his dreams was due to his own subconscious, Jac explained as they conjured their spell.

Inside the house Maurice screamed out, although he didn't know why, and woke with a start, immediately thankful he was still in his bed. How often in these last few days had Daniel appeared again and again, and each time it left him confused and drained of energy. When would it stop? Why had this house begun to trouble him recently? It was as if it was telling him it didn't like him being here. He was not welcome here any more.

Ernestine hurried up from the kitchen and burst into the room, anxious for him, but he waved her away. Not that she took any notice. She could see immediately from his condition what was wrong.

"He has a slight fever. I must send for the doctor," she commented, dispersing the curious children who had gathered at the doorway.

The doctor came the next morning. Apart from medicine to combat the high temperature, he merely prescribed complete rest. But rest meant sleep and sleep meant another confused dream, which was the last thing Maurice wanted.

Once again their dear uncle woke in the middle of the

day, still confused by the fever which would not leave him. He stumbled from the bed, calling out, but no one came. Wrapping his robe around him, he opened the door to bellow again, his voice echoing in the empty corridor, the empty stairs and rooms below. The breakfast room was tidy except for a place laid for one, yet the kitchen was quiet, with no sign of preparation. He staggered from room to room, more perplexed by the minute, more anxious by the second. The place seemed devoid of life. How dare they disappear, just because he was ill? He did not like the house being empty. He sank into the big leather chair in his study and managed unsteadily to pour himself a drink.

The rumbling, stuttering sound of a car came from the yard, breaking the spell, and thankfully clearing all the illusions away. The doctor had come from the village to see how he was, and Maurice was grateful for the timely diversion.

"Everyone's down by the Old Mill celebrating the end of a bumper harvest," said the doctor jovially, sitting down with his patient. "The food looks delicious. It's a shame you're not strong enough to join in, especially when you were so kind as to provide it."

They chatted on about nothing in particular, passing the hour, until the medical man, content that Maurice seemed in better spirits, stood up to leave. Maurice was loath to let him go. It had been the only normal part of the day and he was dreading the return of his hallucinations.

"Well now, you are looking much better," said the doctor. "I won't need to call for a couple of days. It's nothing to worry about. The hallucinations will soon stop, once the fever has gone."

The shutter banged gently in the cool breeze, stirring the curtains and cooling his damp skin. The quiet was broken by the softest of whispers.

"Here lies the body of Ezra Pound, lost at sea and never found."

There was no one else in the house. It did not make sense. It made him shiver. Was Daniel lost at sea and would never be found? Only Daniel would have risked taking that small boat out into the open sea. Only Daniel would risk everything to be free. He had never heard from him, but that had been the arrangement.

He had been lucky that no one had made the connection between the missing boat and Daniel's disappearance. Even the children, who were quite perceptive, had not realised the boat had gone missing on the same day. Everyone had assumed it had drifted off later that week, because it had not been mentioned to the adults until then. Although there had been that one moment of panic when Ernestine had used the idea that he had gone fishing as an excuse for his absence. No, Daniel must be alive, somewhere. He did not want to think differently.

When he voiced his concern to Cleo the next time he saw her, she snuggled up to him, gently comforting him. She sighed deeply and kissed him, then slowly reassured him that Daniel had truly been alive at the time the children had paid for their consultation. He looked at her in utter amazement, while she smiled forgivingly.

"I am not a fraud, Maurice," she said. "I know you never believed I had the gift, but I do. Sometimes it works, sometimes it doesn't. It depends on what I am given to work with. The silver pen they brought with them allowed me to see him briefly. He was in a foreign country somewhere, as I told the children."

Maurice hugged her tightly. He felt so pleased. While she had always brought him these brief moments of happiness, he had never considered or discussed her other talents. This revelation made all the difference to the worries which had surfaced recently. Daniel was safe.

**

Meanwhile the children were still disappointed by their continuing unsuccessful campaign. They had been quite ruthless, putting a concoction into Maurice's wine previously, with no success. Even the hallucinating dreams had not achieved any results. It appeared he did not have a guilty conscience.

"Maybe Maurice, or Magnus, isn't the one we should have concentrated on," Jac wondered.

"We automatically ignored Nevison as a suspect, because we hardly see him," Simon mused thoughtfully.

Nevison had always appeared to be the quieter one and the weaker one, but was he? The quieter ones could be the slyer ones, the more devious and the more dangerous. How would they know until they had challenged him?

"But he rarely leaves the capital," Hicky pointed out.

Nevison lived in an apartment over the Shipping Office and they all realised that weekends were their only opportunity. Anything they did would have to be quick and have immediate results, which meant drastic measures.

"We have to do this, we have to find out," insisted Jac.

Simon looked at his sister, puzzled briefly at her harsh tone and then seeing for the first time that this was not a game any more. It had become something else. Something he was not sure of, and probably would not quite like.

Drastic measures meant a serious change to their normal ways of influencing matters. It meant something nasty, and Jac's rush of ideas soon confirmed what he dreaded. To their astonishment, Jac seemed determined Nevison would suffer.

"Do we have to?" he asked, quite nervous about the prospect.

Jac was determined to get results this time, but the other two seemed set against her intended methods. Hicky even grabbed her arm, pulling and squeezing it painfully, making her wince.

"I don't think we should do this, it's wrong," Hicky protested.

But Jac did not want anything or anyone to stop her. She could not allow her conscience to make her see sense now. She could not afford to pander to their doubts. When needs must, she told herself. They had been patient long enough. They had been good long enough. Although she had previously been unwilling to call upon those other dubious mixtures within her reach, Jac was feeling less squeamish these days. It was time to take control.

CHAPTER 5

"Are you sure we can do this?" Simon whispered. Their steps were hardly detectable on the empty stairs.

"It will be easy. It will be a pleasure," Jac smiled mischievously, which was answer enough.

Half asleep, Nevison saw the dancing rays of the sunlight broken by shadows, silent shapes which drifted into the room. Like some hallucination, the children floated across the floor and came to stand over him, staring at him, waiting for his complete attention. He woke from his afternoon nap to sit up with a jerk, startled to find that the three children were actually in his room, just standing there in a line smiling at him. He thought he had been dreaming.

"How did you get in? I didn't hear you knock. What are you doing here?" he snapped at them, more than a little annoyed that they had had the nerve to invade his private quarters, uninvited.

"Did your uncle send you?"

They did not move. They kept smiling and shook their heads in unison.

"I hope you enjoyed the fruit our uncle sent you," Simon began.

"The fruit? Oh yes, that was very kind. Very thoughtful. I have eaten most of it already."

"Oh, good. We hoped you enjoyed it. But you look quite drained. The fruit didn't make you too lethargic?"

"Really children. How could refreshing fruit make me lethargic?"

"You do look a little pale," Hicky insisted.

"I expect it's the humidity. It affects everyone at times. That's what you get for living in the tropics."

"How is your taste? Did you think the fruit was sour? Or too rich or too sweet? How are you feeling?" asked Jac.

"Oh, I see. It's diagnose the patient time. Playing doctors and nurses, are you?" Nevison laughed. He did not understand what they were hinting at. There was no reason he would. He was not a believer, the island abounded with rumour and suspicion, practices still secret, forbidden and frightening, none of them lacking foundation. It was time to enlighten him, time to make him afraid.

"There are so many herbal remedies and potions which can be used," Jac stated.

"Together with black magic and spells, who knows what could happen," Simon added.

"Oh, children, haven't you got something else to do? There must be other places you would rather be."

"We quite like it here. We are interested in the power of sorcery and what it can achieve," said Hicky.

"You are so silly. Witchcraft is not a suitable subject for

you to play at," Nevis countered, waving his hand to dismiss the whole idea.

"We don't pretend. We have the gift. We can conjure all manner of things."

Nevison stared at them. Surely they did not believe in such ridiculous notions? Yet the simple smile of satisfaction indicated their conviction.

"Don't you feel tired? Are you finding it hard to move?" their voices chanted softly and rhythmically.

He heard their words, far too soft and soothing, but his brain was becoming slow to function, he could not think. He realised his heart was thumping, but he was convinced it was a panic attack, nothing more.

"We thought we might bring you a present as well," Jac told him.

She brought forward her arm and dangled a deliciously bright wiggling snake in front of his face. He jerked backwards in his chair, terrified, his eyes fixed on the creature. He swallowed hard, gulping for air.

"How dare you! Get out of here and take that with you," he stuttered, his voice trembling.

"But this is for you," Jac answered, and she dropped it very deliberately into his lap. Nevison screamed, or tried to, but his body froze, waiting for the snake either to slide away or take a bite. In fact it did neither. It curled up contentedly in his lap, its warmth allowing it to stretch and grow. He gulped hard, unable to take his eyes from it. He could not find the strength to push it away.

"Take it away, please," he pleaded softly.

They still did not move and kept on smiling at him. Nevison, at least, was at their mercy.

"You wait until I tell Maurice about this," he mumbled. He wanted to call for help, but he couldn't move. He was hypnotised by the creature. He could not believe his eyes as the snake seemed to grow longer with every minute, longer and fatter. His face was drained of colour as it curled effortlessly around his waist, then his arms and his chest, until it had him all tied up. Its head was now level with his, swaying back and forth. He could feel the flick of its fangs close to his face. He was sure he was going to die.

"Help me!"

The snake twisted tighter about his limbs.

"Where is Daniel?" the snake hissed in his ear.

Nevison gulped. Snakes didn't talk. This couldn't be real.

"What happened to him? Where did he go?"

"I don't know!"

"How did he leave?"

"I don't know!"

There seemed to be an awful lot Nevison did not know, not that the children had finished letting the illusion work for them.

"The day you arrived on the island. Did you either of you see Daniel?" the snake continued. Nevison could feel its body curling around him, squeezing his lungs. He would have to answer.

"No," he whimpered.

"Are you sure?"

"Yes."

"Did Daniel meet Magnus, even briefly, that morning?"

"Who is Magnus?" Nevison mumbled, not understanding the question.

The children looked at each other and smiled.

The interrogation continued. It transpired that Maurice and Nevison had originally met in Africa, they had built up one business after another, moving to different places and countries where ever the opportunities appeared better. Their investments fluctuated depending on outside influences. They had been in Morocco before coming here. At last they were getting somewhere.

"Why did Maurice come here?" the snake purred, rubbing its soft skin on his cheek.

"To start his business. On Daniel's suggestion. It made good sense."

There were so many more questions which immediately came to mind. How would Daniel have known where to find Maurice? Jac had never seen any previous correspondence between them. Certainly no letters. They didn't often have letters, and even if she had missed the post, it would have lain upstairs on her father's desk for ages, as usual. She would easily have noticed it, because of the foreign stamps.

"How did Daniel contact Maurice?"

"I don't know."

Jacqueline suddenly remembered that she still had not seen the letter from Maurice which he was supposed to have sent to their father before his arrival. But one thing at a time, she must not get sidetracked.

"Did Maurice know of Daniel's intention to leave?"

"I don't know. He never said."

"Did Daniel have an accident that morning?" the snake demanded.

"No, no. I don't know!" cried Nevison.

Jacqueline clutched the whistle in her hand, determined to finish this.

"Is Daniel still alive?" The words were sharp, harsh and intense, and they were repeated again and again in rapid succession. The words made him shiver, they chilled his body and his heart was beating so fast now that he could not control the pounding.

"I don't know! I don't know!"

Nevison wanted this to stop. He could hardly breathe. The words were eating into his brain. He had told the snake everything he could, but that had not made any difference to his plight. The snake had not let go; it remained firmly coiled around him. Nothing made sense. The room spun, tumbling around him, with spooky shadows. He squirmed on the tiled floor of his bedroom, the tropical breeze gently rustling the fine curtains, as he pleaded for the snake to leave him alone. In fact the snake had slithered away ages ago. The children watched with no remorse, guilt or compassion. It didn't bother them, because Jac had reassured them that Nevison would not remember any of this tomorrow. He would fall asleep and wake refreshed, without any memory of the horrifying dream.

They were satisfied and relieved that there was no proof or evidence of foul play connected to their father's disappearance. Especially Jac, who after letting Edwards' doubts find their way into her mind, had begun to doubt her own instincts. After years trying to be as clever as her father, she did not like the idea that she could be influenced by a few casual remarks. Now she could relax. Edward's suspicions were groundless. He had got it wrong.

Jac surveyed her arms, which were covered with a mass of tiny scratches from climbing through the briars and scrub from when she had caught the little grass snake.

"Will you look at all these scratches, they are an instant give away. Rats!"

"Maurice won't suspect the significance of them. He thinks all our minor injuries are natural for this environment," Simon reassured her.

"We're lucky, he doesn't know us as well as he thinks," joked Hicky.

"Maurice hasn't known anything, ever since he arrived," Jac sniggered.

Meanwhile the children had much to think about, much to debate and consider. They needed to be practical. Jac remembered what she had said to Edward, and it was true. They still needed Maurice as a guardian until they were older.

"If only Ernestine had been made our guardian," sighed Simon.

"She knows us too well. We would never have got away with anything," Hicky reminded them.

It was later reported that Nevison had been found on the Monday morning, having died of a heart attack some time over the weekend. No one questioned the matter; the doctor saw nothing odd in the demise and signed the death certificate. To him it was a perfectly ordinary death. And as far as the children were concerned, it meant nothing to them either, and they convinced themselves that they were not to blame for this tragedy. He would have recovered after their visit, and the potion in the fruit would not have contributed to the heart attack he had later. It was highly unlikely that anyone would suspect them of any involvement in this. To them it was just an unfortunate coincidence.

Maurice's own immediate reaction was to resume day-to-day control of the business and see to all the necessary legal requirements for Nevison's funeral. It was not until his friend had been laid to rest that Magnus realised how much he missed his old associate. Nevison, a heart attack - who would have expected that? He took another drink and toasted his friend, thinking of their past together. Well, the prospect of death could not be ignored, he concluded. It could happen any time to anyone. He should seriously re-evaluate his own life on this island and what he really wanted.

Jac took a long, slow walk up to the cliff top, to look out over the sea at the spot where she had often watched her father from. The sea was just the same, but she was not. She was beginning to see that she had been wrong about so much.

She realised that they had wasted too much precious time and energy on trying to outsmart these adults. Even being a nuisance to Maurice had not achieved anything. Nor had their innocent schemes to consult the clairvoyant or send a letter to their grandfather. That had been the worst mistake, because it had inadvertently brought Edward here and his awful theory. And that in turn had meant involving Simon and Hicky in her dreadful plans, because she could not do it on her own. She was the one who had wanted to extract punishment on Nevison, to hit out in her frustration at their failure to find answers. All the previous pent-up anger and need for retribution made her solely responsible for callously frightening an innocent man. The incident had left her with a hollow emptiness inside. She realised now that there had been little need for any of this drama.

She had always trusted her father, loyally trusted his judgement on everything he did. Never questioned his decisions, always accepted that he was right. She had trusted him to use the three words, waited for them. She had waited to hear from him, waited to know he was safe and waited for him to come back. "Wait for me" was the phrase she had kept in her heart. Now she doubted he would come back, doubted she would ever see him again. She had truly given up any hope.

Her whole body shook as sank to the ground and tears streamed down her face, tears she could not stop. She snatched great gulps of air in between the flood of uncontrollable sadness. She was finally grieving for him after all these years. He was never coming back. It was as if he was dead. He did not exist any more. It was time to let go of the past.

Eventually she walked slowly back to the house, still

trying to come to terms with everything. Why her father had left still remained unanswered, but what did it matter? He was not a bad person. He was not a criminal, no one in authority had come to accuse him or question him, No one had come to look for him except Edward, and he had been representing their grandfather, no one official. It was doubtful they ever would have all the answers. There was nothing else they could do.

She scuffed the ground with every step she took back towards the house, knowing that she had to finally rid herself of this obsession concerning her father. It would ruin her life if she didn't. It had to be time to stop. Common sense deserved a chance. She would go and talk to Hannah tomorrow.

Jac finally put her silver whistle into her special drawer of mementos and closed that part of her life. They were going to change, they were going to make Ernestine proud of them by concentrating on their schoolwork. They were going to astound their teachers. They would put all their efforts into expanding their knowledge. There were so many other things to learn.

***

Maurice had become a valued and respected member of the community, having consolidated the town's merchants into the trading company in the capital, and he wanted much more. He needed to be in town, he needed to be on hand to grab any opportunity which came along. He wanted to expand the business further than these islands.

To be honest, after nearly seven years, he was tired of being in Daniel's home. It was never his home. He was sure it had never wanted him here. He hated this house now. He was sure it hated him equally, and he held it responsible for his periods of fluctuating health and low spirits. He wanted to escape its power. And as for the children, they were older and seemed settled enough recently, so they would not miss him. Not that he had contributed much to their lives in any case.

"Oh, Daniel! What did you expect of me? I kept them safe. Have I done enough? They will still have Ernestine to take good care of them," he said aloud.

He had made his decision. He would make that complete break and never have to set foot in here again.

The next morning he forced himself to join them all for breakfast, although no one seemed to take much notice of the effort he made. The children all had their heads buried in books, absently eating in between turning the pages and begrudgingly grunting an acknowledgement as he sat down.

He refused any food, gave a great sigh and banged the top of the table for their attention.

"I have decided to transfer my guardianship to Ernestine, to take place immediately," he said.

Everyone looked at him, all their movements frozen.

"Yes. I see it was a mistake now, to expect you to regard me with any affection. As a bachelor who was not used to children, I was no substitute for a parent. I am and always will be a businessman. I should have realised it was in your interests to have someone you loved and who loved you equally as a guardian. Ernestine has always understood you and known what you needed. I never did. I shall contact the lawyers in town to arrange everything."

The children all sat speechless, gaping as he continued.

"This has never been my home, but it has always been yours and your parents. I want a home of my own, where I feel comfortable, where I can entertain in style. A house in town, a grand house."

His voice soared at the prospect. He sensed he was free.

"The farm and your finances are in a sound situation. Your own family solicitor will take over the management. If you need me for any reason, although I don't expect you will, I won't be too far away. You only have to ask for me at the Shipping Office."

Everyone was stunned by his announcement, but Maurice hadn't been surprised that no one argued with his decision. He got up, actually smiled at them and left the kitchen and its occupants. He was off to live a new life, with no regrets.

A new happiness settled over the house. It was a very strange and enlightening experience. Not that this development meant the children would completely abandon their old ways. There in the jungle forest, the hands met again at the centre of the circle as they re-affirmed their friendship. There the three faces bent in the firelight, the fresh moss from the gorge pressed in their hands, their voices murmuring softly and chanting. Then their laughter would ring out, as they looked at their dirty messy hands, for their old rituals were only taken in fun these days.

***

Maurice moved into Nevison's apartment over the Shipping Office for a while, until his new house was finished. He relished the calm and peace of these temporary quarters. With a deep sigh of relief, he stretched himself out in the comfort of the armchair. His worries were gone. He remembered that initial worry of not instantly responding to his name when the children talked to him, until he realised they thought he was just ignoring them. Then there had been the concern over any contact with their real family and the problem of being exposed as an imposter, but Daniel's imposed isolation and lack of communication had avoided that confrontation. Only Jones had been a brief thorn in his side, and he had gone back to England without causing a fuss.

Maurice was used to the odd business associate calling without having made an appointment, and a welcome drink was always at hand if a satisfactory deal could be made. His next visitor, however, was one he had not been prepared for. Edward Jones had come back to see Magnus.

"Jones! You had to come back!" Magnus began.

"Yes."

"And what are you going to accuse me of this time?"

"Nothing at all. I have come to apologise," Edward replied softly.

Magnus looked surprised.

"You may not be their real uncle, but you are not the villain I first thought you were."

Magnus shrugged.

"You and Daniel were in the special forces together. You developed an instinct between you, you relied on and trusted each other to survive. I firmly believe you came here to help him. Also that you had some hand in his disappearance and that you took care of the children out of loyalty."

Edward waited patiently. He suspected Magnus had supplied a false passport and papers and arranged for money to be left for Daniel somewhere. Edward would never know, Magnus would never tell. He could see that. Edward's new revelations had put a different slant on the whole matter, but if he hoped his latest discoveries would be confirmed, it seemed the opposite.

"Who *do* you work for, Jones?" Magnus asked quite casually, obviously not expecting the truth.

"No one special. Technology has merely improved the access to information which only a few other people originally held."

The choice of words did not seem to bother Maurice.

"Why did you come here the first time?" he asked.

"To find out what had really happened. For Daniel to just disappear for such a long time did seem strange to us. Although apart from checking you out, my main purpose was to make sure the children were all right."

"And who is 'us'?"

"Their grandfather and I. I am a family friend. He trusted me to come, to find out all I could."

"And now?" Magnus asked cautiously.

"I am still a family friend," was all Edward would admit.

"Hmmm."

"Oscar Liscombe would like to thank you for all you have done for the children in the past. The lawyer wrote informing him of the situation. He is pleased that Ernestine is named as their legal guardian for the present and that the lawyer has been given control of the Liscombe finances and the trust fund you kindly had set up for them."

Magnus did not show any interest in his statement. He looked at the keen young man, who was obviously connected to some vague, unnamed administration, and wondered if he would fall into the same trap that Daniel had. Don't become too indispensable, he wanted to tell him, but he didn't. Instead he allowed himself another question.

"You were originally suspicious of my involvement in Daniel's disappearance. Yet you left abruptly. I doubt you were satisfied."

"I was not. You have to thank the children for making me go."

"Ah, yes. The children. That mere children persuaded you, an adult, to leave only proves that I always underestimated them."

While Magnus was not prepared to talk about Daniel, he was not so reticent about his assessment of the children.

"At first I was quite pleased that they were so childish, running around the place and making up rhymes. Although their behaviour was annoying and tedious, I was sure I did not have to worry about them. They seemed just like ordinary children, so I left them alone to enjoy themselves." He sighed and took a drink before continuing. "I had the impression later that the children thought that I might have harmed Daniel. Their taunting poems clearly hinted their beliefs."

"That was my fault. I put that idea into their heads. I'm sorry."

"I don't blame them. But those recent hallucinations, I did not want to believe they were responsible somehow. Were those niggling, strange voices only my imagination getting the better of me?"

It was hard to believe it even now. He remembered that last incident, of being alone in the house, having a headache and hearing a childish giggle from the garden. He assumed the children were playing, but he was tired and he could not be bothered to chase them away. The giggling continued, then silence, and then it came again, giggling and laughter and the sound of another nursery rhyme being chanted. The rhyme repeated, stopping, starting, always with three small voices overlapping.

He had gone out on to the terrace to reprimand them. Except there was no one there and even as he stood on the steps facing the lawn, the same voices came from right in front of him, then from around him, circling him. Invisibly the children danced around and around him, tormenting him.

There was a crooked man, and he walked a crooked mile,
he found a crooked sixpence against a crooked stile,
He bought a crooked cat, which caught a crooked mouse,
and they all lived together in a little crooked house."

Within a few hours, a different rhyme had floated through the house, from nowhere.

"All the birds of the air fell a-sighing and a-sobbing,

When they heard the bell toll for poor Cock Robin."

"There was an old woman, who swallowed a fly, perhaps she'll die."

His head was bursting. He needed a drink, and he ended up finishing the whole bottle. It had been such an unsettling experience.

"Now Ernestine has reported how much they have improved at school, all a little too easily and quickly. They have turned out much cleverer than anyone suspected. It makes me wonder if they were deliberately hiding their ability from the beginning. I wish I had realised the possibility earlier. They could turn out to be too smart for their own good. I just wanted them to be normal children, with normal faults."

Edward made no comment, but it was enough to make him think hard. He remembered Jac's determination when she had persuaded him to leave the island. For one so young, she had an unusually level head. Had they, as Magnus thought, been hiding their acquired skills all the time? If Daniel had already begun training them, what skills had they already been taught? And worse, could they have been smart enough to follow his example and develop their skills further without anyone realising? It was not impossible. Did anyone know how clever they were, and exactly what were they really capable of? Edward was quickly re-evaluating his own conception of these children.

Had Magnus been astute enough to try to curb Daniel's influence on their young lives? Unwilling to indulge them in their father's games and lessons, it certainly seemed to Edward that Magnus's main aim in the beginning had been to stop any of them becoming another Daniel. And who could blame him for that?

Daniel had so much to answer for; he been responsible for so much confusion. What had Daniel been? What had he become? Even the family knew little detail of his previous profession. Had he returned to it? Edward doubted it. To be untraceable, you had to become invisible.

"While you disappeared to Africa with his brother-in-law, Daniel moved to this remote spot," Edward went on. "He was happy here and the need to detach himself from his previous life seemed important. He had distanced himself from his family and the complicated system of any contact with them, acted as some protection."

Magnus remained non-committal. There had always been a darker side to Daniel. That he had quit the dubious world of subterfuge, had married and made his life safely away here, had always really pleased Magnus.

"Am I too close to the truth?" said Edward.

"I think we have finished this conversation. I wish you a safe journey home, Mr Jones."

Magnus had given nothing away. He had not argued, defended himself or corrected his assumptions. There was nothing to gain here, but Edward did believe Daniel was alive and well, somewhere.

Edward left the office. He had arrived with one theory

concerning Magnus and Daniel, and now as he walked back to the hotel he had several completely different ideas concerning the children to consider. Ideas he did not like.

***

Edward had intended to come and go without the children knowing. He had done as instructed and reported back to his agency, just one of many which had been concerned about Daniel's continuing silence over the years. Daniel had contacted no one; he had remained in the unknown, living out his life as someone else. The mystery confounded them all. Their grandfather, a former player of 'games', preferred to concentrate all his energy these days on ensuring that, via his former contacts, the children's welfare received priority consideration and that Edward by default would continue to be the discreet intermediary on their behalf.

"What are you doing here?" Jac asked, almost bumping into him on the street. She was naturally surprised at his presence back on the island.

"I wanted one last word with Maurice."

"I asked you to leave him alone!"

He took her arm and guided her to the familiar coffee shop. This time she was drinking coffee and sat stirring the spoon in the cup, waiting for his explanation. She was growing up, he acknowledged.

"I came to make peace. His only crime was to take a different identity."

"And the real Maurice?"

"He died in Africa in a mine collapse. Magnus was his partner. When they were pulled from the debris, it was easy enough to swap identities. He knew enough about your family from the stories your uncle would have told him during their years together to convince anyone that he was Maurice. But your father and Magnus were also close friends from the past. I believe your father knew what had happened. It was later he saw the benefit of having him come here. As your uncle, he provided the protection Daniel wanted for you."

"Do you know why our father left?" She had to ask.

"No. No one does. I have no idea what happened to make his retreat here no longer safe, what he had done or what he was running from. It will always be an unsolved mystery. Are you all right with that?"

Jac nodded. "We stopped wondering what had happened to father. We stopped thinking about him. He has stopped being part of our lives," Jacqueline admitted sadly.

"Do you have any message for your grandfather? We don't want the letters going astray again," Edward teased, his eyes wide in mischief while a wonderful grin lit his face.

Jac laughed. She was beginning to like Edward and his humour.

"We would love to come to stay when we have finished our schooling here. We would like to go to Europe to continue our education."

"A brilliant idea. He would enjoy that."

"Will you give me his correct address?"

"Yes, I can do that," Edward promised as they parted.

It would be safe to do that now. Family letters and cards were few and far between and the old address book would be of no use to anyone these days. The system which had been put in place to intercept and protect any mail Daniel sent hadn't been used or needed since the day he had left the island. If Maurice had ever been worried about the danger of any family contact causing trouble for him, he need not have, because any communication with England had always been via an indirect and complicated route. It was only Jacqueline's unfortunate letter which had brought Edward on to the scene.

***

Two years had passed. Hicky was the only one of the three of them who never had to pretend she was anything other than what she was. She had always been free to express her love of music and singing. She had flourished in the pleasure and encouragement she had been given. She was happy. She was hoping for a music scholarship, which would eventually mean studying in Europe, either in Paris or Rome, and with that in mind she had taken French and Italian lessons.

Jacqueline and Simon had studied hard during the past two years to catch up and had tasted that same degree of satisfaction. The serious business of improving themselves had them concentrating more on their school lessons. They were more positive about finding their true potential. They had lived under a self- imposed shadow too long. The summer schools on the mainland had given them new experiences and the excitement of travel. They had flourished, becoming the brightest pupils at school. They had excelled in their exams, and Jac was ready for university.

As Jacqueline had casually predicted to Edward, it seemed they were following the careers she had mentioned. Simon intended to take on the challenge of aviation, after having applied himself to mathematics and technology. He had been promised a prestigious apprenticeship with the British Aeronautical Development factory. Although the exciting lure of the sea was a second choice. Jac, with her knowledge of the causes and antidotes of various local conditions, could not decide between horticulture or the more demanding subject of medicine. Law seemed dull.

"Develop your senses, develop yourselves," her father had always told them, and they had. She hoped he would have been proud of them. She only wondered about him now and again, these days. The glimpse of anyone who looked like him had always made her heart miss a beat, but she had stopped hoping, stopped expecting to ever see him again. Stopped waiting.

Jac had often gone to talk to Hannah recently. She was older and wiser these days, and she regretted the stubborn misuse of her logic. There had been no talking or reasoning with her; she had resented the fact that neither of the others felt as strongly as she had. She alone was to blame for coercing the other two into all her schemes and unnecessary games. It was obvious that neither Maurice - she could not think of him as Magnus even now - nor Nevison had harmed their father, just as the pair of them hadn't been responsible for the unnecessary anguish the children had felt whilst growing up. They had done that to themselves, by trying to be too clever, by following Daniel's example. Their own father had done that to them by leaving in the manner he did. Despite all her love for him, he was the one who had hurt them the most. How odd to put it into context, after all these years, Jac thought objectively.

Jac had also accepted that no one was ever perfect, herself least of all. She had learnt early in life that she had been capable of doing anything she had considered necessary. And right or wrong, it was a characteristic of her nature and a philosophy she would stick to. It would see her through the future. She had the determination to get what she wanted. No one would hurt them again. That she had promised.

***

Edward had come back for Poppy, for all of them; it had been agreed he would chaperone them on the journey to England. There they would stay with the grandfather for a while before they all headed off to the next stage of their lives. As Edward waited for them at the house while they packed and repacked their luggage, listening to their eager chatter cheerfully echoing through the house, he could not help thinking about Magnus.

Magnus had expanded his shipping interests and intended to move from the island, and Edward doubted he would see him again. In one way it was the best of conclusions. Magnus deserved to live his own life, travel again, enjoy the rest of the world. He would leave without revealing anything. The truth would go with him. Edward could not help admire his loyalty. The man had never shown any malice towards the children, and despite all their antics, his obligation towards the family had remained unfaltering over these many years. He had done his best for them. His sacrifice had demanded silence, total silence, concerning Daniel. Magnus had been the best friend of all.

Magnus and Cleo's friendship was no longer a secret since he had moved into town. Hicky had seen them often together on the Saturdays when she had been into the capital for her extra music tuition. They had lunch together, talked and walked together in public, and it was obvious they did not mind who saw them these days. She was still as flamboyant and as distinctive as ever, and Magnus seemed to be proud to be her escort. Edward hoped they were happy.

Edward would never reveal his conclusions to the children about Magnus's intention to protect them from Daniel's ways. It was time to let go of the past, yet Daniel continued to haunt even him at moments like this, standing in his house. Where was Daniel? Would he ever be safe? Was he simply waiting to come home? Edward hoped not; he hoped Daniel had the sense not to reappear in their lives. For Poppy's sake more than the others, he hoped their father would to leave his children in peace. Edward shook his head. He must stop thinking about such an awful possibility.

Jac was the last one to drag her suitcase downstairs. To her it seemed strange that after they had conspired so hard and for so long to protect and keep their home, they were now the ones who had chosen to leave it for their respective careers. They were excited about the next adventure; they had to improve themselves, it was part of their very nature, it was in their blood. Their beloved home and all its precious contents would wait for them to return one day. 'Wait for me'; she had written on a piece of paper and left in her drawer. She knew it would.

The three of them walked down to their childhood patch of jungle, with all its memories. Eventually it would be overgrown again, with only the island parrots to echo their perpetual noise through the vast dense vegetation. It had shaped them, sheltered them and been their friend. Good or bad, they were what they were. Their games here were over.

"Kay la la!" they called.

"Kay lay lay!" came the reply.

***

Daniel paused briefly to check the apartment for bugs, as he always did out of habit when he entered the door of the sleek modern glass penthouse overlooking the Thames. Likewise he tapped the outside of his pocket, checking his silver whistle was still there. He would never part with it. It was the only link to the past he had, the only reminder of those bewitching years of love spent with his dearest wife and children.

In his former profession he had never expected the chance to have a life so blissfully different. After the army he had been too eager to please his different employers. He had been drawn in. He had been determined to become one of the best, an expert in intelligence, and before he realised it he had also become too valuable to them for them ever to relinquish their grip on him. Then an assignment had gone terribly wrong. He had killed a man, the wrong man as it turned out, and his agency had been quick to cover up his part in it. To save themselves any embarrassment they had been more than happy to let him retire and later relocate himself in some distant place, well away from the trouble. They had allowed him to live a proper life, out of the way and out of touch. It had been so different, it had taken time to be himself, it was something he had to grow into. With his beautiful understanding Hannah, he had learnt to love, to share, to enjoy the warmth of a family. He had been so happy, and he could not imagine it would ever change.

He should have known better. The organisation wanted him back. He was too good at his job, too clever, too astute, too devious and too good at pretending he was someone else. They owned him, they always had. They mean to control him and exploit him again, but Daniel did not want to return to the game of international intrigue. He knew they would make him comply by threatening his children. He could not risk that type of blackmail. To protect them, he had only one choice, to abandon them and disappear for ever. So he had taken his small boat and gone, with not even Magnus having any idea how or where he was going. He knew there could be no contact with anyone from that day on; he could not afford that mistake.

For nine years he had remained out of their clutches, moving from South Africa to China and Egypt to avoid detection, using money acquired from an untraceable source. Daniel had a new career; he was the master of languages and ancient cyphers, and now an expert with the new technology. He was different, but still cautious, and somehow wealthy.

The coded reports of his old employers were brief and precise, yet he had managed to hack into their system and decipher them. He knew Edward had appeared and who he was. A family friend, a very smart tactical move! He was too handsome, too much like his old self. Who could you trust these days? He also knew the children were coming to England and that thankfully Magnus had kept them safe. Daniel knew he had not deserved his loyalty, he had never earned it. He owed Magnus so much.

Daniel looked at the beautiful clear blue sky, so like the mornings on the island. Today he could have been taking the biggest risk yet, to go to the airport to see his children arrive and be up close as they made their way through the concourse. Unfortunately the surveillance monitoring system would have picked him up even on the approach road. The agency would have been prepared for today, hoping for this one act of stupidity. How long before the authorities gave up on him? Probably never. He would never know.

Today he was going to disappoint them. Today he was going to sit quietly and imagine he was there. The youngsters would look well and happy, linking arms and smiling at everyone.

Suddenly he was hit by a great intake of air. His heart was beating fast and he gulped back tears. His shoulders sagged and his body shook. He hadn't expected to feel so emotional after all this time. He still loved them and missed them, but he would never hear their voices, never touch or hold them in his arms again. He had remembered every birthday with a twinge to his conscience. He shook his head. There was nothing he could do for them. How sad that they did not belong to him any more.

His only consolation now was that he knew they would be fine without him. They were smart and had been taught to question everything. He felt certain they would not make the dreadful mistakes he had. He hoped they would prosper in their chosen careers. He hoped that Jacqueline would not fall in love with Edward.

All he had was memories of the past. Memories of happy children. Children he loved. It would have to be enough.

"Kay la la!" sounded in his head.

"Kay lay lay!" came his soft reply, as if he was actually talking to them again.

ND - #0455 - 270225 - C0 - 203/127/30 - PB - 9781861514752 - Matt Lamination